Silver

Book One of the In-Rel Trilogy

10600997

Michael Stoneburner

Cover: Michael Stoneburner

Interior Design: Ryan Coleman

Editors: Jeremy A. Matthews & Joel Stoneburner

Map: Amy-Alex Campbell

First Published: December 12th 2021
Second Edition: January 12th 2023

Printed in Australia

ISBN 978-0-6453142-2-9
12ink
Sydney, Australia

michaelstoneburner.com

*To all of you who are searching for your voice
and a place in this world to share it,
Rosie, Henry and Silver are for you.*

Table of Contents

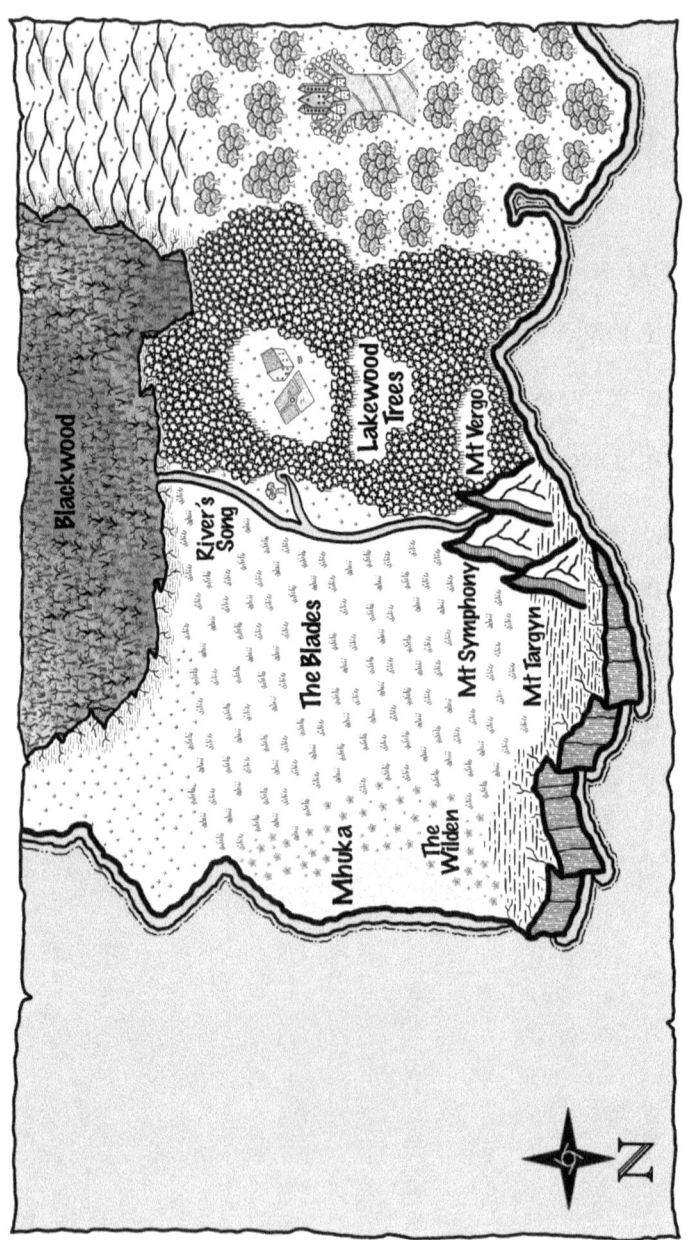

Within the Lakewood Trees

Rosie tucked herself beneath a tree as the rain poured down in unnaturally large droplets. Thunder rumbled in the distance and she clutched her pouch of herbs closer to her cloak. If lightning was coming, this tree would no longer be safe. She was hopeful that she could ride out the rain beneath the thick branches of the Lakewood Trees.

A bolt sketched the sky.

She let the pouch drop to her side as she adjusted the strap around her shoulder and pulled the cloak around her, "Drenched it is."

The heart-shaped leaves failed to keep the luscious green roof she loved about the forest from protecting her against the rain. During the summer months, when the sun poured its heat down upon them, Rosie and her son, Henry, would find refuge in the forest where it stayed cool and inviting. There was no refuge now. The droplets of rain left holes in the canopy where she could look up and see the constant etchings of the lightning.

"The Feygods have a message tonight," she muttered as the ground beneath her started to grow soft and slippery.

The hood to her cloak eventually weighed down against

her unruly hair. When it dried, she knew she'd spend hours trying to calm her brown strands as they acted like wild snakes. Henry would make fun of her until she threatened to razor off his own brown strands and he'd fall silent in one of his moody stupors.

Her heart leapt into her throat as thunder shook the skies and vibrated deep within her chest. It terrified her. She had never been in a storm quite like this one. Her shoes were already soaked through. The cloth was now more of a hindrance rather than protection. She felt slowed by her clothes. A thunderous wave burst ahead of her and every hair on her head felt like it was standing on end. Her button nose tingled and she wiped the line of water running down its bridge. Her nose only tingled when something was wrong. It was usually with Henry and she trusted this intuition.

Through the waterfall of rain and thunder she still heard a boy cry out. She slid around as she tried to pick up pace. Did Henry come out to find her? Did that bolt of lightning strike him? She had a dozen more questions flash through her head as she tore through the thicket and saw the young boy sprawled out in a crater. It was still sizzling from the lightning strike.

"Henry?!"

She rushed to the boy's side. He was face down choking on the collection of rain and mud. She dug her fingers into it and flipped his body around. She wiped a hand across his face as he sputtered out watery sludge. But it wasn't Henry. The rain washed the mud away quickly as the dollops came down. The lightning and thunder had suddenly faded. The clouds were beginning to break and bring out hints of blue and the rays of spring's sun.

The boy looked to be around the same age as her son, 15 or 16. His clothes were torn and singed. They looked to be made of silk. What was someone with wealthy clothing doing out in the middle of the Lakewood Trees? Her house was a few thousand paces from the nearest community and a few more from the nearest town. This boy's clothes had to be from a city that was days away.

"Hello?!" she called out to the black-barked trees around her. "Hello? I have your boy! He's hurt!"

She looked down at him again as the rain completely faded and she felt a breeze dart through the trees. She gasped and raised an arm up in front her. She was completely dry and so was the boy. She looked around. In fact, everything was dry and all that was left as evidence there was a storm was the crater they were sitting in. Her nose tingled and she felt it warm.

The boy's shirt was barely hanging on his torso. He seemed strong but pale. Around his neck was a chain with a locket shaped as a small shell. What was most noticeable about him was that he had short wavy hair that was as silver as the shell and chain around his neck.

"Who are you?" she said, slightly shaking him, "Are you okay?"

His chest was rising and falling and she could feel his heart as she rested a hand on his soot patched chest. The silk shirt he wore was slowly sliding off of him. She'd have to carry him back to the house. There was no way she was going to leave him out here.

She called out again, "Is anyone here? Hello? I found your boy!"

Only the birds' songs in the trees answered her. The world around her didn't seem to notice there had been a monsoon that had just hit. The canopy was shadowing the late morning's sun.

"Alright, Silver," she sighed, speaking to the boy. She had to call him something. "Luckily I'm used to hauling logs to feed the fire through the winter."

She heaved him up into her arms and stood up, "I'm also a mother. I'd carry my son through the pits of Cen-Rel and back to keep him safe. So, I will with you, too."

Her homestead was not far and she knew the forest well. It would only take her longer because she was carrying a teenage boy as if he were a baby. The muscles in her legs were thick. She was a large woman compared to the nearby community's women. They had men that did the labour while the women gathered and cooked. She used to be more like the men so after her husband disappeared, she found herself easing in doing everything around the house. It was dealing with people that Patrick found easy while she shied away. She understood the plants more. People were just complicated.

"I could use you right about now, Patrick," she muttered, despite herself. She hated admitting that sometimes she wished him around, especially in handling Henry.

She replayed the argument they had that night. It was a distraction to the boy growing heavier and heavier in her arms. Patrick was a short man but from what he lacked in size, he had in strength. He worked in lumber and hauled wood daily. In his downtime, he was whittling the wood as extra income for when Rosie used to travel to town to take part in the markets. Although Patrick was more charismatic, Rosie always made the better deals. Patrick was a kind man who would get swept up in other people's issues and would return home empty-handed after giving things away for free. Despite his connection with people, however, he was a soft-spoken man and rarely took part in arguments. Rosie had been caught off guard with his sudden assertiveness.

They had sacrificed all that they had to build their homestead and decide to raise a boy so far away from other children. That night Patrick seemed to be willing to give all that up. He was pleading to her as he wiped the sweat off his balding head, "Rosie, you're not hearing me. I'm not *asking* you if you think we should move to Moon's Edge. I am *telling* you that we are!"

Usually his deep voice was soothing but it became demanding and cold. She was instantly put off by it and threw a shoe at him. "Since when have you told me what to do? Ever?"

He put his hands up and flinched as if he were expecting the other shoe. She waited till he relaxed again before throwing it over his shoulder.

"Rosie!" he hissed, "You'll wake Henry!"

"Well if I do, you can explain to him that all our hard work here has been for nothing. We are just going to abandon our home and the community to go across to the other side of the continent to live gods knows where. And why? Why are we doing that?"

"I can't say, Rosie," he was breathless at this point. His eyes were pleading to her, but she wasn't one to do as she was told unless she understood why.

If Rosie had another shoe, she would have thrown it, "You can't say?"

Then he said something that made Rosie pause, "You'll have to trust me."

She had heard that growing up many times. It was used to make her comply. Patrick knew this. He knew it would have been a trigger. Why was he deliberately trying to upset her?

Then slowly, he added, "Rosie, don't you trust me?"

Rosie flinched. "Right now, Patrick?" she said quickly and harshly, "I don't."

She had pushed him and all he did was slip back into his soft-spoken nature and say, "Then it's done."

There would be many nights thereafter she would mutter better questions and responses. Even now, as she broke through the edge of the Lakewood Trees and shifted the boy's weight in her arms, she muttered, "What's done? Us? Why?"

She could still see the look Patrick gave her. It was regret, but she had been angry to push the argument further and Patrick didn't give her a chance. He had walked out after grabbing his pipe. He only smoked when he had to think.

He never came back.

"It's never done," Rosie hissed, as she looked quickly around the clearing at the edge of Lakewood Trees. Henry was sitting on a stump in the middle of their yard trying to carve a piece of wood. He was trying to find the same talent Patrick had but wasn't having much luck. Henry lacked patience and most of the pieces he was working on ended up in the fire. He didn't look up and Rosie could tell he knew she was coming. He was choosing not to pay any attention to her.

"Get up, boy!" she snapped, "And help me with him!"

Henry looked up and immediately stood. His eyes were staring at the boy. Henry had the same eyes as his father, green like the leaves of Lakewood. In fact, Henry was the spitting image of his father at that age. Sometimes she felt like she was back in the village where they had grown up together, decided to marry and build a home far from her abusive father. Patrick had saved her.

Her arms and legs were burning but she increased her pace towards the house. They had cut the trees and shaped every piece of wood themselves to build the two-storey home. The porch where Patrick whittled was facing her. He had built a long seat where feather pillows cushioned him as he worked. The pillows had not been restuffed in ages and some lay weather worn beneath the table but that was her goal. She would put the silver-haired boy there.

Henry approached her side and matched her pace. He made no movement to help her carry him.

"Who is that?"

Rosie's back muscles were starting to spasm. She grunted a few swear words under her breath that Henry didn't pick up as she heaved Silver up the stairs and dumped him into the chair.

"Hey, mom, watch it! You might hurt him!"

Rosie leaned against the railings of the porch with her hands on her lower back and stared at her son with wide eyes, "I carried him from within Lakewood to here after he got struck by lightning. He's alive. He's here. Let's see you do that!"

Henry was a scrawny teenager who struggled to lift the kettle full of water to hang above the fire. She wasn't sure what she was expecting from the boy and regretted her tone. It was too late. Henry rolled his eyes and stomped back down the stairs to the stump.

"Where are you going? Are you going to help get him in the house?"

Henry put his hands up in the air, "I'm no help remember. Might as well stay out of the way and whittle."

Rosie's body was beginning to recuperate and she took a step down towards Henry, "Now come on, I didn't say that. Come on now. Help me out, please? Besides, we both know whittling isn't for you!"

Henry froze and Rosie instantly regretted her words. She said some awful things sometimes and just didn't know why. The moment Henry's voice started to deepen and he complained that his bedroom was too close to hers, she had somehow lost all connections with him. She went to apologise but she was distracted by sudden movement from the seat on the porch. She spun around and saw the silver haired boy sit up. He looked down at himself and wobbled in his seat. He seemed to be surprised he had no shirt. He stretched and Rosie could hear his joints groan and crack. She even noticed the hair beneath his arms was silver as well.

"What are you?" she wondered aloud.

The boy stood up startled. He scrambled back clutching something in one hand and grabbing at his chain with the other. He tried to speak but nothing came out which made him writhe around in more of a panic.

Rosie held up her arms as if he were a wild animal, "Woah there, Silver, calm down now. You're safe. You were just struck by lightning. I think. I found you and brought you to my home. My son is just over there. I'm Rosie. He's Henry. You're safe."

He didn't move. He couldn't. She could see that he felt ill. It reminded her of last winter when a fever had set in with Henry. Whatever happened to this poor boy had drained him of his energy. His eyes rolled back into his head and he slumped over.

Rosie rushed to him and snapped out to Henry, "Get over here and help me."

"I'm right here," his voice startled Rosie from behind her. He didn't sound pleased with her but that was something she'd have to deal with later.

She ran a hand over Silver's face. It was drenched as if he had been caught in the storm again but this time it was his own sweat. She started to lift him up by one arm and tried to move it over her shoulders. She was much taller than the boys. This wouldn't be easy.

Henry grabbed the other arm and easily put it around his shoulders. Rosie became more of a support and her muscles appreciated it.

"Why is his hair silver?" Henry asked, grunting as he heaved the boy across the porch to the front door. Henry had left it open and a part of Rosie wanted to lecture him for always doing that.

"I don't know," she said, moving to the side so that they could pass the boy easily through the threshold. "Did it rain here?"

"What? No. Why?"

"Never mind. I'm not even sure if it rained at all."

"When? What are you talking about?"

"Never mind," she repeated and nodded her head towards the side room.

"I know where to take him," Henry grunted and continued towards the small room.

They were so far from any communities that Patrick had insisted on building this little room. It had a couple of cots in it, a chamber pot and a small bedside table with one drawer. If travellers were passing through the Lakewood Trees and needed a place to stay they could rent this room out or if someone was hurt they could tend to their wounds there. There was no window for this room so it was always incredibly dark. A thick single candle rested on top of the table. As soon as they were inside, Rosie let the boy go and lit the candle. It sizzled and popped but lit the room nicely.

Henry grunted as he slowly slid the other boy into a cot and stood over him, "There. Nice and soft. I'm not my mom. I don't throw around someone like they're a piece of meat."

Rosie rolled her eyes, "Quiet you," and left the room. She

walked through the room that Patrick kept calling the Great Hall. It was the largest room on the ground floor. It held a long table made from the Lakewood Trees with chairs where only two were being used. They were on opposite ends of the table. The four remaining chairs were stacked upside down along the sides of it.

"Three extras in case of visitors," Rosie muttered, repeating Patrick's reasoning in making the useless things. No one came to visit now that Patrick was gone. It was as if their random travellers were only coming through because they knew Patrick was there.

Rosie took a moment to lean against the table and stare into the empty fireplace that filled up most of the wall. The mantle held small wooden figurines Patrick had whittled. It was the stages of their lives. On the far left were two young figures representing Rosie and Patrick. They were beautiful, even then. Patrick had made them at Henry's age. He had a talent that was for sure. The next figures were Rosie with a hammer and Patrick with a saw, representing when they built the house. The third set was of Rosie holding a baby and Patrick hugging her from the side looking up at them both. He was really that short. The last set was incomplete. It was of Patrick whittling with Henry as a boy. Patrick didn't get to finish her figure before he disappeared.

Rosie looked out the windows that stood on either side of the fireplace. The Lakewood Trees were a few paces away. "What am I doing?"

"Mom," Henry called from the door of the spare room.

She stood and walked towards the kitchen, "I'll be right back. I'm just getting some water and a washcloth to wash away his fever."

The kitchen was built in the back of the house leading out of Patrick's Great Hall. It was Patrick's pride and joy. He loved cooking on the iron stove he had brought in from a blacksmith he knew. There was another fireplace here that held a large pot for boiling water or soups. Henry tried to insist he keep the pot filled with water but he wasn't as strong as his parents. He hadn't reached the age in which he would start growing and be able to contribute more.

There were many cupboards that aligned the kitchen where Patrick had somehow managed to organise each one and keep it filled. It had been a beautiful menagerie of dried fruits, herbs and cutlery that within a few rotations of his absence had become neglected. Rosie tried but never managed to fill it like he did. Henry would always mutter his disapproval of the place whenever he couldn't find what he wanted.

Rosie grabbed a large bowl from one of the counters and used the ladle coming out of the pot in the fireplace to scoop out some water. She reached into a drawer of one of the cupboards and grabbed an unused wash cloth. She headed back towards the doorway leading back to Patrick's Great Hall. She stopped once again and stared towards nothing in particular.

"What am I doing?"

The backdoor rattled with the wind. It was on the opposite wall of the doorway leading back towards Henry and the boy. She took a moment to look out the windows to the backyard. Most of the Lakewood Trees had been cut in that area to make room for Rosie's garden. She loved that garden and when she wasn't out looking for herbs and berries that grew best in the shadows of Lakewood, she would be tending to the vegetables and fruits that grew there. Back in the village where she grew up with Patrick, she was always mocked for the way that she ploughed and tended to the gardens. She was the only female that stepped out into the sun and overturned the ground. During harvesting, everyone pitched in to gather the food but that was because they were taking their share before the rest was sent to the markets.

A draft howled up from the cellar stairs where the food and wine storage rested. It snapped her out of her thoughts and she turned back towards the door and hustled through Patrick's Great Hall and into the spare room.

"What were you doing? It shouldn't take that long," Henry said and tried to reach for the bowl.

Rosie moved it out of his reach, which was easy with her height. She sat on the edge of the cot and soaked the cloth into the water.

"I could do that, you know," Henry hissed but didn't wait for her reply, "His left hand is clutching something. I couldn't pry it open to see what it was."

"Never mind that," Rosie said, "His business is his business. I just need to break this fever and find out who he is and where he's from. Just give him some space and mind yourself."

Henry sat on the other cot, "I'm not leaving."

"Oh?" Rosie looked over at him, "And what will we do for lunch, then? You're always complaining I don't let you in Patrick's kitchen. So, there you go. Get a broth going for Silver and put some food together for us."

Henry couldn't help but smile at her request and get up

off the cot quickly before he recomposed himself and frowned, "You don't have to call it that you know."

"Call it what?" Rosie said, still washing the boy's face gently.

"Patrick's kitchen. It's our kitchen too."

Henry stood there waiting for a response but she had moved the wash cloth to the boy's chest. It looked as if he had soot patches all over him, as if he had been in a fire. Henry watched his mother clean the smooth chest for a moment before he snapped himself out of it and left the room.

Rosie waited till Henry left before she moved her free hand to the boy's left hand. Henry wasn't wrong. The hand was clenched tight and protecting something. She could see a hint of metal between the thumb and forefinger.

"What do you got there?" she asked and tried to push a finger through to touch the metal.

The boy's eyes flickered open and he quickly sat up and moved his left hand closer to his chest. He opened his mouth but no words came out before he snapped it shut.

"Sorry. Sorry," Rosie said, placing the bowl of water next to the lit candle. It flickered with her movement. "I was just trying to get you to relax. I was washing you up. I think you were hit by lightning."

The boy shook his head slowly to Rosie's surprise.

"You can understand me?"

He nodded.

"Well, I'll be…alright, that's good. What's your name?"

He opened his mouth again only to show his white teeth. She almost forgot that he had been in a silken shirt. His pants were of a different material but just as soft, almost velvet. He scratched at his head absentmindedly and then shrugged.

"You don't know your name. Well, I've been calling you Silver. Because, well," she waved at his hair, "you have a unique shade of hair I have not ever seen before."

The boy tried to play with his bangs but it wasn't long enough to pull into his view.

"Trust me," Rosie giggled, "It's Silver."

"It's silver everywhere," Henry said as he entered the room again carrying a bowl of broth and a chunk of hard bread.

"What do you mean?" Rosie snapped her face towards Henry before her eyes widened, "Oh gods, Henry, you didn't?!"

Henry suddenly went red and he pushed the bowl of water aside to put the broth down, "I mean no of course I didn't. Well, maybe just a peek. I was curious!"

Rosie turned back to the boy who was giving Henry an odd look, "I am so sorry. Henry is just, well, he hasn't been around boys his age. I guess he was just curious. Oh gods, anyway, I'll organise the table for our food. Henry, make sure he stays resting…"

Rosie got up and rushed to the doorway. Henry moved over and sat where she had been on the boy's cot.

"It really was just a peek. Why is your hair silver?"

She shook her head silently as Silver took a peek under the covers and shrugged. She quickly left the room. Henry used to come to her to ask questions of the changes he was going through but she had answered quickly and brushed any further questions aside. She knew nothing about boys. Patrick was always the one answering his questions. It just seemed easier for him to sit there and answer all the whys and whats and hows. It didn't come naturally for Rosie. She just couldn't find the words.

When she returned with her hands full of two bowls of vegetables, some dried meat and bread, she found Silver taking down the chairs off the table awkwardly with one hand with Henry copying him with the other two chairs.

"What are you doing? He shouldn't be doing that. He has a fever," she explained but looking over Silver, he suddenly appeared to be fine.

Henry shrugged, "I don't control what he does. He took down a chair for himself and then started to take the others down. It's not a bad idea. Chairs are meant to be sat in."

"Oh? Is that what they are for?" Rosie walked over to the end of the table closest to the front door and put Henry's bowl down and returned to her bowl and sat. "I didn't realise how hungry I was until I started picking at the meat in the kitchen. We're running low. I might have to go hunt soon. If I am able…"

Silver disappeared back into the spare room and brought out the broth and bread Henry had brought him. He looked at Henry eating at one end of the table and then looked at Rosie eating from the other. He seemed confused.

Rosie froze mid-bite and looked around at the table. There were four empty chairs.

"What's wrong?" she asked him.

Silver motioned with the hand with the bread in it across the table.

"Yes. This is a table. And those are chairs. There's four of them. Pick one."

Henry looked between the two and then talked with his mouth full, "He's probably confused as to why we are sitting so far away. We didn't used to."

"What's wrong with where we are sitting? This is where Patrick used to sit. Now I do. You're the one that moved all the way over there."

"She means my father," Henry explained to Silver, "She always says his name like that."

"I don't say Patrick's name in any way he doesn't deserve," Rosie snapped.

"Doesn't change he is my father," Henry muttered.

Rosie pushed her teeth together before saying, "He was. And Silver doesn't need to hear this old argument. Now. Eat."

"She means, 'Shut up, Henry,'" he said to Silver.

"No, I meant eat. If I meant shut up, I'd say it. Now shut up and eat."

Silver watched the two. Henry was scowling as if he had

23

tasted something bad. Rosie looked amused as if the two had just shared a joke. Silver turned around and returned to the spare room.

"Good job, mom," Henry grumbled, "Now the guest doesn't even want to sit with us."

"Well, you did make it awkward. Always making things a bigger deal than they are. As you do," she sighed, "As you do."

Lunch was eaten in silence but that wasn't abnormal. It was the talking beforehand that wasn't natural. Rosie and Henry ate in peace until he walked back out front to the stump to try at whittling again. Rosie checked in with Silver in the spare room. His bowl was empty. The bread was gone. At some point the candle had gone out.

"I can take your bowl. You don't need to be sitting in the dark. There's plenty of daylight," she felt his forehead and nodded, "You seem to be free of that fever. It came and went as quickly as that storm. Oh well. Maybe you can help me in the garden and we can try and see if you remember anything. Or you can go hang with Henry and watch him slice up a poor unfortunate chunk of wood. This house is your house. We'll figure all this out, okay?"

Silver stood up and followed Rosie out of the door. She looked back at him and thought she saw a look of relief spread across his face.

"The room is depressing, I agree. It's not a room to spend a lot of time in. Patrick insisted on adding it to the house in case we had visitors who needed to stop in or needed help. He wasn't wrong. Since we have lived here we've had quite the guests. Patrick would love the whole mystery surrounding you."

She looked down at Silver, who took a few fast steps to walk alongside her.

"This is Patrick's Great Hall. It's nothing like a Great Hall I've ever been to but it amused him, so the name sort of stuck. Those stairs leading up next to the spare room. That heads up to Henry's room and mine. If it isn't a problem with you, I might have you camp up there with him. No need to keep putting you in that cot cage, aye?"

Silver looked around the Great Hall, then to the stairs and then up at her and nodded.

"You are such a mystery, Silver," she said quietly and then continued towards the kitchen, "It's a shame we don't know your real name but I think Silver suits you. Don't you?"

Silver tilted his head for a moment and then nodded. He looked around the kitchen and then out the back window.

"That's the garden. I planted every single thing in that beautiful place. The flowers along the edges I use to sort of set up a border. Make it look nice. The bushes. The hedges. Those trees there? See them? I planted those. I didn't think they'd grow amongst the Lakewood Trees but they do. The one there at the far end of the garden. That's Patrick's favourite. It only grows in Moon's Edge. It's a Moongrove. Its leaves illuminate in the moonlight."

Silver opened the backdoor and stepped out. Rosie followed him. The garden was rotations of work and she had it segmented into seasons. At the beginning of each season, she'd harvest the previous ones and plough what would grow next. This garden made up most of their food. As she started to walk through with Silver, her mind forgot about everything else but her plants. They spent hours going through each part until they were resting beneath the Moongrove. Silver had insisted.

"Henry has never walked through this garden with me. Patrick used to every so often. He said I had this connection with the plants that he was envious of. I always joked and said if he didn't spend so much of his time cutting them down maybe they'd connect with him, too. But it's just the way our world works. My mother always said, 'We need to end something now before we can begin something new.'"

Silver let out a small snore from his spot underneath the Moongrove and Rosie laughed, "We'll need to get you some suitable clothes. You are about the same size as Henry so I'm sure he'll have something for you."

Rosie spent the rest of the day finishing off the Spring segment of the garden and clearing out the Winter one. Henry eventually came looking for Silver and the three ended up back in the kitchen preparing for dinner. Rosie kept tripping over both of them as she tried to get things done but she held her tongue when wanting to send them away. She watched as Henry and Silver carried in fresh water from the well to boil. They both lit the fire and stoked it until it continued on its own. She was surprised when Henry offered to cut up the vegetables. It was then she could no longer hold her tongue.

"Now, Silver, I want to point out he never offers to help. He's showing off for you."

Henry shook his head, "No, Silver, she never let me help before. She's trying to act like she's all nice and not controlling."

Rosie asked Silver to set up the table while she poured the hot stew they had made into bowls. She would pass a bowl over to Henry who would take it out to Silver. Once she had all their helpings, she put the lid on the pot.

"Definitely more for tomorrow. I might have made a bit too much with Silver here. It's been awhile since I've made something for three," she said as she walked into Patrick's Great Hall and froze.

Silver was standing behind her chair holding it out for her with a big grin. Henry was sitting at the chair on the left while a setting waited for Silver on the right.

"What?" Henry said looking up at her after smelling the stew, "Silver set the table like you said. I guess this is how he wanted it."

Rosie slowly nodded, "Thank you, Silver. I mean, if you're comfortable there, Henry."

"I'm fine."

Rosie sat down and watched Silver take his seat and start to dig in. Henry was already eating. She just sat there a moment. Every part of her body was tight. She even realised she was holding her breath. She shook her head and took in a breath and let out a sigh.

"I guess this is how it is now," Rosie said to no one in particular, "Oh, Henry, I'm not sure how long Silver will be staying with us so instead of him sitting in the Cot Cage-"

"The Cot Cage?" Henry asked automatically before thinking about it and nodding.

"I came up with that as I was describing it to Silver. I don't know, I think it works. Anyway, I was thinking Silver could camp up in your room. You might find him some clothes he can wear."

Henry nodded eagerly, "That will be fine."

Rosie was relieved when they fell into silence once again while they finished eating. She didn't realise how much she had been talking since Silver had been there. A different kind of exhaustion swept over her. She almost preferred the tired she felt over heavy labour than this.

Henry and Silver finished first as the light disappeared beyond the Lakewood Trees. Henry had brought out a few candlesticks. They were each stuck into a holder carved by wood. Rosie's candle holder had carved vines and roses. Patrick's had trees and Henry's had a single bird on it. Patrick had always said he'd finish it when Henry grew and learnt who he was.

As she finished her meal and stared at the chairs that were down off the table, there was a knock at the door. Her eyes slowly moved to the steps that lead upstairs where the boys had disappeared to Henry's room. She slowly pushed herself up from her chair and slowly made her way to the front door. There was a slab of wood to bolt it closed in the corner next to the door but they had never needed to use it. Lakewood was a peaceful forest. The dangerous areas were deeper into Blackwood where only the most skilled hunters went to bring back furs and meats. She looked through the front window but whoever knocked at the door was making sure not to peek through. They had at least some manners whoever it was. The fireplace crackled with the light as she opened the door.

Rosie looked at the small wrinkled man that held a sealed parchment. He looked up at her with big round eyes over a long hairy nose.

"For you, Lady Edwards."

"I'm no Lady. Rosie is fine," eyeing him warily.

She took the parchment from his shaky hands. He bowed once his hands were emptied and turned. She watched him skip back to a horse that awaited him along the start of the path, "It's late!" she called, "I do have a room and a place for your horse!"

The scrawny man waved back at her from atop his horse, "I couldn't impose, Lady Edwards! And from here on out, I would not give such an invitation! I will be the last welcomed guest upon your door!"

Rosie looked up from the parchment with wide eyes, "I said call me-wait-what did you say?"

But the horse had galloped away with unnatural speed and it did not follow the path towards the community. It turned and disappeared into the Lakewood Trees exactly in the direction she had found Silver.

She closed the door and for the first time lifted the plank of wood and put it into the grooves that would latch the door. She broke the waxed seal that kept the parchment curled up. Her eyes quickly scrolled the words carefully written on the page. Something rose up in her throat and she choked it back down and forced her eyes to read it again but slowly:

My Dearest Rosie,

I am pleased you received my gift the other day. We have much to discuss. Meet me at Moon's Edge in 200 days. No sooner. No later.

Yours,
Lord Patrick Edwards

The Pawprint in the Blades

Henry's eyes burst open. Instinctually, he held his breath and listened. He felt his wolf skin blanket tug as a shape rose from his bed and stretched in front of a curtained window. Sunlight was forcing itself in through the partial gap in between. Henry watched the silver haired boy scratch at the seashell pendant on the chain around his neck. It hadn't been a dream.

Last night as Henry was about to put wool down on the floor with an extra wolf skin, Silver had crawled into his bed and looked at Henry in expectation. Henry just put the coverings on the floor and crawled in next to him. Silver didn't blink an eye. He just held his clenched hand closed and fell asleep next to Henry as if this is what they had been doing for rotations.

Henry watched as Silver peered back over to the bed quickly. The room was dark enough to hide Henry's face but he closed his eyes slightly anyway. He watched Silver go back to the window and peek out. This window was right next to the bed and looked out over the yard where Henry's father used to whittle. The forest beyond that yard was where Rosie had found Silver.

Henry opened his eyes so that he could see fully and watched Silver open his fisted hand. Henry felt his heart jump into his throat. One of the many mysteries of this boy was what was in his hand he guarded so carefully. Even at dinner last night, he ate with one hand as the other rested in his lap. Henry tried to see what was in his hand but at this angle he could only see that Silver switched a small object into his right hand. Henry dared to sit up slowly but Silver heard him almost instantly and he spun around and put his right hand behind his back.

"Are you okay, Silver?" Henry asked, pretending that he wasn't just trying to creep on him but just wake up and stretch in bed. "Did you sleep well? It's great that my clothes fit you. It gets pretty cold in here even in summer. My father treated the wood with something to protect from the elements. I didn't get a chance to learn what it was."

Silver just stared at him with his eyes like ice. Henry slid out of bed and didn't stop talking. He tried to stay quiet but couldn't. There was something about this boy.

"My mom and father cut down the trees, shaped the wood and built this house. This area used to be full of Lakewood Trees. Listen to me, I'm rambling. If you're like my mom, she can't stand talking first thing in the morning until she has her grounded coffee beans. She grows them. She grows a lot of things. I'm still talking and you're still staring at me."

By this time, Henry had gotten out of bed, grabbed clothes for both of them and headed towards the door. All the while, he tried to catch a glimpse of what Silver was hiding behind his back. Silver didn't speak of course. Sometimes it looked like he was going to by opening his mouth and taking in a breath, but it just turned into a sigh.

"I'm going to go get water from the well in the garden to heat up so we can clean. You can just wear the nightclothes for now. It shouldn't take long. Until then you can stay in here if you want. I've got Tabs to play. They're in my top drawer."

Silver frowned and looked at the drawer Henry pointed to.

"You know Tabs, right? I thought everyone played them. My father got them from town. Said everyone played it. That was rotations ago though when he—never mind. Maybe kids don't play it anymore. There's a bag in there. It's full of coins. Most are wooden but my father got me a couple of other sets so they could play with me. My father used the wooden ones. My mom was the gold ones because that set is rare. I was silver…hey! You can be silver. It makes sense with all your hair being—"

Henry took a deep breath as he caught Silver staring at him again in awe. Henry nodded, "Right. I'm talking too much. I know. I'll get the water ready. Then we can bathe."

Henry ignored Silver as he rushed out of his room and closed the door behind him. He didn't care if Silver wanted to leave the room. He just needed time to remember how to breathe normally. He closed his eyes for a bit. There was a large window to his left at the end of the hallway that overlooked the garden. He was tempted to sit in the chair his father had built and just hope to forget the last few minutes of his life.

A noise down the other end of the hall startled him. It was coming from his mother's room. Her door was ajar and he thought he heard her crying. The last time he heard his mother crying was the day after his father disappeared.

Henry never saw her cry since.

He stepped up to the door and knocked lightly before pushing it open, "I'm going to go heat up the water…"

Rosie suddenly stood from her four posted bed and crumbled the letter she had gotten last night at the door. She had refused to talk about it with Henry. He instantly frowned and felt his own anger bubble in his gut.

"Henry, I," she had already been dressed. In fact, she looked dressed to leave.

"Where are you going?"

Rosie shoved the crumpled up letter into the pocket of her thick trousers, "I'm going to the Blackwood today. I need to hunt. We're going to need to restock on food. Dry out some meat for us."

"The pantry is fine," Henry folded his arms, "What am I supposed to do with Silver all day? Let us go with you."

"I have never let you come to Blackwood. Why would I start now?"

"I don't know. Maybe to teach me how to hunt?"

Rosie threw her hands up in the air and grabbed a bow and quiver tucked in the corner of her room. "I'm not having this argument with you again, Henry."

"If my father was here…" Henry started.

"But he's not!" she snapped and pushed past him into the hallway. Henry followed closely, still clutching both of the boys' clothes. "He left us. So, he's not. I'm here. Sorry to disappoint."

Henry jogged down the stairs after his mother, "You don't know what happened to him. And stop saying that! You don't know what I think. You never ask!"

Rosie stormed through the Great Hall and grabbed Patrick's walking stick with a pouch tied to the top of it. She didn't say another word and walked out the front door. Henry stood there in the doorway and watched her round the house past the stump and towards her garden. Henry slammed the front door and rushed through the Great Hall back through the kitchen and opened up the back door.

"Mom!" Henry called out to her, "Mom!"

She just kept walking past her garden and disappeared beyond the Lakewood Trees heading south to Blackwood. He closed the door much like he did the front and muttered to himself, "Why don't you ever—"

He froze as he saw Silver standing in the kitchen doorway just staring at him.

"You're pretty good at that. You know, staring all the time. If you don't have anything to say, why are you even here?"

Silver tilted his head slightly. His lips slowly curled downwards.

"Sorry," Henry sighed, throwing the clothes partially on the counter space, "My mom left. She's heading to Blackwood to hunt. Apparently, we need more food even though we have plenty."

Silver tilted his head the other way. His lips relaxed.

Henry blinked rapidly, "I mean, there are three of us again. Maybe it would go quicker."

Silver gathered the clothes up into a bundle and looked back at Henry.

Henry cleared his throat, "So maybe she should have gone. And you were struck by lightning, so you couldn't really make the trip. And we don't know if you hunt. I don't hunt yet. You can't even speak, so there's that too."

Silver just kept staring at him until Henry groaned, "Alright, fine, Silver, my mom was right. But she could at least tell me what that letter was all about last night."

Silver shrugged.

"Yeah. She has her secrets and you have yours. Maybe I should come up with a secret for myself, too."

Silver cracked a smile and rolled his eyes before stepping out the backdoor. Henry watched him wander through the garden before sitting on the edge of the cobblestone well. Silver flicked at the handle and watched as the rod rolled a bit with the thick rope tied to it that held the bucket. He seemed amused by its mechanics. Henry watched him a bit longer. He noticed his left hand was in a fist again and held the clothes tightly to his chest. Silver stood and with his right hand turned the handle until the bucket lowered into the depth of the well. He looked to the house and Henry snapped out of it and grabbed the iron pot from the fire his mother had left stoking.

The well was smack dab in the middle of the garden

surrounded by the different seasonal segments. All pathways led to the well. He set the pot on the edge and reached for the handle Silver struggled to wind back up with one hand.

"It'd be easier if you weren't so protective of whatever it is you're holding," Henry grunted as he wound up the bucket.

Silver took a step back and was bemused at how much Henry seemed to be struggling using both of his hands.

"I think it's snagged on something," Henry grunted.

The sun was not even halfway above the tree line and Henry started to break into a sweat on his upper lip and forehead. He had done this many times and yet the bucket full of water never felt this heavy. He was pulling something else up with it.

Silver's eyes looked amused and disbelieving.

"Okay, fine, anyone could pull this up with one arm. I just wanted to see what you are holding. You've ate and slept in our house. Slept in my bed, even. Surely you can trust us."

Silver reached out and for a moment Henry's heart fluttered until Silver gripped the handle with him and they rotated it together. Silver's hand was cold to the touch. They pulled the bucket up to the top and held it. Both of them lingered at the sight.

A black clump of feathers filled the bucket with a limp wing hanging over the edge and a bent head resting over the breast of the bird. Henry cursed and pulled at the handle until it locked into place.

"The water won't be safe to drink or bathe in. We'll have to wait till my mom gets back from Blackwood. Until then, we'll have to walk to the stream. It's not far east. I'm sure you won't be hit by lightning along the way."

Silver stared at the bird.

Henry eyed it again, "It's just a bird. Looks to be a raven. Usually they're messengers. This one must have gotten thirsty. It happens sometimes in the summer. Dumb birds. My mom has crystals she makes that can purify the well again. Come on. Don't worry."

Silver didn't budge.

The silence was uncomfortable for Henry. He hated it with his mom, too, but he didn't have a choice there. She was never much of a talker and Silver was a mute. He missed his father's chatter. They'd always be talking about something random. Henry just wasn't sure if it was because of the lightning strike or if Silver was just like that. Same as the hair colour. Elders had white hair, but silver, that was usually only seen in tools, weapons or jewellery.

"I'm sorry about the lightning comment. I was just joking. My mom doesn't have a sense of humour either."

Silver shook his head and then nodded his chin towards the raven.

"Fine," Henry sighed and reached for the rope to swing the bucket over, "I'll take care of the bird. Unlatch the handle. Just give it a push."

Silver did as Henry instructed and Henry set the bucket next to the pot and grabbed the bird by the neck. The face pointed upwards as Henry pulled it out and gasped.

"Heavy bird. Unnatural. Look at its beak!" Henry held it out to Silver, who cautiously leaned over and looked.

Jagged teeth outlined the black pointed beak. There were even hook-like claws that grew out from the tip of the wings.

"What sort of creature is this? I thought it a raven but ravens don't have these," Henry gasped and used his other hands to take a look at the claws. "Look at these."

Silver took a step closer behind Henry and leaned his chin on Henry's shoulder. Henry was taken aback but allowed it. He played with each claw of the bird.

"The claws have been filed back as if it were someone's pet. There's an old man in the community who has an owl like this. My mom doesn't like it. But the teeth and claws on the wings? That's new to me. What about you?"

Silver lifted his head and shook it.

"I'll leave it near the compost and have my mom look at it when she gets back. Come on, though. I smell and so do you. I think you smell a bit burnt from yesterday. No joke. I smell like my mom's feet after a good hunt. You'll see when she gets back. Let's get to the river."

Henry tried to laugh again but Silver only quietly followed. "I've met a few people who were mute. They talked with their hands or drew pictures. Can you do that?" Henry asked as he held the backdoor open and Silver walked inside.

Silver stood in the middle of the kitchen and held out the clothes.

"I'm thinking we should eat before we go. My mom has some great conserves to go with some bread. The bread will be stale though. The river isn't far. Just through the trees a bit till we get to the Blades. It runs along that."

Silver's head was tilted again. Henry didn't realise it but he copied him for a moment as he looked Silver up and down. He was so interesting and mysterious and Henry wanted to know everything about him. It was frustrating not knowing. He hated that feeling. It was a feeling Henry had since his father disappeared.

"My mom would say my father left us. But I think something happened to him," Henry held a hand up to his mouth, "I don't know why I said that. I was just thinking about his disappearance. There's so much I don't know and there's so much I don't know about you."

Henry disappeared from the kitchen, leaving Silver to stand there with his mouth hanging open before reappearing again with a couple of backpacks. He opened one and set it on the counter.

"Here, stuff one of the pairs of clothes in here. Put the other in yours. I'll get the bread and conserve. You have a preference? I like strawberry myself. But my mom makes a great banana one. We got them in town last summer. A trade came in from the coast. Pretty rare my dad says. He likes to boast about the things he finds. I mean, he liked to…"

Henry snapped his mouth shut and disappeared down the stairs from the kitchen. He grabbed a candle holder on his way down and quickly lit it before he descended into darkness. The pantry was full of meats and other things the cold ground protected. Henry hated the cold. He much preferred the heat. He was miserable in winter. Even when his dad was around, he couldn't understand why his parents liked to go outside and throw snowballs or make shapes out of the snow.

"The snow is like whittling," Henry said aloud what his father would always say to him, "Probably why I wasn't good at that either."

When Henry returned upstairs, Silver was no longer in the kitchen. Henry peeked into the Great Hall and called for him but there was no answer. That's when he saw Silver out the windows heading down the steps towards the stump where Henry kept his own whittling.

Silver had both bags one on each shoulder and stopped at the stump and stared down at a single carving left on the stump with a small knife. He let the bags slide to the ground and knelt down. He went to reach for the carving but his fist reminded him to use his right. Henry watched it quietly as he slowly descended the steps. Silver touched the handle of the knife with a single finger before picking up the carving.

"It's going to be my mom," Henry spoke quietly as he approached, "My dad didn't get to finish it. So, I'm trying to. He told me all I have to do is picture whatever it is I want to see in the wood and then carve it. I try. I picture it. I just can't do it."

Silver nodded and put the carving back down. It was just a lump with barely formed shoulders. There were indents and cuts that Henry didn't want there.

"So many mistakes, but another thing my dad said was that mistakes can add character. He says that my favourite carvings of his are full of mistakes. He's never shown me where but he says they are there. I just see perfection and he says I'm just blinded by sentiment. I have them upstairs in my drawer if you want to see them. They're with my Tabs. I can show you them if you want."

Silver nodded and started walking through the yard. Henry picked up the knife and held it in his hands. He could see where the blade was dulling and the scratches in the handle but the knife was sentimental to him, so he couldn't understand what his father meant. Henry tucked the knife into the sash that tied the night clothes together. They hadn't bothered to change.

"No, we aren't going back to the garden. That's south. That's where Blackwood is and we aren't going there. It isn't safe. That's where my mom goes to get wolf pelts. One rotation, she even brought back a bear."

Henry looked to Silver as if to impress him but Silver just kept walking. Henry could tell that the silver-haired boy was listening from the expressions on his face. Sometimes the expressions just weren't what Henry was expecting or hoping.

"The Blades are to the east of here. Just through those trees. Not far. It's a beautiful field. You'll see. The river is nice, too. Crystal clear water. My mom goes this way when she needs certain petals for salves. My dad says the water that runs through here is the purest in all the continent. It's the best water I've seen. The one that runs along the community is murky and the one near town is even worse."

Henry took in a deep breath and willed himself to stop talking. They stepped through the black-barked trees and weaved around a cluster of bushes and shrubs. Silver kept going, listening to the birds in the distance that grew silent as they approached. Sometimes a few bushes would shuffle and Henry would point to a rabbit or a squirrel. Silver seemed to be absorbing it all in as he gazed at everything longingly.

"The trees are starting to thin out already. In a little bit you'll see Blades. It's one of my favourite places to go to. I think you'll like it as well."

Silver and Henry didn't have to veer as much around the trees. They were thinning out just as Henry explained it until Silver stepped out into a field where the grass grew up to his knees. Orange and yellow flowers popped up randomly with their petals spread out like fans.

"My dad said that the Blades is a battlefield of beauty. The grass are the swords of the earth while the flowers are their shields. He told me that my mom was born here."

Silver gave Henry a look of disbelief and Henry laughed, "I know, right? He was always sweet like that with her. I would always pretend to vomit, but I really liked it. They were good together. That's why I know he wouldn't just leave."

Silver tilted his head but Henry pressed on and started walking through the fields before stopping again, "I almost forgot. Silver, if you duck down into the grass and look beyond the blades of grass, you'll see something more."

Silver wrinkled his forehead and ducked down before popping back up with a grin. Henry laughed and ducked down himself. Little bushels of purple and blue flowers appeared everywhere. Their petals as small as moss.

Silver crawled over to where Henry was picking a handful and shoving it into his mouth. He tried to explain to Silver what he was doing but ended up spitting a few petals out of his mouth. Silver went to laugh but Henry shoved a handful into his mouth.

"Chew."

Silver chewed and his eyes lit up. It wasn't hard for his eyes to light up, Henry thought to himself. They were the brightest blue Henry had ever seen. He looked deep into his eyes as he watched Silver swallow the petals.

"Oh no. Don't eat them. Just chew. Tastes like honey, don't they? If you eat too much of them, you'll have trouble shitting later."

Silver spit out the rest.

"If my mom was here, she'd want the chewed-up petals. She can make a lotion with them but she'd need the sap out of them anyway. That's how I knew we could chew on them. They're a special treat. My mom calls them Fairy Moss. Only grows here in Blades. The lotion helps heal burns."

Silver brushed against something in the dirt and Henry leaned over to see. It was a large paw print as big as Silver's hand. Henry put a hand on Silver's arm.

"A dog? No, it's bigger than a dog. I don't think it's a wolf. They don't come this far out of Blackwood. If my mom would take me hunting, I could learn to track like she does."

Silver stood up and Henry joined him. The shadow of the

grass had blocked them from the sun so both of them put a hand over their eyes to shade from the glare. Henry looked at the clenched fist against Silver's forehead and sighed.

"Come on, the river is further through Blades. The field will dip down and the grass will shorten until we hit the riverbed. It's nice to lay there and let your feet dabble in the water. We can do that while eating our conserve and bread. I'm starving."

Silver nodded but kept looking around them as if expecting someone or something.

"Don't worry about the pawprint. Sometimes the community can travel this way. They have pets like I said. Some have dogs, too. My mom says no animal should be a pet unless it chooses to be one. I don't think that's real. No animal is going to want to live with a human."

They waded through the long grass and stopped to smell the Shields every now and then. The sky was cloudless and a soft breeze tickled the tops of the blades. By the time they had reached the riverbed, Henry had taken off his shirt and dropped it just out of reach of the water. Silver got down on his knees and took handfuls of the water to drink. His eyes rolled in the back of his head.

"It's good, aye?" Henry grinned.

Silver nodded and pulled off his shirt first and just as suddenly his pants. Henry flinched and quickly looked away until he heard a loud splash and Silver was wading out into the middle of the river. The current slowly took him further downstream until he started to swim back. Henry pulled out some balms his mother had created and held one up in the air.

"Silver!" Henry called, "Come use this! My mom made it to help wash!"

Silver slowly stepped out of the water again and walked towards Henry unabashed. The balm smelt like Fairy Moss. The boys took a moment to enjoy the scent before Silver started to rub himself with it. Henry turned away and dropped his pants and walked to the water's edge with his balm. He was about halfway in before he started to wash himself. His back was still to Silver.

"My mom won't teach me how to make these either!" Henry called back to Silver, "I asked her if it was because it was as dangerous as Blackwood! She wanted to laugh. I could see it but she yelled at me instead!"

Henry turned around to an empty riverbed. Their clothes were still piled up near their bags but Silver was nowhere in sight. Henry took a few steps towards the shore before the water in front of him exploded and Silver lurched out and tackled Henry into the water. They writhed around together until both of them sputtered up and Henry made his escape to the shoreline. He laughed all the way.

The sun warmed Henry quickly as he lay in the grass at the edge of Blades. He used his hands as a pillow and watched Silver hover over him and join him at his side.

"I'll get you for that," Henry said quietly, turning his head towards Silver.

Silver was on his belly propping himself up with his elbows and grinning from ear to ear. His seashell chain swung back and forth against him.

"You shouldn't have gone into the water with that. It

might have slipped off."

Silver looked down at the pendant and lifted it up with his right hand. His left hand still held whatever it was he was desperate to keep on his person. Silver looked at the seashell as if it were a stranger.

"Silver," Henry said, shifting his body to be on his belly, too, "are you from around here?"

Silver shrugged.

"I don't think you are. Do you know where you got that necklace?"

Silver shrugged again.

Henry thought for a moment and gasped, "Silver, do you even know who you are?"

Silver looked up from the seashell and into Henry's eyes. Water drowned his pupils before he shook his head slowly. They laid there in silence until the sun had dried them and their bellies growled in protest.

"Let's get dressed and eat," Henry finally said. Silver nodded and followed Henry to the bags and they each pulled out their clothes and put them on. They were comfortable clothes enough to keep cool during the spring days but dry and warm when it rained.

"My mom says it rained the day that she found you," Henry said after swallowing a large bite of bread he had dipped into the strawberry conserve. "I was whittling when she went out. We had just gotten into an argument. It didn't rain at the house. The sky was blue. Do you remember it raining?"

Silver nodded, already finishing his bread and a portion of the conserve.

Henry laughed, "I should have fed you earlier. I'm sorry. When we get back to the house, we'll have lunch. I can show you how not to whittle. Or we can play Tabs!"

Silver nodded to everything and stood up and put the strap of his bag on his shoulder. The river eased them with its song as it flowed soft towards Blackwood. Across the river was more of the Blades as it spread unending towards the east. The north held deeper and higher Lakewood Trees and the horizon hinted to three mountain peaks in the distance. Henry pointed to the third and told him that that's where the river started from.

"My dad says the river had many names, but this part he says is River's Song."

Silver pointed across the river where Blades continued.

"I haven't crossed the river. As you can see the river gets pretty deep and I can't swim. I guess you can."

Silver looked surprised, almost startled.

"There are a lot of things my parents said they'd teach me that they haven't. Everything stopped when my dad left."

Silver put his right arm around Henry's shoulder and gazed over the river.

"My mom says the Blades beyond the river is a bit more dangerous. My mom went once and she said the grass grew so tall that she honestly thought she was shrinking.

I overheard her tell my dad that there were strange people that lived within the blades and had not seen the sun. Their eyes were as white as snow."

Silver shivered but then pointed south to where River's Song ended up disappearing into Lakewood Trees.

"That's Blackwood. The trees grow as thick as the grass in Blades. They grow taller and taller the further south you travel until they're so tall it blocks out the sun entirely and all it does is rain. The deeper you go the greater the beasts. As I said, my mom brought home a bear once. It's the largest thing she has brought home and even then, I overheard her tell my dad that it almost killed her."

Silver turned and walked up the riverbed and towards the Blades that they had come from. The horizon was hidden behind the trees and the sun hovered directly overhead of them.

"We're going to get hungry pretty quickly," Henry added, "It's midday. There's some more stew from last night we can have."

Silver nodded and pointed towards the west and waved his hand.

"Beyond our home there's a trail that leads out in the community. Not many people live there but they're a nice folk. They keep to themselves mostly. They'll trade with us and other communities but refuse to enter town. Further along the trail is Lakewood. The town claims all these lands except ours. My mom and dad made a deal with them. I'm not sure what but they got this part of Lakewood Trees. I've never been to town but I've been to the community a lot. They're mostly quiet, almost like you."

They started towards the Blades when a section of the grass shook and a low growl came out of them. Henry shifted backwards and slowly looked at Silver, who also took a step back.

Henry was scared but he didn't want to be. This area was safe. It had to be a dog or something. None of the wilds from Blackwood ever stepped near their home.

"Silver, it's okay, it has to be—" Henry said, reaching a hand out to him.

The grass shook violently before a large dark shape leapt out and slammed into Silver. Both of them went rolling into the riverbed. Henry felt weak in the knees as the form darted a few feet away from Silver and growled again. It was a wolf. He had seen one brought home before. He had helped skin it. He knew how to make meals and clothes and other things from its parts but this wolf was alive and real and moving. Its eyes held a spark of life Henry had not seen before and the mouth seemed much more dangerous here on the riverbed.

Henry pulled out his whittling knife and shouted, "Silver, are you okay?"

Silver was struggling to get back to his feet. He seemed disorientated, looking around as if he didn't know where he was. His eyes just kept glancing at the wolf and the area around him.

The wolf crouched again and Henry understood somehow that it meant to leap at Silver once again. Henry couldn't let that happen. He was supposed to be looking after Silver, so Henry tried to growl as well. It sounded more like a gargled shout before he ran forward with a fierce speed and slashed at the wolf with the small blade. It hissed across the wolf's flank and left a red streak. With that same speed, Henry darted to Silver's side and perched against the ground with one hand supporting him up and the other holding the knife in front of him. He tried to growl again and imagined if the wolf could laugh it would.

The wolf snarled, showing a glint of something between its teeth. Henry gasped and looked to Silver who was still looking around. In the teeth of the wolf was Silver's seashell pendant. Henry darted forward to try and get it back but the wolf spun around quickly and ran southward along the riverbank before disappearing. Henry took a moment, still propped on the ground again, to catch a breath. He dropped his head and inhaled deeply. His eyes dropped to the smooth stones that gathered around parts of the river. Amongst the stones was a key, oddly carved from metal. It was uniquely made with one single tooth to fit in a lock and a perfect circle for its eye. Henry picked it up and turned to Silver.

Silver's shoulders were heaving as he stared at the key in Henry's hand. His eyes flashed silver like his hair and he flashed his teeth before running at Henry and screaming,

"MINE!"

Into Blackwood

Rosie leaned against one of the Lakewood Trees listening to Henry calling after her. She closed her eyes and listened to the frustration in his voice. He had a right to be and she knew it. If it wasn't for the note jammed into her pocket, she might have surrendered and brought them along. It would have given her time to interrogate Silver. What was a boy dressed up like him doing way out here? Why was his hair silver? Why couldn't he speak? What was around his neck and in his hand that he was so guarded with? She stood there until Henry fell silent and heard him walk away.

"Well, Patrick, you, hair from a Treenut sac," Rosie muttered, pushing herself away from the black tree and heading deeper into the forest that practically surrounded her home, "You really did it this time. First you walk out. Then you write me a letter rotations later."

Usually she was careful with the sound of her steps through the forest. Even though there were no savage creatures that lived amongst these trees. Silent. Watchful. But also, careful not to trudge along important herbs that could be useful.

"Dearest Rosie?" she sneered, "Is that how you address me? The last time we spoke your boy was still a boy. Now he's becoming a man. And worse for it, too, because, you rat, I have no clue how to take over from where you left off..."

She broke free from the Lakewood Trees for only a moment. There was a small clearing they had cut the trees from. Even the saplings they replanted were in their teenage rotations. Patrick had insisted they grew them in a particular pattern, even though she had no clue what that pattern was. It all looked random to her.

She stood in the clearing. It used to give her comfort. Then he left and it became a place of waiting. She grew mushrooms soon after. So instead of just another reminder of what she no longer had, the place held purpose.

"I am pleased you received my gift the other day," she muttered, gathering a few large mushrooms for her satchel and being careful not to step on the plethora of shrooms growing beneath and around the base of each tree. "What gift? The note isn't old. Parchment fresh. Ink legible. It was written a few days ago. So, sac, you're a few days away and couldn't hand deliver your message yourself? Too scared to face me, sac?"

Rosie squeezed the mushroom in her hand to pulp, "Well, damn."

She put it in her satchel anyway. She repeated the line in the letter. She knew it off by heart. She had read it a hundred times during the night. She had slept barely a wink and even in her dreams she had the words swimming around her. The clearing disappeared quickly as she stepped beyond the Lakewood Trees. She'd reach the Blackwood by the time the sun was at its highest.

"We have much to discuss," she hissed and she leapt over a fallen tree. She wondered for only a moment what might have caused that tree to fall before returning to the letter. "Yes, sac, we do have a lot to discuss. Let's talk about the son you left behind. The promises you broke. The fact that I'm the one that will come back to this tree and make it our firewood. How the garden is slowly falling apart because I'm doing your workload too."

She pushed through the incline of the hill that gradually appeared before her. At one point, she needed to use the trees as leverage before the landscape smoothed again. "We have much to discuss? Oh, so when it's convenient for you, you mean? Well, what could you possibly want to talk about? How about you tell me why you left, sac?"

She stopped. The birds were silent. The Lakewood Trees blocked out any possible breeze. The sunlight seemed to find a way still but even that was growing dim. She needed to pay attention now. But first, she'd have to learn how to breathe again.

Her muscles tensed and she so badly wanted to hit a tree, but it would be nowhere near as satisfying as Patrick's face. She hated him.

"I hate you," she muttered and lifted a thick finger to wipe a tear away, "I hate that you make me cry. I hate that I have no idea how to raise our son the way you wanted. I hate that I can't spend the day in my garden or discover new herbs and create new salves. I hate our stupid fight because you wanted to leave our home. I hate that—"

She choked on her words and slammed her fist into the tree over and over again, "I hate that I still love you."

"Meet me at Moon's Edge in 200 days. No sooner. No later," she whispered until she hit the tree one more time

with the side of her arm this time and stood upright,
"No. No, you little sac, you don't get to command me.
You never could. Meet you? No, you'll meet us. We won't
come. You'll come. Begging. Explaining. Looking both of
us in the eye until your neck aches from gazing up at us.
Yes, Patrick, your son has grown. I've grown. You don't get
to command anyone…not after all these rotations of the
moon."

She pushed off of the tree and stomped forward. Her unruly
hair whipped around her face and she picked up speed. In
a blink of an eye, Rosie sprinted through the trees. Her
feet echoed around her and she knew it wasn't wise to do
but she had to. She had to run off the ache the words had
caused. She wasn't prepared to give up Lakewood so many
rotations ago for Moon's Edge. She wasn't about to now
over a letter given to her by a little old man.

She ran until the sun was at its highest. She could tell
from the streams of light that poured into the forest. She
could have run for ages after but she had regained her
senses and froze for a moment. She wondered how much
foliage she destroyed in her tantrum, how many animals
she frightened away or how much closer she had come to
Blackwood and into immediate danger without realising
it.

The trees stood like tall towers around her. Unmoving and
unyielding the sky above her. In the distance, she could
see the darkness calling to her. The flora around her grew
wild and unruly. She imagined the treasure trove of plants
she could harvest from beneath the sea of green. Thunder
echoed across the area and Rosie swore and looked
upwards.

"Am I going to find another silver haired child?"

She swallowed her words as the thunder grew louder and she hugged herself up to the nearest tree. It wasn't thunder she was hearing but a type of stampede. Something from the darkness ahead was running towards her. Heaps of something.

She put her back to the tree and pulled her feet close. She clasped her hands onto the black bark and watched intently at the shadows ahead until they took shape.

"Oh, sac," she swore before slipping her way around the tree until she was facing away from the impending trample.

She felt the tree she dug her fingers into shake with the ground as the stampede reached them. Tears filled her eyes as her nose twitched and itched. She so badly wanted to let go of the tree and run. Blinking away the tears, she saw them pass as their shoulders slammed into a few of the trees. Rosie worried hers would be uprooted.

They were Entmen. Mostly talked about in legends. Entmen stood tall and still like the trees. Grew leaves and branches like the trees, but their red eyes are what gave them away. Yes, she had seen them before, but not here. For her, their eyes always gave them away. They were bright and unblinking. They were the watchers of Blackwood. The legends told that a group of aging roamers travelled into the Blackwood and decided to set up their final resting places within the mist-filled forest. Slowly the Blackwood consumed them, creating the tree-like creatures that stood like sentries amongst the trees. Rosie had never seen them on the move. She had only seen a couple in passing as she hunted. She knew how to read their omens. If more than one Entmen were gathered together, a traveller must not pass. There were stories of people getting ripped apart by an Entmen and never seen again, but Rosie believed they were just tales to scare the children from exploring the dangerous woods. The Entmen were gentle creatures who merely warned.

Or ran apparently, right passed Rosie and towards the northeast. She watched the Entmen barrel through, their roots clawing at the ground in front of them and behind them as they moved. Their tree bodies swaying their branches like running arms. Her nose twitched. Were they running to or from something?

As soon as the ground stopped shaking and the Entmen disappeared beyond the real Lakewood Trees, Rosie stepped away from the tree and stood there for a moment. Her nose was still bothering her and she wasn't about to ignore her intuition. But she had to understand what had just happened. If they were running to something, Rosie should follow and see what omen they warned, but if they were running from something, Rosie had to go see for the same reason.

"In all my rotations living here, you haven't left your home. Why now?" Rosie scratched her chin and turned towards the direction of Blackwood. "Let's see what's there now."

As she walked past a few of the trees, one of them blinked at her and Rosie froze. Its red eyes stared at her coldly. Rosie could see it breathing. The bark expanded every so often. She kept eye contact with the Entmen and bowed her head a bit.

"I am just here to hunt, Entmen, just as I have done before. But if I am not to enter Blackwood today, I can go home now."

A branch lowered from somewhere above and revealed a tip with smaller branches with about 8 fingers. All of them curled up except for one, which pointed more towards the southwest.

"Want me to stay away, Entmen?" Another branch came down and nudged her towards the area and Rosie nodded, "No, you want me to go there."

The Entmen turned away from her and that's when she saw a deep gash in the back of it. Red sap-like blood seeped down it as it moved further away from her. She went to grab her satchel and chase after it but she stopped.

"An Entmen tells you to go, you don't ignore them," she warned herself.

She followed the direction the Entmen had indicated and noticed a light mist was starting to form on the forest walls. She didn't need her nose to tell her something was wrong. She had not passed through to Blackwood yet. The mists never passed beyond its borders and now they were crawling their way through the Lakewood Trees.

She pulled the bow and an arrow from the quiver that she had strapped to her back. She nocked an arrow and held her bow tightly in her ebony hands as she held it up in front of her and slowly made her way forward. She looked for the signs that she had stepped over into Blackwood. The foliage would be a darker green and further into the depths she went, it would soon be as black as the bark of the trees. The mist would start to deepen until it completely filled the trees. All light would be banished by the jagged branches and the large thorns that began to grow from the body of each tree. Patrick only ever cut one tree down but it was a hollowed tree filled with maggots and sludge.

Rosie sidestepped a raspberry bush that had quite a few ripe ones. Momentarily distracted, she only just jumped out of the way as a large shape burst towards her but was still distracted enough to lose her bow and arrow. She rolled twice before getting back up to her hands and feet and darted her eyes around her. A low growl almost laughed at her from behind and she ducked and rolled so that she could spin around with a dagger in her hand.

The hind end of a wolf disappeared behind a few trees. She still hadn't seen signs she was in Blackwood. This wolf was out of bounds and Rosie couldn't understand why. The Entmen would not run from such a native creature to Blackwood.

She slowly used her leg muscles to stand up. Her right hand outstretched with the silver hilted dagger. Her left hand balanced her. She allowed her eyes to survey the ground around her until her peripheral spotted her bow. She hoped her little roll around the forest didn't damage the arrows in her quiver.

Side step by side step, she made her way over to her bow. A snarl came from her left and she spun. The wolf was circling her to try and confuse her. Rosie grinned.

"Try harder, wolf."

She ducked behind a tree quickly and hugged it with her left arm as she swung the dagger down and pointed it offhand. Her left hand sunk into a mound of oozing sap and she leaned back to gaze up into sad, red eyes. She let her eyes rest there for a moment before looking over the tree. It had slash marks up and down its side. She pulled away her hand as the sap stubbornly clung to it. Movement from her side startled her to jump back as the wolf dived through. Claw marks appeared along the front of the Entmen and the forest filled with a low groan.

Rosie hissed and screamed out into the tears, "Here I am, wolf! You want me. Come and have me!"

A wolf stepped out between two trees and snarled, showing long fangs. Rosie gasped at the sight of long spikes growing out of its spine. She had seen nothing like this wolf. It took a few more steps towards her as it howled a low taunt and started to walk towards her left. She switched her dagger and the wolf turned towards the right. It knew! Its fur didn't seem as shiny and alive. She would not have hunted this wolf normally. Its skin would not fetch a price and it looked sickly, not to mention the spikes coming out of its back. Rosie carefully slid off her satchel and sat it at the foot of the Entmen.

"Hold this," she hissed and roared as the wolf finally took a leap at her. They both went flying backwards with Rosie pounding a fist into the side of the wolf with one hand and stabbing it with her dagger in the other. The thick leather hide she wore under her clothes barely kept the claws from digging into her. She hissed between clench teeth as she took her fist and opened it to find one of the spikes and pull at it. It seemed to be bone and she heard a crunch as they tumbled over the forest floor until finally all was quiet.

The Entmen tilted against another tree and used its branches to prop itself up as the slashes up and down its body oozed with sap. Its red eyes weren't as vibrant but it made its way over to the heap that was the wolf on top of Rosie. As soon as it was within reach, the Entmen brought a branch down and twisted around the wolf before hurdling it through some trees and cracking it against a trunk. It gazed down at the motionless woman.

"Lady Edwards?" a voice emanated out of the Entmen like its slow, bleeding sap.

Rosie snapped her eyes open and looked up at the fading red eyes of the Entmen and thought to herself, "What is with this lady crap all of a sudden?"

She sat up as a branch handed her a satchel and the other a bow, "Thank you. I didn't know Entmen could speak."

The branches helped her up despite the fact that others struggled to keep the tree standing. "I'm starting to think that collapsed tree I passed might have been one of you."

"Warning," a low but deliberate voice waned.

"Let me help you," Rosie immediately said as she put her bow away and opened her satchel, "In the garden, the Moongrove trees struggled to grow at first. A huge storm came and damaged their luminescent bark. Within days I watched the trees repair the damage and grow stronger because of it. That's when I learnt if I cut away its branches they grew back bigger and the trunk stronger."

The Entmen moved away from Rosie until she laughed and held out a hand covered in salve, "Oh I won't be cutting away your branches, Entmen. I just learnt that if I peeled off their bark and shredded it, I could make a mixture that helps heal plants." She spread the salve over some of the wounds, "What are these wolves and why are they attacking you?"

The Entmen's eyes were closed as the salve almost healed the slashes instantly to even Rosie's surprise. When it reopened their eyes, the red seemed brighter and the whole tree shuddered, "We watch. They find."

"I can understand you watching Blackwood. But what are these spiked wolves trying to find?"

"Us."

"They were hunting the Entmen in Blackwood. They could sense you and were trying to kill you."

The tree wavered front and back a bit which led Rosie to believe it was a nod.

"But why?" Rosie asked as she continued to stuff the salve into the rest of the wounds. If she came across another Entmen, she wouldn't have enough of the salve for them. "I guess that's part of the mystery. Like the mist. Like Silver."

The Entmen stood on its own and its red eyes flashed, "Thank you, Lady Edwards."

"You really need to stop calling me that," her eyes widened, "but how do you know me?"

"We watch."

Rosie wiped her hands on her hips and packed away her satchel and returned it to her shoulder. "If I go into Blackwood, are there more of these spiked wolves?"

"All over."

Rosie slowly walked over to the carcass of the one they had just killed, "Look at these spikes. I tried to snap one off but they're like iron. The teeth are larger and longer too. I have never seen them before. I mean, I've seen wolves but not these."

"All wolves."

Rosie looked up to the Entmen who had followed,

"They've turned to this?"

The Entmen wavered front and back, "North not safe. We cannot watch."

"And the mist travelling beyond Blackwood means something too. Everything the Entmen were holding back will be free to travel south. And south just happens to be my home."

"Yes."

"What will you do, Entmen?"

"East. We watch."

"You're going to think I'm crazy, Entmen, but I'm going into Blackwood." She turned south and looked beyond the trees into the darkness, "I need to see for myself. If things are going to get so bad I can't hunt, that's going to cause a food shortage."

She turned back around only to find the Entmen slowly walking northeast and then blending with the trees. She shrugged and walked forward, but not as foolishly as she had done before. Her travel was delicate this time. She moved from tree to tree and at times stayed in one place and listened. One of the spiked wolves was enough. She wasn't about to fight a whole pack.

She rubbed her nose and took in a deep breath as the plants around her started to darken. The trees thinned but grew thorns and the mist was lifted quickly up to her hips. Blackwood would soon slope down into a wide valley where the trees would thin out, but the beasts roamed as freely as the mist, which didn't seem to bother them.

At the height of the decline, she could see over the valley. The tips of the thorned Blackwood trees peeked out like sharks of the mist. Beneath the sea of moisture lay bears and wolves as they hunted each other or the other fauna that thrived in the gloom. When Patrick first brought her there, she always wondered why the deer thrived in the valley. She accused the wolves of finishing them off.

"Let me put it this way," he had said to her on a bluff they had found near the edge of the valley. Rosie started walking slowly to it as his words echoed within her head, "Each creature in Blackwood is like a root to a tree. The roots don't strangle each other out. They all know that with each root the tree survives. They coexist and take the nutrients when they need it."

"You're stretching," Rosie dared to whisper aloud what she had said to him until he stretched out and took her beneath the stars right on that bluff. A part of her didn't want to return there, but she knew it was the safest place. She wasn't going to see much of Blackwood anyway. She never did with the fog. It was all about finding spots to set up camp and stay in until eventually the prey came to them.

The bluff's location was marked by symbols drawn into the thorned trees. It was of a rose, a flower Patrick mistakenly thought she was named after. If it wasn't before, it was now. She weaved through the trees. They had travelled this way enough throughout the rotations so there was a path now. Those who dared to travel to the Blackwood could easily be led to the bluff, but they didn't care. It was better than finding their bodies spread throughout the valley after being eaten. They found the bluff by accident after Patrick sprained his ankle trying to scale the cliffs of the valley above. Rosie watched as he tried to act like a circus performer and then fall over the edge into the valley below. She had always been more serious between the two and she made that very clear when she scaled the cliff face down to the bluff and found Patrick still alive nursing a sore ankle.

Rosie reached the point above the valley by nightfall. She could find the crevices blind if she had to. It used to be a rope that was tied to a post but that became too dangerous when the rope broke and there was no way up. So, Rosie had dug in small crevices into the sides to climb their way up. Eventually Patrick added his craft and soon there was a safe and secure ladder leading down to the bluff. Small walls were built with circular windows that could be opened and closed and a balcony that could be used as a perch to hunt prey down below.

She lit up the torches along the walls and it crackled and hissed. The mist that had swallowed the hut whole dissipated. It was a few dried herbs she had mixed together that when burnt sucked the moisture of the mist right out of the air. The only downside was dry eyes, throat and nose, but it made things clearer. She'd take an extra torch back with her. She hadn't planned on actually coming to Blackwood when she told Henry. It was out of anger and a reaction to the letter. She panicked for a moment and patted her pocket until she found it. A part of her wanted to burn it or tear it up and throw it away but her panic surprised herself.

Rosie looked around the room. Everything reminded her of Patrick. The chair for two he made. The bed frame. The mid-sized table in front of the chair. The cupboard. The chest. She sighed and walked out into the balcony and leaned on the railing and gazed down into the valley. She knew she wouldn't see anything. It was absolutely dark.

She wondered what Henry was doing and if he was taking care of the mysterious Silver.

Above the bluff on the cliff's edge making the shape of the valley she heard them. It sounded like hundreds of howls and snarls. She looked up into the darkness where the makeshift ladder would be that led down into the small entrance of the hut. Rocks and dirt fell into the light and onto the roof where it slid into the balcony.

"No," she hissed," they can't be."

She rushed back into the hut and ran to the entrance where the door stood collecting dust. She had made fun of Patrick for making it but he insisted.

"You'll never know when you'll need safety in solitude," he had said and Rosie cursed him for being right again. She pulled at the door but it was stuck. Outside the entrance she could see more rocks and dirt fall and the howls and snarls get closer. The door had never been closed. The hinges screamed as the door dug against the floor as she slammed it shut and brought down the barricade. Something landed on the other side of it and the whole door shuddered. She backed away, shaking her head.

"Wolves can't climb down like that," she whispered as the torches around her flickered with her sudden moments. That's when the roof started banging as if a couple of large things landed on top. She heard scuttling across the roof top and she turned to the balcony door. It, too, had a door for it. She bolted across the small area and slammed the door just as the creatures landed on the balcony.

"Spiked wolves can," she slid the barricade down and backed away till she was in the middle of the hut. The windows were already clasped closed and the doors rattled as the beasts tried to make their way through. "This was a bad idea."

Rosie watched both doors as they rattled and thumped each time the beasts jumped on them. Sometimes the roof would have more bangs as more leapt off of the ladder onto the hut. Wolves that could take a ladder wasn't something Rosie thought she'd ever see. These wolves had an intelligence beyond their natural one, which was already clever enough.

"The doors will hold," she said aloud and the pounding stopped. They were listening. She wondered if they understood what she was saying. She moved slowly to the small circular windows that were merely used for ventilation and light. They were not large enough for even a child to crawl through. She hadn't opened them in ages, so they'd probably be a struggle to open. Rosie tapped the latch of one of the four windows and the latch rattled as barking and growls thumped from the other side. They could probably sense her. Two of the windows were on either side of the balcony. One faced outward to the valley. There was no ledge or perch for that window. She moved towards it and tapped the latch of this one. There was running along the roof and terrible scratches coming from the wall before this window's latch rattle as well.

"So, you can climb along walls like a spider," Rosie said, replacing one of the torches that was dimming. The chest held a few dozen more. She'd last till the morning if she needed to. She just couldn't stay in there forever. She only had enough food and water for a couple of days. She listened to all the noises around her. One was on the side of the hut trying to claw its way in. There were two in the balcony that she had seen leap down to her. A couple more were still on the roof and at least one was at the entrance.

Rosie suddenly thought of the Entmen and the deep gashes along their sides. These spiked wolves could cause a lot of damage to the wooden construct around her.

"Fine. I have a shorter amount of time in here than I realise."

The balcony door cracked and she could see a long claw jut through. It disappeared and then there was another crack and a few more claws made their way through. Rosie pulled out her dagger in her offhand and reached for one of Patrick's tools. It was a thick axe he had created to help him improve the hut. Patrick always had ideas to improve the house and the hut didn't escape his scrutiny. It took every ounce of her patience and nerve to prevent Patrick from adding on an attic to the house or a sub-basement to the food cellar they already had. Even with the hut, he wanted to make more entry points and exits.

"I could turn the ladder into a pulley system," Patrick had said one night at the hut. Both of them were sprawled out on a large wolf skin. "Hold a handle at the top and it lowers us down slowly from the lesser weight on the other side."

"That would get us down," Rosie muttered to herself as she stared at the old dusty wolf skin lying on the middle of the floor. "How would we get out?"

Rosie pulled away the wolf skin and grinned, "Irony." She snuffed out all the torches.

The mist took over the bluff within moments and it seemed to activate the spiked spider wolves in a frenzy.

Within moments the balcony door shattered and two of the wolves came in and tore apart the place to get to Rosie. The ones on the roof clambered over each other and leapt down onto the balcony to join the others. The entrance door was soon obliterated and the window facing the wall began to show cracks. The bluff hideaway was lost.

Rosie slid a few feet down a makeshift chute until she landed on a smaller balcony further down the valley underneath the bluff. Pulling away the wolf skin had revealed a trap door and an idea Patrick had that he obviously had completed.

"You clever sac," she dared to say aloud as if Patrick could hear it. She listened to the sound of the destruction of the hut somewhere above her in the dark mist. The bluff was the first place she looked to find Patrick after he disappeared. He had been there. The torches were lit when she arrived. Food was left half eaten on the table as well as a spilt drink. She believed he had heard her coming and fled further. For days she went from hideaway to hideaway in the Blackwood, but the bluff was the only place she found clues of his departure. Doubt started to sink in. Perhaps he had died in the Blackwood. Foolish in his anger. But the letter in the pocket confirmed it. He had just left. "So, when you went off hunting alone in the Blackwood and didn't want me to come, you weren't just proving yourself. You were building things like this."

She wasn't grateful like she knew she should be. She wanted to punch him square in the jaw and call him a liar. She wanted to follow that up with a knee to the gut and tell him that's how wrenching it felt to watch their son fall asleep crying in her arms. And lastly, she'd upper cut directly into his groin to show him just how much of a Treenut sac he truly was now.

A curled-up rope ladder sat on the end of the small balcony. She kicked it and watched it disappear down into the dark mist below. She watched as a corner of the ladder sparked against the edge of a railing and a small trail of rope ignited. The mist around the rope hissed away as the small fire travelled along the rope and back up to the bluff. Rosie watched in interest.

"Patrick, what did you do?" her eyes followed it up. It was causing all mist to retreat on its way up as it disappeared over the ledge.

An eerie silence followed. The destruction up above ceased and the howls and snarls of the beasts fell mute.

BOOM!

Rosie flew backwards off of the balcony and tumbled in the air before she stretched out her hand and luckily found the ladder. Her shoulder screamed at her as it felt like a knife entered her. She found her footing and had her left hand hold her place as the right arm dangled painfully. She looked up to see a few beasts fall off the bluff in a blaze of glory. The hideaway was completely in flames and all mist retreated into the distance. She'd be able to find her way home with no problems. The light would keep the mist at bay and hopefully attract so much attention, she'd be able to slip out of Blackwood unfollowed.

She made her way slowly down and looked up at the bluff one last time. It seemed to say goodbye to her. She could easily return if she wanted. Rebuild. It was a great spot, but there was something about these flames that told her that's not what she would be doing. She nodded her head and slowly made her face to the base of the valley and slammed her arm into the stone wall. There was a click and the stabbing pain subsided. She blinked rapidly for a few moments. Not a sound escaped her lips. She was done playing now. It was time for a silent retreat home. If Blackwood wasn't safe before, it was impossible now. Not alone anyway. They'd have to hope that by the time their food reserve ran out, things would change. She'd seek the closest community for guidance later.

A spiked spider wolf landed behind her in a heap. Its body still sizzling from the fire. She wanted to inspect it a bit more, try and understand where it might have come from but howls in the distance told her that would be foolish. She would not be getting answers that night. Besides, travelling in Blackwood during this time would only be permissible with the bluff fire. She wasn't sure how long it would last. It was still blazing strong. She still had her dagger, but the axe had been lost along the way. She reached back and checked her quiver with her bow and arrows. It seemed to be alright. Her satchel was tapping against her hip as she pushed herself up the incline until she was at the edge of Blackwood once more. A loud crack echoed from deep beyond the valley. It made her turn one last time. The fire had spread the mist quite a ways. For the first time the moon and the stars were able to bring light to it. This was certainly going to bring attention. In the far-off distance Rosie saw the peaks of trees disappear as the echoes of a loud crack reached her. Something was coming and it was large. Howls of wolves responded to the snaps of the trees. A dark shadow loomed over the horizon. Rosie clenched her fists and willed herself to turn and run. She lit a torch she had stuffed in her satchel. The torch was meant to last longer. The cloth that wrapped around it had been soaked in a special salve that red its flame slowly but still allowed it to light her way.

She reached her mushroom clearing in record time and took a moment to rest there as the torch went out. She didn't need it. She could walk through Lakewood Trees blind from here on out until the Moongrove tree became a beacon for her. Something inside of her willed her forward. The feeling was unfamiliar to her. Usually it was the other way around. She had the ache to get lost in the trees as she harvested and hunted and avoid the emptiness the house seemed to give her. But now, she wanted to burst through the door and see Henry and Silver safely inside.

By the time the Moongrove tree's leaves illuminated in the distance, hours had passed and Rosie was finally feeling the waves of exhaustion. It didn't stop her stride. She kept it constant. She willed the speed out of her as she crossed the seasons of her garden and burst through the backdoor like she had imagined. The house was dark and silent, as it always was at this time of night. She closed the backdoor and dropped her quiver against the wall beside it. Her satchel found its home on a hook in the Great Hall. She made her way upstairs and entered the small hallways that separated their bedrooms.

Henry's door was open and the beds were bare. She took a giant step inside and looked around. The room was empty.

"Henry?" Rosie called as she stepped back out of his room and went to check hers. They shouldn't be in there but she did have the largest bed. Perhaps they were sleeping there. It wouldn't be the first time she'd have to kick Henry out of this room.

But her room was empty as well and by the time she was back downstairs and even searched the newly named Cot Cage, Rosie's heart was in her throat.

She stepped out of the front door and grabbed an empty torch that rested in its socket. She lit it and closed the door behind her before stepping onto the stairs leading down to the grassy area. She could see that the whittling stump was empty but she walked over to it anyway.

"Henry?! Silver?!" she yelled as loud as she could. Henry wasn't one for camping out but perhaps Silver convinced him.

"Or…" she said aloud but stopped herself. She didn't want to think about the other. That she didn't know a thing about Silver. Perhaps someone had come looking for him. Or that the spiked spider wolves had made their way here, though she lost all trails and sounds from them back at the bluff. The fire had done its job.

She was just about to turn back to the house when two shapes stepped into the range of light from the torch. They were coming from the east where the Blades grew and beyond that River's Song. Silver and Henry both looked as if they had been in a fight. Both boys had black eyes and bloodied lips. Their clothes were torn and muddy. Unsalvageable from the looks of them. Silver was looking at Henry's face as they walked. Rosie wasn't sure if it was a look of worry or guilt but she started to scratch at her nose. Something wasn't right. Henry looked up at her and as soon as he saw her he tried to run, even push away at Silver, but something was wrong with his right leg. She walked over to them and stabbed the torch into the ground and, still kneeling, reached for her son.

Henry fell into her and sobbed into her shoulder. She held him tight. Her eyes met with Silver, "Shhh. Henry, it's alright. What happened?"

Henry tried to speak but the tears were making it impossible for her to understand so she just held him. She didn't know what else she should be doing. Should she pull him away from her? Tell him to calm down. Grow up and explain why they were out so late. Is that what Henry needed? Or should she keep holding him and try to find answers from the mute silver-haired boy whose eyes were a hauntingly pale blue?

Silver opened his mouth but chose to close it again. He held out his fist instead. The one with the key in it and held it open. Rosie could barely make the details out but she understood that it was a key. Was that what he was holding this entire time and why was he showing it to her now?

Silver looked around and pointed to the house. Rosie followed his finger with her eyes and nodded, "Yes, let's take this inside. I have a lot to tell you. Blackwood isn't safe."

Henry seemed to sober up some and pushed himself away and wiped the tears from his eyes. He looked down at his mom, "There was a wolf at River's Song. It tried to kill us. It had…it had…these…"

"Spikes?" Rosie finished for him and he nodded, "Coming out of its spine?"

Silver walked past them, picking the torch up along the way, towards the porch. He waved for them to follow.

"Let's get inside," she stood up and followed Silver but when she stepped up onto the porch she realised Henry didn't follow. He was still standing in the shadows near the whittling stump. She snatched the torch from Silver and held it out and over her, "Henry, come on."

"I don't know if it's safe!" Henry called, his silhouette sending a chill down the bridge of Rosie's nose.

"Safe? In the house? From what?"

"Him."

Rosie turned around to the front door where Silver stood. His hand outstretched again showing his key, "I'm sorry, but it's mine."

Rosie's eyes widened, "You little sac."

The Raven in the Well

The Great Hall flickered with the blaze of the fireplace. For a moment, only the sound of crackling wood filled the room. Shadows danced behind the unfinished wooden carvings standing on the mantle. Silver sat at the large table. Rosie was to his left staring at him intently. He could feel the heat of her gaze. His silvery eyes stared across the table at Henry, who in turn was avoiding his gaze and looking to his mother. Rosie rapped her knuckles on the table but Silver refused to end his gaze.

"Are you listening, boy? You can talk, so how about you tell me what's been going on and who you are."

Silver's whole body twitched. He could hear the frustration in her voice and every part of him wanted to answer, but his eyes narrowed as his hand clutched the key nestled against his chest. His other arm cradled it like a baby.

Henry's eyes tried to stay intently on his mother but despite his will, they darted over to Silver.

Silver's lips parted at once, "I'm sorry."

Henry's eyes danced between the two for a moment, subconsciously rubbing at some of his wounds on his shoulder. "You bit me."

Rosie's eyes widened and looked over her son. He looked as if he had been dragged through the dirt. Scrapes appeared where his skin was showing and his clothes were pretty much not worth saving. They were as much rags as Silver's attire had been when she first found him. She looked back over to Silver.

"You did this?"

Silver's eyes never left Henry's, "It is mine. You took it from me. I had to get it back. I'm sorry."

Henry blinked rapidly, "You dropped it when the wolf attacked us. I was picking it up for you."

Rosie looked back over to her son, "A wolf attacked you?" She put her hands on top of the table and spread her fingers out.

Silver didn't blink. His eyes almost seemed to glow. "I. I needed to have it. It. It needed to be back in my possession. I. I could not stop myself. I'm sorry."

Henry's face darkened, "I was going to give it back to you. I wasn't going to keep it."

"It. It didn't know that."

"What do you mean, *It didn't know that*?"

Silver finally blinked, "The key. It didn't know you were going to give it back."

Rosie's head snapped back to Silver, "The key talks to you?"

"You didn't have to bite me," Henry snapped, "Or tackle

me to the ground. Or twist my arm behind my back. Or try and break my fingers to get to the key."

"Wait," Rosie said, raising her hands to her temples.

Silver blinked again, "I'm sorry. I. I didn't want to do those things. It wanted me to."

Henry flung his hands up in exasperation, "Keys don't talk to people unless they're crazy! Are you crazy?"

"Wait a minute, guys."

Silver put his clenched fist on the table, "Keys can't talk?"

"Wait."

Henry sighed, "I think you're crazy."

Rosie slammed her fists onto the table, "Will you two just wait a minute, please?!"

Only the crackling fire dared to make a sound as Rosie spread her hands out flat against the table and pushed herself up. Henry looked wide-eyed at Rosie. He had never seen her like this. Sure, she grew impatient and demanding at times, but he could see the frustration pouring out into her hands.

Silver took his eyes away from Henry and slowly turned his gaze to Rosie. They stared at each other for a moment and Rosie could see how tired and drained he looked. She closed her eyes and leaned her head backwards.

"Silver, start from the very beginning. I want to hear all of it."

Silver slowly nodded and opened his hand up and revealed the key nestled inside of it. The key glowed the same silvery hew that his hair and eyes did. "I would have spoken sooner, but you terrified me. Both of you. I had no idea who either of you were. I awoke in your arms, Rosie. You spoke to me but I couldn't hear you. There was a ringing in my ear. Almost like a scream. It did not stop until we stepped out of the forest."

Rosie sat back down and Henry leaned in to listen closely.

Silver stared down at the key, "That's when I heard the voice. It broke through the ringing and it soothed me. A soft voice. A gentle voice. It told me that I needed to stay silent. Then you called me Silver and I thought you knew who I was. I almost spoke to you then."

Silver allowed the key to slide on the table. He watched it sit there a moment before the ringing returned. He winced and snatched the key back up before the sound consumed him. "I am Silver. It is a name you have given me. That is all I know. So, the voice told me to watch and listen. It guided me to help you. It told me that as long as I wore the shell, they couldn't find me."

"They?" Henry asked but Rosie shook her head at him.

She asked instead, "The shell you wore around your neck?"

Silver continued, "Then the wolf came and I lost the shell. I could feel the wind again. Sounds were brighter and louder. Colours returned to me. I saw you Henry. Saving me. Coming to me and picking up the key."

Silver dropped the key onto the table again and the ringing started to rise, "That's when it screamed. It warned me that you were going to take it. That something terrible would happen if I didn't get it back."

The ringing slammed around in Silver's head as he forced himself to just watch the key rest on the table. He sat on his hands and stared, "I'm sorry, Henry."

"Silver."

The ringing grew louder until eventually it was a scream. "It so desperately wanted to be back with me. I tried to warn you. I tried to tell you it was mine."

"Silver!"

Silver felt a wetness slide out of his ears. The scream almost blinded him.

Rosie snapped her fingers in front of his face and held up the key to him, "SILVER! Take it back!"

Silver pulled his hands out from beneath him and snatched at the key and held it to his chest. He felt Rosie grab at his chin with one hand as she dabbed at his ears with another.

"The blood is silver," he heard Henry whisper.

"Who are you, young one?" Rosie whispered and stroked his chin tenderly.

"I am Silver. That's all I know."

Henry pushed himself up and slowly walked around the table and headed upstairs without another world. Rosie finished cleaning up Silver's ears with her handkerchief and let go of his chin.

"We'll figure this out. You and I. I promise."

Silver looked up into her eyes and for the first time, since he had appeared in the Lakewood Trees, Rosie saw his strength crack and melt away as a scared little boy leaned into her. She bit her lower lip and awkwardly patted his shoulders as Henry returned from upstairs. He paused at the bottom of the landing and stared at them for a moment before taking a deep breath.

He marched over to them, "Silver."

Silver pulled away from Rosie and both of them looked over to Henry. Rosie took a step away from Silver. A heat appeared around her neck. She was relieved the boy had let her go.

Henry reached out a hand, "Give me the key, Silver."

Rosie lowered her eyebrows, "Henry, no. We just saw what happens when he's apart from it."

Henry turned to his mother and shot her a dirty look before returning his gaze to Silver, "Give me the key."

Silver wiped his tears away. They almost looked like tiny little diamonds. "Why?"

"You need to start trusting me," Henry said to both of them.

"You think I'm crazy."

"You're not crazy."

Silver held out his hand and fought to open his fist. Rosie

could tell he was hearing a voice. She could see the conflict flicker in Silver's eyes but the silver-haired boy handed the key over to Henry.

Rosie gave him a look as if to say, "What are you up to?"

Henry pulled out a silver chain from his pocket and looped it through the hole in the key. The chain suddenly hummed softly until it grew to a higher pitch and Rosie and Henry winced as the sound turned into a horrific scream. Henry held out the key chain and Silver snatched it up and the room slipped into silence.

Silver lifted the chain up and stared at the key dangling from it. "It is content."

Rosie put her little finger in each ear and shook it, "I'm so happy for it. Meanwhile, my ears aren't."

"Mom," Henry said, staring at the key chain. "The chain. It's—"

Rosie looked at him and then at the chain before tears threatened to burn her eyes. She swallowed deeply.

Henry felt an emptiness as he watched Silver put it around his head and down his neck. The key disappeared beneath his shirt. Henry remembered when he got that chain. It was the night of the big fight. Patrick had appeared at Henry's bedroom door with a box. His father sat at the edge of the bed and placed it on Henry's lap.

"A present," Patrick had said.

Henry remembered being confused, wondering why his father was giving him a gift. It wasn't his birthday. It wasn't a feast in the community or a new rotation. He had asked him what it was for as he pulled out a silver chain from the box.

Patrick had already gotten up and was moving back to the door, "Just in case I miss a few."
Henry had watched his door close and never got a chance to ask him anything further. That night he had woken to the sound of shouting and the slam of the front door. He never saw his father again.

Rosie reached out a hand and looped a finger around the chain, "That little sac."

"Mom!" Henry gasped. Silver just stared blankly up at the two as they still hovered over his seat.

"Sit back down, Henry," Rosie groaned, "It's time I tell you what I found in the Blackwood."

Both of the boys listened as Rosie filled them in about the Entmen and answered Silver's questions along the way. When she got to the part of the spiked wolves, the boys babbled on about the wolf that they had seen and how it was the same kind. Rosie talked about the bluff, the fire and the large, looming shadow that approached in the distance. She especially talked about Patrick's little tricks and pointed to the chain.

"The little sac knew," she snapped and Henry gasped again before they had to explain to Silver what that meant. He laughed so long at the explanation that Rosie and Henry found themselves laughing along with him.

Rosie sobered up first and slapped a letter on the table, "And then there's this."

They read the letter in silence. Even Silver.

Rosie noted, "So you can read as well."

Rosie and Henry had fallen into a solemn silence. Silver kept trying to ask questions. He didn't know who Patrick was or where they were. He didn't know why Patrick affected them like this.

It was Rosie who ended his plethora of questions by getting up and walking over to the fireplace. She opened a small tin with grounded herbs in them. She took a pinch and sprinkled it over the fire. It instantly started to slowly die out.

"We shall sleep on it," Rosie sighed.

Henry had already gotten some candle holders, lit them and passed them out. Each of them made their way to the stairs and to their rooms. Silver followed Henry closely and barely walked into his room before Henry closed the door. Silver watched Henry stride across the room and throw a few bed coverings on the floor and a pillow stuffed with feathers and straw.

Silver waited till their eyes met before asking, "Who is Patrick?"

"He is my father."

Silver wanted to ask more but Henry pushed past him and climbed into bed. Silver walked over to the bed coverings on the floor and stood there with his candle as Henry blew out his.

Silver spoke into the darkness beyond his candle light, "Where is he?"

"I don't know," came Henry's voice, growing uncontrollably impatient with each question. He didn't feel like talking about him.

Silver slowly sunk into his bed and blew out the candle. While his eyes adjusted, he sought refuge beneath the wolf skin that kept him warm at night. It got surprisingly cold in the house.

There was a spark that flicked Silver's eyes back open and Henry's face appeared above a lit candle. He was sitting up in his bed gazing down at Silver.

"We don't talk about it much. The argument they had. I don't even know what it was about. My parents never argued. They worked so well together. My mom and dad weren't people who got angry. They'd have these looks that showed they meant business. Or a tone in their voice."

Henry went quiet and stared into the darkness where he imagined Silver was still laying there. Henry wasn't even sure if the silver-haired boy was even awake anymore. He sighed and continued, "My father was acting weird ever since he came back from the nearest community. He wasn't much of a talker to begin with but we couldn't get him to stop. He had so much to say and most of it was in private with my mom. Then he gave me that silver chain. It was the last thing he ever gave to me. He said that it was in case he missed a few birthdays or celebrations. I didn't get to ask him what he meant."

Henry almost dropped his candle as Silver walked into the light and sat next to him on the bed. Henry was mesmerised for a moment, as Silver's hair seemed to absorb the light and reflect it with tiny sparkles. Silver noticed his stare and they both softly smiled.

"I awoke to them screaming. At first, I thought something was wrong and I ran to the door and opened it. I still couldn't hear all of what they were saying but my mom kept shouting out, 'No, Patrick, we will not!' The last thing I heard was the slam of the front door and someone putting out the fire downstairs. I slipped back into my room, closing the door quietly and slipped into bed. Underneath the wolf skin, I could hear someone walking down the hallway and into my parent's room. When the sun rose, I found myself home alone and by the time my mom came back all she said to me was, 'Your father left us.'"

Silver put a hand on Henry's leg and that's when Henry realised he was crying. He quickly wiped away the tears and apologised.

Silver was confused by the apology, "Why?"

"I shouldn't cry."

"Why not?"

Henry thought a moment and shrugged, "I don't know. But anyway, my mom says he left, but he wouldn't do that. For a while, I thought he had gone for a walk and something happened and he was hurt. I tried to go look for him but it made my mom insane with anger. She didn't let me go far at all for a long time. The more that the days passed, the more I believed he was dead. So, I kept this chain hidden away. I only look at it when it's my birthday. We don't go to any festivals anymore."

Henry's eyes widened as Silver wrapped his arms around him tightly before quickly letting go and resting a hand back on Henry's leg. The darkness hid Henry's blush that left his ears burning.

He cleared his throat and continued, "But the letter. The bluff. And now your key. I think my father knew. Somehow he knew."

"He knew about me?"

"He wrote about a gift. Maybe you are our gift?" Henry felt his heart skip a bit hearing his own words.

Silver and Henry looked into each other's eyes until the candle suddenly flickered out.
Silver's hand left Henry's leg and up to Henry's chin like Rosie had done to Silver, "I really didn't want to hurt you. The key. It. It doesn't want to leave me. It's scared to leave my side."

"When we put it on the chain, we both heard the scream. It was coming from the key. It was so scared it hurt."

"You heard it? I'm not crazy?"

"No. I don't know. You might be." He grinned but the silent response worried him, "No, Silver. You're not crazy. But you are weird."

Silver nodded as if accepting that and slid off the bed slowly. Henry was surprised the moon wasn't lighting up the room. The sky must have been full of clouds. He listened as he heard Silver rustle around with the bed coverings. Henry felt guilty he had thrown them there. He went to speak but closed his mouth. He wondered if this is how Silver felt when they first met him. He had a lot of questions but just didn't know if they were right to say. He drifted into sleep thinking of his new roommate on the floor and how the boy really did seem to be made of silver.

"Rosie."

Rosie sat up with sweat dripping from her brow. The sun was beaming through her window. She looked around in a panic and called out, "Patrick?"

The emptiness of the room replied to her. She sat there until her heart calmed and the sweat evaporated away. No matter how much she tried to replace Patrick's things in the room with her own, it still felt empty. She slid out of bed and slipped into the day's clothing. It was pretty much always the same. Boots that were made to trample around in the forest and the hills. Pants and shirt protected her from the ailments, thorns or bristles of the flora. Her satchel was always close by and even now, as she knew she'd mostly be in the house or around it till the boys were ready, she still put it around her shoulder. She slipped out into the hallway and passed Henry's door.

She paused for a moment before knocking. She sometimes did that. Patrick would be the one knocking. He'd joke that a teenage boy would sleep all day if they let him. But there was something awkward about it all. She never knocked. She always passed by and started her day knowing he'd eventually come down.

Rosie knocked.

Henry's eyes snapped open and he sat up in bed, "Dad?"

There was a moment of silence as Henry stared at the two shadows of feet beyond the space beneath his door. Silver had sat up as well. "No, Henry, it's me. I was just—I was going to start breakfast and thought you two would want to help."

Silver and Henry looked at each other as they heard Rosie mutter, "What are you doing, Rosie? Just walk away."

The shadows disappeared and Henry slipped out of bed, "Mom!"

The shadows returned and Rosie knocked again and heard her hiss, "Why are you knocking again?"

Henry, looking over at Silver, shared a silent laugh. Henry walked over to the door and opened it. Rosie stood there with a hand raised behind her head scratching it. She looked extremely uncomfortable. "Mom. It's okay. We're coming. We just need to get dressed."

Rosie nodded and took that as her cue to scramble away down the stairs. Henry turned around to find a nude Silver starting to pull on some clothes he found in the wardrobe. Henry blushed and looked down at his feet.

"I'm glad my clothes fit you."

Silver said, "Oh. Yeah, is it okay that I put on whatever?"

Henry nodded and slowly made his way over to his bed and organised it. He usually didn't do this but he felt more comfortable with his back to Silver.

"What do I do with these? Should I take them down to the Cot Cage?"

Henry spun around and was relieved to see Silver dressed but saddened as he had bundled up his bedding from the floor. "I mean, if you want to."

Silver nodded slowly and made his way to the door.

"Or they can stay here! I don't mind. There's room. If the floor is too hard, we can share — I mean, we can both use the bed."

Silver turned back and smiled, "Okay," and returned the bedding to the bed.

Henry put a hand to his chest and wondered why his heart was beating so fast. He made his way to the door, "There's some scones left over from a few days ago. If they aren't too hard, we can heat those up. It's great with conserves."

Silver's eyes lit up, "Oh yes please. I enjoyed that yesterday."

They both slowly made their way to the kitchen searching for Rosie. The backdoor was open and a stern voice called to both of them, "Boys? What is this?"

Henry frowned and jogged his way out the backdoor and down the garden to the middle where Rosie stood next to the well. Silver was closely following.

Henry stopped when she saw her looking down into the bucket that she had rested on the ground next to the well. Henry groaned. He had forgotten about the black bird they had left in the bucket. With everything that happened afterwards, it had slipped his mind. A wing was still hanging limp over the edge of the bucket and Henry could just make out the head resting over its breast.

"We found it in there yesterday. It slipped my mind. We didn't use the water. I knew your crystals could purify it again."

Rosie nodded and used a stick she had found to nudge the head, "Did you see its beak?"

Henry shook his head and stepped closer. He knelt down

and followed the stick with his eyes to the beak and gasped, "It has teeth. Ravens don't have teeth."

"No," Rosie said and moved the stick to the limp wing and used the stick to lift the wing up, "And their wings don't have long, sharp claws either. But look at its feet. The talons are trimmed. As if it were tamed."

Henry nodded, "I had noticed the talons."

Rosie stood up and tipped the bucket over with her foot and the raven rolled out of it. She reached into her satchel and pulled out a blue tinted crystal the size of a finger and dropped it into the well. They could hear the plunk of it as it hit the water and the sound of boiling water as it dissolved, "The water will be fine, but we'll need to clean the bucket. The bird will need to be taken care of. There are gloves in the cellar."

"I'll take care of the bird," Henry said and ran back towards the house.

"I can clean the bucket," Silver offered but Rosie shook her head.

"No. Let Henry do it. There's something else I wanted to show you."

Rosie walked past the gardens towards the east where the Lakewood Trees were starting to thin out to the grassy plains called Blades. Silver followed. He hesitated at first remembering what had happened in the Blades just beyond where the river flowed through.

When Henry returned, he watched as Rosie and Silver walked into the trees to the east. He almost followed but he knew he had to take care of the raven. If it started to rot, whatever disease it may have would go into the garden. He decided he'd take it to the edge of the southern trees that led to Blackwood and bury it there. He had brought some salts with him to sprinkle over the body.

He had pulled on his father's gloves on the way back, so he reached down to the raven to pick it up. Its breast moved. He held his breath. Something was moving from within the raven's body. His hand slowly reached for it again and that's when the feathers of the bird started to part. The thin layer of skin that hid the insides of the raven started to tear. Something black and smooth started to poke out and the dead raven started to expand.

Henry took a step back and looked up towards where Rosie and Silver had gone. He wanted to call out to them but no sound came out. He looked back down in time to see the rest of the breast tear open and the head of another raven burst out. Two black, beady eyes blinked at him as the head tilted to each side before the beak opened up and a loud cry made him wince.

"CAW! CAW CAW!"

Henry watched as two claws ripped open the rest of the bird and two, feathery wings burst out and flapped madly. With each flap, the new raven pulled itself upwards and a body as large as the first raven appeared. The new raven cried out again and hopped on top of the dead one a few times still flapping its wings madly. Henry stumbled backwards in surprise and fell hard on his backside.

"CAW CAW CAW! CAW!"

Henry screamed and tried to crawl backwards as the raven rose up into the air and dived towards his face. Its jagged teeth glaring at him as its beak opened wide. He lifted up his hands to block his face and the bird slammed into the gloves. It tore at them with its teeth and clawed wings.

"Henry!" he heard his mother scream from somewhere in the distance. He screamed out more. His voice cracked. He tried to grab at the bird to get it to stop. The oversized gloves protected him from the sharp beak. He only felt the pressure of the bird. He actually didn't feel it nor did it break through the material of the gloves.

The bird retreated back up into the air as Henry took that time to crawl around and get up onto his hands and feet. He crawled a few steps before pushing him up and started running towards the house. The backdoor had been left open and he was grateful for that.

"Henry, duck!" his mother screamed out at him again. This time she sounded closer, but he spun around and swung a hand out to the sound of the raven's beating wings. His hand made contact and the bird slammed into the ground with a crunch. He stood over it as Rosie ran up and slammed a foot down on its head quickly.

"I thought it was dead," Rosie gasped, "I'm sorry, Henry."

"It was dead," Henry stared down at the nearly headless raven, "This came out of it."

Rosie checked Henry's face over and then proceeded to wipe her shoe along the ground to remove leftover raven. "Where did you get those gloves, Henry?"

"In the cellar. Why does it matter?"

"Those are your father's gloves. I've been looking for them. They disappeared when he—"
"When he did," Henry finished. "He really did leave us,

didn't he?"

Rosie stared down at her obviously fuming son. She could see the burning tears that had filled her eyes for rotations. She knew what he was feeling. She could actually relate to this and with that, she pulled her son into her arms and joined him in his tears.

"I know, Henry, I know."

"He really is a sac," he sobbed.

Rosie nodded, "Come inside, Henry. We have a lot to say to each other."

Silver watched as the two retreated through the backdoor. Rosie called out to him, "Silver, take care of the birds. Take them beyond the garden to the edge of the trees. Cover them with salt."

Henry untied a pouch on his belt and threw it onto the ground as they both disappeared inside. Silver stood there for a moment and watched. His lips pierced together. His eyes glaring at the open door. He clenched his fists together as he slowly walked to the pouch and picked it up. He grabbed the ravens and he trudged through the garden towards the trees that bordered the Blackwood. He dropped the birds. One of them was barely being held together. The other one was headless. He opened the pouch and poured all of it onto the birds. Little white crystals piled onto the corpses and some drifted with the slight breeze. He looked back towards the garden and beyond it to the house before turning back towards the trees that thickened to Blackwood.

"Mine," he growled. His eyes flaring into two beacons of light.

* * *

Rosie lit the fire in the fireplace that held the large pot. She pulled it off of its hook and replaced it with a kettle. Henry rested against the counter, pulling the gloves off and tossing them onto it.

"He knew I'd find these gloves," Henry glared at them as if they were his father. "Why didn't he stay? Where has he been? Why didn't he come back himself?"

"That night," Rosie leaned against the mantle of the kitchen's fireplace. Her fingers whitened as she clenched at the wood and stone. "He wanted us to move. To leave everything behind. He wanted to take us to Moon's Edge."

"But why?" Henry pushed himself away from the counter and slowly approached her.

"He wouldn't say and the more I wanted answers the angrier he became. And you know your father…"

"…he never got angry," they both whispered to each other.

"He said some things he knew would upset me. It did. He stormed out the front door and left. I said some things…I wish I hadn't and there were things…I wish I had said."

Henry stood behind his mother and stared at her back. It seemed to be heaving. He used to catch her crying during the first rotation his father had disappeared and then there were the times after he pretended he didn't notice. But there was a time when the tears stopped and he hadn't seen her do it since. He just stood there slowly raising a hand and wondering if he should touch her, if he should reach out and comfort her.

Henry dropped his hand.

A shadow stood in front of the window near the front door in the Great Hall. It was an oddly, tall shape that seemed to have to bend over to see into the window. Long arms perched themselves against the glass with jagged nails that left little white lines as they slowly moved down. It watched as the boy moved further into the kitchen. Two perfectly round, silver-globed eyes blinked rapidly as its hands reached for the door's handle.

"Mine," it hissed.

Silver

The Worms in the Garden

Rosie played with the cloth in her hands, "A blindfold?"

"What do you expect? I can't walk out behind you with my hands covering your eyes. You're too damn tall!"

Rosie smirked and started to wrap the cloth around her head, "You're just too damn short, Patrick. You could always ride on my shoulders."

Patrick only felt short when Rosie was near. He was eye level to her bulging stomach. He placed a hand on it and felt their baby kick. "She says, 'Don't be a whiff of dung.'"

Rosie raised the blindfold off of one eye and looked down at him, "Oh, does he now? You're teaching him to swear already."

"She," Patrick corrected. "I can feel it in my bones."

"Oh, do you now? Do you?" she rolled her visible eye and put the blindfold back on, "Alright, little Patty, show me your surprise."

Patrick spun her around, "Not sure if you deserve it now, but our child does. So you're lucky she's with you."

"He," Rosie corrected, "I can feel it in my bones."

Patrick led her through the empty room to the kitchen's entry way. They had just finished with that room. "Watch the doorway. Don't worry. You don't have to duck your head in your own house. It's made for you, remember?"

Rosie blushed beneath her blindfold. She was careful not to let Patrick see by covering her face with the crook of her arm and pretending to cough. Sentimentality always made her feel uncomfortable. With her other arm, she held it out before her to ensure she didn't run into anything. She also trusted Patrick and wasn't surprised when she was led out the backdoor without any issues. She did the blindfold to humour him because he was so excited about it all. As soon as she stepped out of the house, her nose started to twitch. Her hands could feel the electricity in the air. Before she took the blindfold off, she knew that she had stepped foot into a garden.

"Patrick, you didn't?" Rosie gasped and pulled off her blindfold.

Patrick didn't bother protesting. He knew she could sense the garden as soon as her feet touched its grounds. He watched as she walked down a cobbled footpath into the depths of the garden. It wasn't finished. Many of the plants had only just arrived throughout the night so that Patrick would be able to share this moment with her.

"Four sections, just as you envisioned. The plants' roots are covered and protected by your own mulch. I had to slowly steal it out of the cellar."

Rosie stopped at the centre of the garden where a well was slowly being built.

"I haven't finished it all," Patrick grinned, "Just like the house. But it's enough for you to take over and make it your own. Summer. Fall. Winter. Spring. You'll have it all here thanks to your gift. That mulch of yours."

Rosie wobbled next to the half-finished well as she tried to sink closer to the ground. Patrick rushed to her. Beads of sweat instantly started to form on his forehead and dampen his thick head of hair.

"Are you going to faint?"

"Me? Faint? When have I ever fainted?" she smirked, "Get over yourself. It's lovely and you know I love it. I've got a lot of work to do. I was just trying to bend over to kiss you. But forget it. You're not worth the effort."

Patrick pretended to be hurt and grabbed one of her hands. He kissed the top of it, "I love you." He pulled at her arm and then kissed the top of her wrist, "I love you." He continued to tug and kiss a few more times with each time repeating those three words.

She pulled her hand away in fake disgust and then brushed her fingers across his lips, "This garden will be glorious. It will feed us. It will feed the community. It will feed the Lakewood Trees around us. We will spend the rest of our days here until our son can take over."

Patrick nodded slowly as he hesitated for a moment before taking a few steps back. He spun on his heels and headed back towards the house and called back out to her, "You mean our daughter!"

Rosie looked around her and rubbed her belly slowly. She knew she wasn't wrong. They were going to have a son. She took a few steps around the well and pointed, "This will be winter. Over there will be spring. Summer and Fall over there."

She kept rubbing her belly as she walked further away from the house into the borders of her garden. Patrick had put up a wooden fence. She'd lace it with vines that would chase the vermin away. Her mulch would keep the grounds purified and rich with nutrients.

The Lakewood Trees loomed around her and she stopped at the furthest edge of the garden and looked back over it again towards the house. A raven glided across the sky and she followed it before it disappeared over the horizon towards River's Song. They had walked that way a few days ago. The river was beautiful.

"You're so lucky, my boy," she spoke to her belly, "To grow within such beauty. Safe. Forever if you want. I'll make sure of it. My last breath will be here for you. Now, come on now, Henry, we've got a lot of work to do. Wake up. Wake up, Henry." Rosie hissed as she held the candle above his bed, "Henry, get up!"

A bit of wax dripped down onto his pillow. Silver sat up on the other side of Henry and Rosie couldn't hide how startled she had been.

"Sorry, Rosie," Silver whispered, rubbing his eyes with one of his hands, "What's wrong?"

Henry rolled over until his face was into his pillow and he muttered something. It wasn't until there was a loud crack of thunder that shook the whole house that Henry bolted awake. The rain could be heard on the roof already but as soon as the thunder shook the sky, it seemed to shake the rest of the rain out of it as well.
Rosie had to shout, "I need your help!"

"The garden!" Henry shouted back and threw aside the

blankets. They piled up over Silver, who fought them off as he joined the other two.

They followed the light from Rosie's candle out into the small hallway and down the stairs. The Great Hall was already lit up but it was the smoke in the fireplace that was beginning to become a problem. Rosie rushed over and reached up into the fireplace and pulled a lever that closed the flue. Her arm was drenched from the rain starting to pour in.

"Last time I saw rain like this…" Rosie muttered, stepping away from the fireplace and turning around to see Silver standing alone near the table. He was staring out into the kitchen. Rosie approached him and asked him where Henry had gone to but the sound of rain was louder as the back door hung open from beyond the kitchen. Rosie put her hands on Silver's shoulders as she passed and took big steps to get through the kitchen and out into the rain. There were only a few times in their life there that the rain caused flooding and damage to the garden. The paths throughout the garden helped with the overflow and acted as gutters that would take the water beyond the borders of the garden. As each flash of lightning crossed the sky, she grew closer to the well. It was the middle of the garden and the well's level would tell her how much trouble the garden could be in. There was a slight incline to the well. The land flowed away from each. Each section of the garden was outlined by a cobble path. The path she was on was already flowing with water. She had trouble keeping her balance.

"Mom!" a voice called out to her. She turned back towards the house and saw Henry struggling to pull a boot on he must have gotten from the cellar. Silver was there holding up a lantern struggling to keep its light. His face was gazing

103

up at the sky and Rosie could have sworn his eyes lit up with each flash of lightning. The light certainly reflected off of his hair.

She turned back to the well. She'd normally light a match and drop it down to see the water level. It would tell her how high up River's Song was getting. As long as the paths could drain the water out, her garden would be fine. She'd just need to grab some sand bags to help with the flow. The rain kept growing thicker and thicker. She knew her small plants would be pelted into the ground, but after all this, they'd still thrive. The smaller the plant, the more will it had to live.

She turned when she saw movement out of the corner of her eyes. Silver and Henry were carrying sandbags from the cellar to the outer edges that led to River's Song. It had never reached them before, but there had been a time where it had come close. That was when all of Blades was underwater. If it weren't for the trees between them, the river would not have been held back. After that, Rosie put the sandbags out if the rains grew torrential just in case. Henry seemed to remember that and she felt a sense of pride watching him work.

Rosie gasped as lightning flashed the well into view. She wiped the water from her face and waited for another flash to confirm her fears. A couple of bolts etched the sky and confirmed it. The well was overflowing. But there was something else Rosie could see. She pushed through the rain and managed the slippery cobble before finding herself closer to the well. Lightning flashed a few more times and the thunder made her ears ring. She couldn't quite make it out but there seemed to be something in the water. Almost like little stones or a bunch of leaves. The water was not clear like her crystals should have made it.

"Mom!" she heard again, but just barely. She turned and with a few flashes of lighting and the lantern Silver was holding onto, she saw Silver wave to her and Henry pointing to the trees. She wiped the rain away from her face again, even though it made no difference. The trees seemed to be moving. She could see the red eyes blinking madly.

"Entmen?" Rosie gasped and ran towards Silver and Henry. The rain continued to pelt down and the water flowed along the paths like miniature rivers. She felt as if she were walking on tiny marbles, not from the cobblestone but from whatever was flowing out of the well with the water.

The Entmen all walked out from the trees along the eastern border of her property. They stood there for a moment. Their eyes followed them as all three of them returned to the back door. One by one they tilted over until they crashed into the ground. Side by side and on top of each other, the Entmen fell until a large wave crashed from behind them. Rosie pushed the boys into the house and looked back from the doorway. The red eyes closed one by one. They had stopped the river from coming.

Rosie whispered, "Thank you," and closed the door.

Rosie took the boys to the Great Hall where they stayed until the rain stopped. Henry paced back and forth.

"Did you see that?!" he exclaimed "Those were the Entmen! Mom, you've told me about them! They were here!"

Rosie was wringing the water off of her as she made her way to the fireplace. The candles in the Great Hall were still lit, "Don't slip on the water. I'll need to dry out the fireplace. Grab my satchel on the post. I've got some powder in there that will help."

Silver grabbed the pouch and brought it to her.

"Go get changed into dryer clothes. Both of you. We don't need to be getting ill."

"I saw them," Silver quietly said as he stood next to Rosie and watched her rifle through her satchel until she pulled out a small pouch and looked up at him, "Those trees. I saw them when I went to take care of the birds."

Rosie nodded and sprinkled what looked like ash onto the hearth where the moisture sizzled into steam. The wood crackled as it dried.

"I thought they were bad," Silver continued, "So I told them to go away. That you were mine."

Rosie looked up, "Yours?"

Henry called from the stairs as he made his way back to his room, "Silver, let's go. I'm wet to the bone. Oh gods, did you see how large they were? It was amazing the way they just made themselves into the dam! And the water just crashed into them and they didn't budge!"

Silver's eyes never left Rosie's, "I don't know who I am. I only know what you named me. I only see what you've shown me. Henry is your son. You are his mother. I am your silver-haired boy. I am what you see. I am yours. So, you are mine."

There was a tenderness in Silver's tone that touched Rosie's heart but she only nodded and returned to lighting the fire, "Go dry up, Silver, and try to calm that son of mine.

He's acting as if he hasn't seen Entmen before."

"They are our friends?"

Rosie struck a fire and the wood ignited. She reached up and pulled the lever to open the flue again. "For now. Let's try and keep it that way."

Silver nodded and left her staring at the fire. He was just about to disappear up the part of the stairs that turned to the left when she called out to him. He turned to find her leaning against the table and looking over at him.

"You remember the storm that brought you here?"

Silver shook his head.

"It was very much like this one. Shorter. It disappeared the moment I found you. It was as if it had never rained."

Silver just stood there frozen in place.

"The wolves. The ravens. The Entmen. All of it. All of this," she motioned towards the front window and the back door. "started after you showed up."

Rosie cracked her knuckles against the table and straightened up, "I'll get the hot water going. I could use a tea. We could all probably use a bath."

Silver watched her disappear into the kitchen before he started to breathe again and slowly made his way up the rest of the stairs. He pushed open the door and found Henry pulling on a shirt and then pointing to a pile of clothing on the bed. Silver stripped off his wet clothes and threw them onto Henry's. The cool air left over from the storm sent goosebumps across Silver's skin. He stood there and let the air dry him.

"I'm sorry," Silver broke the silence and turned to face Henry.

Henry's eyes went wide and he struggled between embarrassment and curiosity. He scratched at his chin and decided to gather up the wet clothes, "It's—I mean— natural. I guess—I just—not everyone is comfortable— you know—being nude."

Silver squeezed his eyebrows together and frowned, "What?"

Henry was squatting to scoop up the clothes and looked up before his head spun back around at the sudden view change, "OH! I mean—no, it's fine. You don't need to apologise for being nude. I'm just—not used to it."

Silver looked down at himself, "What's wrong with me?"

Henry gulped, "There's nothing wrong with you. You just said you were sorry."

Silver looked back at Henry with confusion, "I was apologising if I caused all of these problems here. But if you need me to…"

Henry closed his eyes and squeezed at the wet clothes in a hug. He'd have to change again, "No. No, Silver. You're fine. Just don't let my mom see. Keep yourself covered. She'll be all motherly and lecture you. And you don't want that. She doesn't stop."

"Oh, don't I?" Rosie said at the door. "If Silver wants to

strut around this house like a rooster and catch a fever, that's his decision. He can mop up his own sweat. Henry, stop playing with those clothes and get them to the wash basin in the kitchen. And stop gaping at Silver. He's got what you got. We get it."

Henry's face burnt and his mouth snapped shut. He stomped past his mother with the wet clothes in his arms. He refused to look at Rosie and missed her wink. She ordered Silver to get dressed before she turned to head towards her room to change.

"Give the clothes a good soak before adding in the shaving to wash them. I've got a few crystals, too," Rosie called out and when Henry didn't answer, "Did you hear me, Henry?"

"Yes!" Henry barked back from somewhere downstairs.

Rosie rolled her eyes and lit a few candles around her room. Her bedroom windows reflected the light and her image against the backdrop of night. Only droplets of water on the glass was what was left of the storm. She was halfway changing when she turned around and found Silver at her door. She quickly finished getting dressed and walked towards him, "Okay, Silver, Henry has a point. You need to know that if a door is closed it's because someone wants privacy. You knock first and only enter if the person behind the door says it's okay."

Silver nodded, "Are we supposed to be going to bed? Because I'm not tired."

Rosie sat at the edge of her bed and studied Silver for a few moments. He really was just learning. His eyes always seemed to study everything. He was taking their words at face value. Though he seemed to be around the same age as her son, his mind was craving for knowledge like a younger child. He seemed to be searching for the answers to everything without ever asking, "Why?" Here she was trying to figure the kid out and he didn't even have the answers himself. The longer she studied him the more Silver studied her back. He didn't grow uncomfortable at her gaze. It was as if he understood what it was she was doing and he decided to do the same with her.

"I'm not good at this," Rosie didn't move. She just sat there looking over at him. "You want me to talk. I can tell. Henry wants me to, too. But that's not what I do. You seek answers, so do I, but I can't give them. I probably won't even find them. All I can do is keep this place running. Keep this place going because it keeps me going. You kept silent at first. Well, silence is where I like to stay."

Silver just watched her with his pale blue eyes.

Even though she had just told Silver she wasn't much of a talker, she felt inclined to speak, as if Silver was drawing it from her, "When my hus—when Patrick left, I just picked up where he left off. That was easy. Having you here seeking answers…me seeking answers…Henry seeking—"

"You," he paused. Silver's eyes seemed to glow in her dimly lit candled room, "talk more than you know."

"I guess we both do."

"Mom!" Henry called from down below, "Silver! I've made us some tea and the fire is warming up the Great Hall. Come!"

Rosie stood up and walked to each candle and snuffed

them out before picking up the one she had entered with. Silver still hadn't moved and his gaze kept with her. She went to reach out to him but stopped. Where was this tenderness coming from? It made her feel nauseous. She just walked past Silver and headed down the hall to the stairs. She heard Silver follow her.

As she took the first few steps, she commented, "If Patrick were here, he'd comfort us with his words. He'd tell us that we were going to be okay. He'd probably have you all figured out already Silver."

Henry was still at the bottom of the stairs listening as they made their way down the stairs. Rosie took a mug from Henry's hands and continued to the fire, where Henry had pulled some of the chairs to overlook it.

Silver took the other mug of tea, but lingered at the bottom of the stairs waiting for Henry to join his mother, "I'm dressed now."

Henry almost looked displeased and this confused Silver even more. Henry just nodded and went to the table where his tea was waiting for him and joined his mother at the chairs. He left the middle chair for Silver.

The fire was popping and crackling and Rosie stared into the depths of the fire as if something was inside it. Henry just side glanced her before sitting down, but his gaze fell to the whittled figures on the mantle. His father had amazing talent that Henry felt he'd never have. He loved each stage and when he got to the last few figurines his heart sank again. Silver sat between them, something he was getting used to doing. He wasn't sure why but he felt that the distance they put between each other shouldn't exist. They lingered in these chairs as the night ended and the dawn brought light and promise that the storm had, in fact, left them.

Rosie stood. She had let the fire die out within the last hour. No one looked tired. The storm had brought an energy with it that still lingered. She had enjoyed the small talk Silver and Henry had every now and then but she refused to admit it to them. She just stared off into the fire and imagined where Patrick was at that very moment. A lingering thought she had well before the arrival of his letter. Henry had just accepted his father went off and died, so she could only imagine what it was like to suddenly accept the fact that Rosie had been right all along. Patrick had left them and chose not to come back.

Silver had asked at some point during the night, "What if Patrick didn't send the letter?"

But she was so sure that it was from him that she would bet her life on it and was surprised to hear Henry agree with her.

As light started to seep through the windows, Rosie stood up. "I'm going to go see the damage this storm did to the garden. I suspect I'll have a lot of work to do," Rosie sighed and grabbed her satchel and slipped on her boots that lay near the stairs where she had left them.

She turned to see the boys quietly talking about the whittled miniatures. Henry was holding on to the last two figures Patrick had worked on. Hers was missing. It had been one of many things left unfinished. She wasn't sure why she lingered or why she even turned to them. She had never had Henry work too much in the garden anyway. She shook her head slowly and left them, quickening her pace through the kitchen and opening the back door. She stopped for a moment and again listened to the boys. It was an almost involuntary reaction. The boy's laughter sent her outside and down the cobbled path a few steps before she froze.

Rosie's understanding of the flora around her helped understand the soil beneath her feet as well. She had travelled around enough in her childhood to understand that what grows in a tundra would not grow along the coasts or deep within the forests. But all of them still had a connection and it was what connected all life together in all its roots, the soil. So, Rosie spent rotations creating a mulch that would connect all life together so that no matter where they grew, that connection of life would be strong enough to keep them. Some called what she did magic, but she had seen magic, even from the Feygods themselves. She just felt she had an understanding. She wasn't just some rumoured mystical woman in the woods. But as she gazed across her garden, no amount of mulch was going to save them now.

Sometimes when the rains came, worms would writhe their way to the top soil and pop themselves out as if to wave to the world above. Patrick and Henry would grab a handful each and head to River's Song to fish. Those worms were thick and natural. The worms Rosie found writhing throughout her garden were long black ones that had spent the rest of the night chewing at her vegetation. She could hear the sounds of thousands of worms sloshing around the mud and stone to reach the next plant and begin devouring it, but what alarmed her the most was their size seemed to be growing the more that they ate. Some were the size of her feet and Patrick always made fun of how giant they were. At the end of each worm was their gaping mouths with tiny sharp teeth that sawed away at the plants and looked sharp enough to damage her.

They didn't seem to show any interest she was there but if allowed, they'd tear her garden down to nothing.

She turned and quickly ran through the back door. The cellar's stairs groaned under the pressure of her run as she skipped a few steps and made large steps to a large sack of salts. One rotation she had trouble with slugs and came up with her crystalline salts that took care of them quickly. She hoped they'd do the trick.

* * *

Henry and Silver stood on the front porch staring at the stump that still looked damp from last night's rain. Henry pointed to a bunch of small blocks of wood scattered around the yard, "He'd spend a lot of his free time on that stump whittling away at his little figurines. He'd sell most of them during the markets and festivals of the community nearby. Sometimes he'd go into town and sell a few of the more detailed ones. He never came back with leftovers. Those are the ones I've tried. My mom has stepped on a few too many so she hates that I leave them around. I can't whittle. My dad was showing me how right before he di—he left."

Silver tilted his head, "Show me."

Henry looked over at him as he stood on the top step leading down to the yard, "I told you I can't whittle."

Silver smiled, "Show me anyway?"

Henry couldn't help but smile back and put a hand over his stomach as the butterflies began. "Maybe we should eat first?"

"No," Silver stepped away from the front door and put a

hand on Henry's shoulder, "Show me now."

Henry nodded, "We'll have to find his whittling knife. Throughout all the stuff that's been happening and me using it on that wolf, I'm not sure where I put it."

Silver frowned, "I know you had it with you when we came back. It was with you when your mom cleaned you up. Maybe you left it in the Cot Cage?"

Henry took a step back onto the porch and said, "Yeah, maybe it's in there."

"I'll go check," Silver offered and dashed back into the house just in time to see Rosie through the kitchen doorway carrying a large sack out. She heaved it onto the counter and their eyes met.

"Silver, get the door," Rosie nodded towards the backdoor and Silver jogged through the house and held it open for her. His eyes fell on the garden and he gasped. "No, Silver, don't worry. This will do the trick. Try and keep Henry away from back here though. I don't know how vicious these sacs will be."

Silver stared in silence at the horrific scene of black slithering bile crawling through the garden and Rosie hefted the back up one last time and turned to him, "Silver, you hear me?"

Silver nodded and closed the door quickly and walked back inside. It wasn't till he was near the spare room's door that he muttered, "Oh the Cot Cage, right. Patrick's knife."

He stepped towards the door and grabbed the handle. "Silver!" Henry called from out front, "I found it! It was near the stump!"

Silver let go of the handle and walked out the front door and closed it behind him. He jumped over the three steps leading off of the porch and made his way over to the stump where Henry was sitting and already trying to carve away at a misshapen chunk of wood. He sat down and listened as Henry started to explain the techniques his father always talked about and Silver tried to listen, but his mind wandered to the sight of Rosie's beautiful garden. It was one of the most amazing things he had ever remembered seeing. He looked at Henry's lips as he spoke but he no longer heard his words. His mind thought of the worms that now covered the garden's beauty and wondered if it would ever be the same again.

* * *

Rosie dropped the large sack on the cobblestone and untied it quickly to shove a hand inside and grab a handful of the crystalline salt. The smell of it filled the air and if she closed her eyes, she could imagine the smell of the ocean.

"You don't have time for sentiment," she told herself and flung the salt over a nearby patch of worms that were finishing off the last of her Echinacea. The salt bounced over them and landed on the ground. As soon as they touched the soil, it liquidated.

At first, nothing seemed to happen to the worms. They continued eating the stems until the flowering plant fell and they ate at the spiky core and long petals. Her face grew flush until one of the worms exploded and then her face was covered in guts instead. She blinked slowly at first and then darted away as each of the worms combusted. The ground was splattered with their innards. The other worms froze. The sound of their hacking died down and the ends with their tiny, sharp teeth all pointed to Rosie.

"Well, dung," Rosie thrusted both hands into the salts as the worms quickly started to slither towards her. She flung out the salts in an arc way in front of her and dug her hands in again. As the salts sprinkled across the worms, each one slowly started to combust until the air was full of guts and the sounds of, *"Sploog!"*

The salts were working but that wasn't the problem. The problem was that she couldn't gather them and toss them out fast enough. She regretted not keeping Silver at her side, but she was too determined now to retreat. She could imagine the damage they could do to the rest of the flora around her. She had never seen creatures like this before. They were as twisted as the ravens and the wolves. It wasn't until the worms reached her and jumped up onto her legs and tore at her skin like she was shredding a cheese wheel that she finally screamed out, "Silver! Silver! Henry!"

"Did you hear that?" Silver asked, his chin still leaning on Henry's shoulder looking down at the piece of wood. He had been watching Henry show how the knife needed to be held as it scraped against the wood and how the shavings could be used for Rosie's mulch.

Henry couldn't hear anything except the beating of his heart, but he stopped mid-carve to listen. They heard their names faintly and coming from the back.

Silver gasped and instantly stood, "The worms!"

Henry pocketed his father's knife and sat the wood piece down as he stood, "What worms?"

"Your mom had me open the back door for her and I saw

them. Hundreds of worms the size of our heads, I think. Well, some of them. They were all over the garden. Your mom told me to keep you away."

Henry looked defeated, "Oh, you didn't—never mind, it sounds like she might want us, after all."

Silver nodded and they ran around the eastern side of the house where the Entmen were still on their sides acting like a dam to the water that was already quickly retreating. Rosie was fighting off a bunch of worms that were making their way up her body. Her legs were dripping with blood. She looked as if she were going to topple over like the Entmen had done.

"MOM!" Henry screamed, his voice cracking. He pulled out his father's knife again and sliced at a few slithering up her sides. They exploded as soon as he broke their slimy skin as if they were just bubbled foam created by the sea against the sands.

Silver stomped on a few but they were already starting to crawl up his legs.

Rosie screamed at both of them, "The salts! Spread the salts on them all!"

The black worms had steered clear of the bag. It was as if an imaginary boundary was preventing them from nearing it. Silver was the closest to it and reached a hand in and grabbed a handful of the salts and flung them onto Rosie. She winced as the salts touched her wounds as each of the worms on her exploded into a gooey mess. She limped back over to the sack and with bloodied hands helped Silver throw more salts on him, Henry and around them. Henry quickly joined in but noticed his mom's legs were wobbling as she struggled to stay standing.

"You need salves!" Henry yelled as he tossed a small handful out into the clew of worms.

"Don't worry about it, Henry, now grab a bigger handful!"

Henry ignored her order and grabbed at the satchel that hung around her neck and shoulder. He fought to find the healing salves as Rosie continued to move down to the sack and throw out the salts at the diminishing onslaught of worms. Each explosion sent a burst of salts and innards over the garden, killing other worms and layering the garden with the mess. Henry darted and weaved to slap the salves onto his mother's legs. She swore but kept battling with the salts and watched Silver rush forward to stomp on a few, almost slipping on his way back.

"Stay close, Silver, don't be a fool!" Rosie snapped, as the wobbling of her legs strengthened as the salves worked their magic. The sting of tiny cuts dissipated. She looked down at Henry, who seemed content that his mother was fine. He return to the salts and before long all that was left of the worms were their splatters spewed across the garden.

* * *

The door to the Cot Cage rattled. It was a room forgotten unless needed. Dust already started to collect on the side table where an old wash cloth lay abandoned. The tall, slender shadow filled the room. Its silvery eyes glowed fiercely at the door daring it to open. Its sharp nails continued to dig into the wood of the ceiling, creating its glyphs. When it was finished with one, the glyph would glow. There were a dozen already scribbled along the walls. Each one symbolised a different summoning and those yet to come:

The ravens. The wolves. The water. The worms. The Silver Eyes.

Silver

The Song Inside

Patrick stared down into the scrying pool blankly. His calloused hands squeezed the edges of the large bowl as he leaned over. His bald head glistened with sweat as his focus concentrated into the depth of the water.

A voice roared out of its waters, "Let go of my son!"

Patrick watched as his wife ran roaring towards the shadow that held up Henry by his throat and squeezed. The shadow's claws drew blood as Rosie approached with Patrick's whittling knife in her hand. Silver's body lay cold near the stump that Patrick knew well.

He closed his eyes and started to hum. The scrying pool flickered with small circular ripples. When he reopened his eyes, they flashed with silver and his hum turned into a song,

> *"You'll raise a bird who'll hunt you down*
> *the huntress will come after,*
> *the silver tongue will guide their path*
> *and the gift you give thereafter."*

Silver bolted from the bed, sending Henry clunking onto the floor.

"What the hell?" Henry mumbled, squinting his eyes from the light of dawn. "Silver? What is it?"

Silver looked around the room bewildered and then up at the ceiling, "He's watching! I saw him! The man! He was watching us!"

Henry's bedroom slammed open and Rosie stood there with her fists ready, "What is it now?! Twelve-legged spiders but instead of eyes it has mouths with teeth?"

Henry moaned, "What? Mom? No. Silver had a dream."

Silver was pacing, pointing above them and around them. His words rushed together, "And the shadow it was here and it had you Henry and I was dead and Rosie didn't get to you in time and then the singing-the sky was singing and through the pools I saw him watching the bald man."

Rosie leaned against the door frame with a smile of relief, "Can we just have a day where all that happens is Silver having a bad dream?"

Henry pushed himself off the floor and groaned, "Even they are dangerous. I think I broke my butt."

Rosie disappeared back to her room despite Silver's continuous rambles. He fell silent at her disappearance and Henry didn't appear to be worried, "But I saw…"

Henry laughed, "Silver, it was just a dream. With everything going on, I'm surprised all of us aren't waking up screaming and flinging each other out of our beds."

"Dream?"

Henry paused for a moment, scratching his underarm

absentmindedly, "Huh. I keep forgetting that you don't know who you are or where you're from. I shouldn't be surprised you don't know about dreams. I'm sorry, Silver."

Henry sat down next to Silver and explained.

* * *

Rosie made her bed before heading downstairs to the kitchen and boiled some water for washing. She stared out of the backdoor into the garden and surveyed the damage. She made herself a tea and wandered around the remains of her garden. Her heart ached at the sight. Some areas would take rotations of work to regrow. Other parts would take many more seasons beyond that.

"What were those things?" she asked her remaining plants. "First the wolves and then the ravens. What do these creatures have to do with Silver?"

Her eyes wandered towards the Entmen's dam, "And what is it you know? The water from River's Song is gone and yet you still remain. Far from Blackwood."

She headed back towards the house before turning back to them, "Thank you, by the way."

The rest of the morning found them sitting around the table eating breakfast. They had all washed and clothed themselves. Silver looked like a galvanised version of Henry all dressed in his clothes. Rosie finished off the last of her oats and folded her hands together.

"We'll need to take it easy on the foods that come directly from the garden. It will take another season to bring some of the vegetables back."

Silver and Henry nodded sadly as visions of the black worms slithered around in their heads.

"What's happening, mom?"

She didn't answer. Instead, she watched Silver eat the last of his oats in silence. He avoided her gaze. Eventually, Rosie unfolded her hands and picked up her bowl and returned it to the kitchen. Silver absentmindedly scraped at the contents of his bowl. Henry frowned. He shouldn't have asked, but he was always full of questions.

"Why is this happening, Silver?"

Silver shrugged and began to hum to himself. Henry recognised it almost immediately. Rosie returned and started to gather Henry's bowl before she stopped and slowly looked over at Silver. She, too, started humming along the same song.

Henry reached across the table at Silver, "Where did you learn that song?"

Silver looked up and then over at Rosie, who was staring at him with wide eyes, her hand to her throat. He tilted his head as he watched their reactions. They almost appeared to be hypnotised. He intently watched them. His eyes flashing silver as he continued to hum.

"Dad hummed that to me to get me to sleep," Henry whispered.

Rosie slowly sat down and stared at Silver, "He told me that it helped the plants grow."

Henry laughed, "You always told him his singing would kill your plants."

Henry and Rosie shared a small laugh before Silver's humming grew louder and formed into words.

"You'll raise a bird," he began and closed his eyes, "who'll hunt you down. The huntress will come after."

Henry and Rosie looked over at each other and then back to Silver, who continued, "The silver tongue will guide their path and the gift you give thereafter."

Silver stopped singing. His eyes opened and flashed silver before settling back down to their pale blue, "He sang it to me. The man in front of the pool. He was short but strong. His head glistened with sweat. He was bald. His hands held the edge of this cauldron as if he were being forced to watch. Watch us. Watch me die."

Rosie reached a hand out to Silver's arm and Henry flinched at the affection, "We will not let you die, Silver. We promise."

Rosie's other arm stretched so that her other hand met Henry's arm. He looked down at her hand as if it were foreign to him.

"I don't think he was dreaming," Henry whispered, "He's describing father. That tune."

"Silver," Rosie squeezed his arm, "the man in your dream, did he seem familiar to you? Have you met him before?"

Silver squeezed his eyebrows together until he finally shook his head. "Both of you are all I know."

Rosie stood up and walked abruptly towards the kitchen door, "The garden won't fix itself."

Henry watched her go before he stood up and headed towards the front door, "I'm going to do some whittling."

Silver stared at the arm that Rosie had touched as he slowly pulled it closer to his body. Tears burnt in the corner of his eyes as the frustration began to grow deep inside of him.

"Are you coming?" Silver heard and looked over at Henry standing on the porch. The door swung slightly in the breeze. Silver could see the Lakewood Trees sway in the distance. He grinned and stood up, following Henry out to the stump.

* * *

The door to the Cot Cage opened. Long, slender fingers spilled outwards. The frame around the door cracked along the sides as the shadow creature spread itself out into the Great Hall before dashing out the front door and sliding itself along the left side of the house. Its silver eyes looked back at the boys huddled together at the stump and then dashed around the house along the Lakewood Trees towards Blackwood. It paused for a moment, watching the woman stare around bewildered at her garden and it sneered, showing long, piercing teeth. The glyphs were working and soon the household would fall.

"Come," it hissed and disappeared amongst the trees. Hundreds of howls erupted around them.

* * *

Rosie snapped her head upwards at the sound of the howling. The air around her echoed with the wails of the spiked wolves and a low rumble followed it. The Blackwood was calling to her and she knew it brought danger. She turned and ran towards the backdoor just as the first of the spiked wolves bounded out of the southern borders of Lakewood Trees. They were already halfway through her garden trampling over the rest of the flora that survived the black worms. She spun around and slammed the door until it latched into place. She dashed out into the Great Hall. The front door hung open and she could hear the screams of Henry and Silver outside.

Panic gripped her throat, "Do not touch my boys."

The backdoor banged as the wolves slammed into it. The glass in the door shattered and Rosie could hear the barks and growls as more and more slams hit the backdoor. By the time she reached the front door, a wolf had lodged itself into the broken remains of the backdoor's window.

She leaned out into the porch and screamed, "Henry! Silver! Get inside!"

The stump was empty except for the occasional wolf that leapt over it. She looked towards the northern border of the Lakewood Trees and saw Henry look back at her as Silver pulled him into the ferns and bushes blanketing the forest's floor. She stepped out to follow but on either side of the house came large packs of the mutated beasts. She backed away into the Great Hall, slamming the door behind her. Two wolves leapt through the front window and rolled along the Great Hall's floor. She screamed in rage and started to run back towards the kitchen. She had to get to the cellar.

The backdoor shattered and wolves began toppling over each other to get to her. She swore and leapt over a couple of steps on her way upstairs instead. The small hallways seemed so much bigger now as she took giant leaps to get to her room. She could hear the clawing of the wolves as they made their way after her. She dashed into her bedroom, twisting her body around to slam the door and bring the latch down to brace it. The door groaned and shook with each pounding of the wolves that hit it. She backed away slowly until she reached the wall filled with windows showing a front yard full of howling and snarling monsters. They were pouring into the house and the rest were heading north.

"Where are you going?" she hissed.

* * *

Silver panicked. He had put his hands over Henry's and glided them to carve off a groove into the wood.

"I think I see her," Henry grinned was just about to nestle himself into the almost embrace of Silver when the howls shook the air around them.

Silver looked to Henry's face before his eyes focused beyond him towards the garden. The wolves were snarling at the backdoor and more were heading their way. He stood up and pulled Henry with him and ran. He wasn't even sure where he was running. He just knew they had to get away. The Lakewood Trees were closer. Maybe he'd be able to lose them amongst the trees.

Henry jerked upwards off of the stool. His father's dagger fell into the grass surrounding it but he was able to hold on to the carving of his mother. At first he went to yell at Silver to return to the house but even he understood their best bet were the trees. He looked behind him to see his mother stand on the porch. She was screaming out their names, but the wolves were already getting too close.

The ferns and trees blurred around them as they ran together. The snarls of the wolves were getting closer. Henry knew these trees well. They held most of the herbs Rosie needed to put into her satchel. They had travelled days to collect the things she needed before. There were plenty of places to hide but he wasn't sure if they could hide from the wolves. Henry had a feeling he and Silver would get tired first before the wolves did.

"Silver," Henry called out, already out of breath and the silver-haired boy nodded and turned to the left. Now the wolves' threats were coming from their left instead of behind them. Whatever Silver was planning had better work or they were going to be wolf food.

Silver was trying not to panic. Henry was relying on him. He frantically looked around the unfamiliar trees until he found himself tumbling into a crevice. Silver landed face first and Henry on top of him. He pushed Henry off and struggled to stand up again.

"Henry," Silver moaned, standing up and spinning around slowly. He was almost relieved he recognised the area. But would this help them? This was the place that Rosie had found him. The howls of the wolves were getting dangerously close. Henry grabbed one of Silver's hands and held it tightly as they stood there. It would have been easy to climb out of the crevice but the canines were too close now.

A wolf leapt out from between two trees. Its mouth spread open in hopes that its teeth would sink into one of the boys. A thick branch swung out and sent the wolf flying backwards and snapping in half against another tree. Silver and Henry slid into each other's arms as more and more trees moved around them.

129

"Entmen," Henry watched in fascination as the trees made a wall surrounding the crevice. All light soon vanished except for the slight splinters of sun through the Entmen's canopies. Sometimes the tree trunks trembled as they heard the loud whoosh of their branches swing and the yelps of the wolves as they made contact. Some of them groaned as the boys heard what sounded like axes hitting them as the wolves' claws made contact.

"Silver," Henry whispered, trembling against his body.

Silver whispered back, "I'm here."

"My mom," Henry's voice cracked and Silver held him tighter.

* * *

Rosie's bedroom door held firm as the ornate carvings around the doorframe suddenly lit up and pulsated as the wolves slammed into the door.

"Patrick," Rosie whispered.

She could almost feel his hands in his as he led her around the upstairs. His carpentry skills were amazing, but the ornate carvings were more than that. They held importance she recognised immediately.

The ivy carvings ran up the length of the door as if the frame was a thick tree. Instead of leaves on the ivy, it held small dragons. He had done the same with Henry's room but instead the leaves had little birds flying upwards.

"From the story," Rosie whispered to Patrick, tears gathering in her eyes despite herself.

"Of course," Patrick whispered, pulling her into his arms, "The little girl out gathering comes face to face with a purple dragon. Her people cowered in terror, but she stood and gently touched it. It bowed to her before taking flight."

"Fairy tales," Rosie whispered, as the wolves slammed themselves against the door. "Alright, little Patty, your tricks have saved me again."

She trusted Patrick's frames as she casually walked over to the bed and reached underneath it, pulling out a long wooden case, "I should have used you ages ago. You were the last gift he gave me before he aban… before I… I should have listened."

She opened the case and pulled out a long, sturdy staff and a bow with a quiver of arrows. A leather belt with straps lay curled up in between. The staff, bow and quiver waited for her on the bed. She put on the leather and felt it attune itself to her form. There were two loops along the back strap that ran along her right shoulder down to her left hip. She lifted the staff and slipped it into the loops. Patrick preferred carpentry but even he couldn't ignore his innate talent for smithing.

The quiver had a metal hoop that she could squeeze and it came apart enough for her to attach around the back strap and hang in such a way that she could either reach for the staff or the quiver. The bow she picked up and held tightly to it. She wandered over to the window opposite of the door.

The window frames held the same ornate carvings as the door did. It was no wonder the glass never broke. In a few drunken nights after Patrick disappeared, she had tried to

131

throw his things through the glass. It didn't work and she passed out trying. She unlatched the window and pulled an arrow out of its quiver. She had twelve but that was more than enough. Although the garden was destroyed, she had plenty of the toxin she used on the arrows to make more. The Curet flower blossomed on the edge of midnight in between the limbs of the Blackwood and could be used to add an exotic flavour to soups if used in small amounts. But if the seeds were quantified and concentrated, it became a deadly toxin that if put into a blood stream could make the infected feral and lash out at anything in sight. trees. She couldn't even grow those flowers in the garden. She tried, frustratingly so.

She positioned herself firmly on two feet, nocked an arrow on the bow and heaved her shoulder muscles to pull the bow string back. She closed one eye and aimed out the open window to the sea of wolves that went in and out of the Lakewood Trees and her house. She aimed at one of the spiked wolves and fired. The arrow bounced off one of their spikes and landed in the grass.

"Sac," she nocked another arrow, "Don't get ahead of yourself. Breathe. Take it slow."
She closed an eye again, aimed and took a breath like she instructed herself to do and held it. She fired. The arrow found its way between a shoulder blade and chest of one of the wolves. She knew there would be solid muscle and fat there, unless the wolves had changed more than she knew. The arrow wasn't made to go deep but just enough to pierce the flesh and inject the toxin into the bloodstream.

The spiked wolf yelped as the arrow pierced its flesh and rattled to the ground. It stood for a moment licking its wound until it started twitching and convulsing to the ground. When it stood up again, it started its attack on the pack around it.

Rosie shot another arrow and another wolf. The arrow hit its mark and soon she had two wolves teaming up to destroy the others. The Curet toxin would not attack itself. After a few more arrows, Rosie had 5 other wolves tearing the others apart. It caused a confusion in the pack and they started to attack each other, unaware of where their own loyalties lay. Henry and Silver just had to stay out of their way.

Rosie left the other half of the arrows safely in the quiver and threw her bow on the bed. She pulled the staff out and held it firmly in two hands and faced her bedroom door.

"Sorry, Patrick" Rosie hissed.

She stepped towards the door and opened it.

* * *

All Henry and Silver heard were the yelps of the wolves as the Entmen held their defense. They would hear the occasional wolf try and pry itself between two trees as their claws dug away at the bark. Some of the Entmen groaned in pain. Most of them creaked in anger and determination. It was obvious they were not going to let the spiked wolves through no matter the cost.

Occasionally a tree would rotate and two large, red blinking eyes would look down at them, "Stay. Safe. We will not fall." While a few of the other trees would groan and their barks would lighten in colour like an old tree and stand still.

In moments, all but one of the Entmen had gone still when the spiked wolves fell silent. A single Entmen moved away from the silent trees surrounding them. Its long branches beckoned to them, "Come. Safe. Come."

133

Silver stepped out first and gasped at the lifeless bodies of dozens of wolves that had been flattened or bludgeoned to death.

The Entmen had old scars and new wounds as it creaked a few more steps before stopping, "She saved me. I saved you."

Henry looked up to find two red eyes peering down at him, "Thank you."

"They come from above," the Entmen wheezed, "You must go to her, little bird."

Silver ran a hand along one of the Entmen's wounds, "Will you be okay? You're hurt."

"I am. But I will not be. Go."

A branch swung lightly from above and nudged them back towards the south. Silver grabbed Henry's hand and both of them ran towards the house where they could still hear the howls of the wolves on the horizon. Henry could feel his heart return to his ears. They were running back into danger and without the Entmen, the guardians of not only Blackwood but of the Lakewood Trees as well. Henry felt vulnerable and even more so when they broke free from the forest and found wolves fighting wolves in his own backyard.

"Henry! Silver!" Rosie screamed from the Great Hall. She was almost where the front door used to be as she swung a long staff and cracked a wolf's head open.

A dark cloud suddenly seemed to black out the sun as it passed over momentarily.

"They come from above," Silver hissed and pointed upwards. Henry followed his finger to the sky where the cries of ravens suddenly pierced the air.

"The ravens!" Henry gasped. He remembered their taloned wings and teethed beaks and bolted towards his mother. The wolves seemed preoccupied with themselves and ignored him. He didn't question it until he reached the porch and Rosie pulled him inside, "The wolves…"

"Curet," Rosie snapped and pushed him towards the stairs, "Get to your room. You'll be safe there. Where's Silver?"

Henry's eyes widened, "He was just behind me! Where is he, mom? He was just there!"

Rosie nodded and pushed him again but he stayed. She didn't have time to argue with him. The door seemed to explode and dozens of ravens burst inside and filled the room up. She yelled out in pain as their talons ripped into her arms. She felt warmth trickle down her forehead and her right eye closed instinctively as red liquid tried to pour into it. Henry backed up as the unkindness of ravens swarmed around him. He felt their unnatural teeth sink into his back and shoulders. He was blinded by black feathers and deaf from their sounds.

Two hands grasped Henry's waste and pulled him backwards and a warm, haunting voice mumbled in his ear, "Crows caw and Ravens croak. But you'll still scream when they come for your throat."

Henry flew backwards and rolled across the floor where Silver knelt down from the backdoor and pointed to the stairs leading down, "The cellar!"

Henry scrambled to get up, "Where were you?!"

135

Silver held the whittling knife out toward Henry and shoved its handle into his hand. They both scrambled down the stairs and pulled aside the door that kept the cellar cool and dry. Rosie suddenly appeared at the top of the stairs and clambered down after them, pushing them inside and slid the cellar door closed and latched it.

"I always wondered why dad made a latch for the cellar," Henry mumbled.

"I wonder about a lot of things when it comes to your dad," Rosie snapped, lighting up a black candle from her satchel. It lit brighter than normal candles. She held it out until she found Silver, standing further into the room staring back at them.

"What did you mean?" Rosie slowly stepped towards him.

Silver whimpered, "When?"

"You know when. When you pulled me from the ravens. You said, 'No matter their feathers and no louder their cries, you linger much longer and the bird, he dies!' What did you mean?"

Henry stepped in her view, "He didn't pull you out. He saved me."

Silver watched them both silently. His eyes flickering silver from the candlelight.

Henry whispered, "Crows caw and Ravens croak. But you'll still scream when they come for your throat," and Rosie finished, "No matter their feathers and no louder their cries, you linger much longer and the bird, he dies!"

They heard footsteps run along the floor above them. They

fell silent and listened. Someone was up there running about and slowly the sound of the ravens diminished.

Rosie swore and Henry gasped as they ran back to the cellar door, both scrambling for the latch and handle and both shouting out, "Patrick?" "Dad?"

They both started to lift up the big wooden board that held the door firmly closed when Silver screamed. They both spun around and watched as Silver clutched at the key hanging around his neck on the silver chain. His nose was bleeding. His eyes were clenched shut in pain. They both froze and watched as the boy opened his eyes and thrusted out the hand that still clenched the key.

His eyes poured out silver mist as his mouth opened and a voice boomed around them, "I am the probabilities between the stars! The guiding hand in the rotation of worlds! I am the messenger and I am your end!"

Silver collapsed and the house fell silent. Henry went to rush to him but Rosie put a hand up to stop him. They both stared at the smoking, young boy. A couple of footsteps from above broke the silence and Silver's smoking stopped. The footsteps lingered for a moment before running across the floor above them towards the Great Hall until the house fell silent again.

Rosie turned and scrambled to open the cellar door and rushed up the stairs, "Patrick! Patrick!"

Henry slowly walked to Silver and knelt over him with a hand just hovering over his back. He wavered for a moment before he turned Silver onto his back and looked into the boy's face. His face looked paler. His lips were as silver as his hair. Henry's heart sank and he allowed his hand to stay on Silver's chest.

Silver coughed.

Henry's eyes burnt with tears and he slammed himself down into Silver's body and hugged him tightly. By the time he released Silver, Rosie had returned and she just slowly shook her head.

"The wolves? The ravens?" Henry helped Silver sit up.

Rosie sighed, "They're dead. They're all dead. A big mess to clean up."

"Mom."

Rosie shook her head, "No sign of him."

Henry returned his tender gaze back down to Silver, "What did you do?"

"I doubt he'll even know," Rosie helped stand him up. "Or not tell us."

Henry glared at her for a moment. She just shrugged and stared suspiciously down at Silver.

Silver's eyes kept fluttering as his head wobbled back and forth. They struggled to get him up the stairs and into the Great Hall where Rosie pointed to the Cot Cage's door, "Let's put him in there."

"No," Henry said, "We can get him to my room. You said it was safe there."

Rosie nodded, "The frames. Your father's frames. They couldn't pass through."

Henry nodded. He wanted to ask more questions but he

knew they'd just frustrate her. Sometimes even his own questions frustrated him. Why couldn't he just know things like his mother seemed to or his father? He almost felt like he knew as much as Silver seemed to. Life appeared to be a bunch of questions without answers. He had defended his father's disappearance for rotations as Rosie blamed him for abandoning them. But now, after all they've been through with Silver, and all these puzzles Patrick had left behind, he was running out of excuses for the man.

Long after they put Silver to bed, and long after they emptied the house of the countless number of ravens, Rosie and Henry still hadn't spoken to each other. It was as if the world had fallen into silence. Henry couldn't remember the last sound he heard as he started to drag a wolf over to the pile his mother was starting not far from the whittling stump. The sun was setting and neither of them had eaten. They had no urge to do so, although they both found themselves drinking from the well together. It was still full from the flooding and they still had no need for the bucket.

Finally, the last wolf they could find was dragged into the pile and Rosie lit it on fire. They both gathered old shaving left around the stump and started to toss them in until Henry saw a familiar carving in Rosie's hand as she headed towards the fire.

"Mom, wait!" Henry called, "That one is mine! Leave it! I must have dropped it."

Rosie looked down at it a moment and then back at Henry, "You do not need to replace your father. Do you really want to? After all that we have learnt? All of his secrets?"

"No, but I—" Henry began but stopped as he watched

Rosie throw the carving into the fire. His body felt numb and the burning tears that had threatened to come all day finally poured down his face.

"Don't cry for him," Rosie muttered.

"That was for you!" Henry snapped.

"What?"

"I was making that for you! The last piece for the mantel! The most important one! I was making it for you!"

Rosie's gaze returned to the fire with only a moment of regret before she shook her head, "What is done is done." She turned towards Henry but he was storming off towards the house. She sighed and returned to watching the fire. She imagined going after Henry and apologising but she wasn't wrong. What was done was done and there was no coming back from ash. Henry had to learn that there would be some things in this world that cannot be replaced. Sometimes there wasn't room for sentimentality.

Henry returned to her side and emptied his arms full of figurines into the fire. Rosie stared at them as she watched them burn. She stayed silent. She had lost her right to speak and she refused to admit that it hurt watching them burn. It is not what she had wanted to happen. Even though her anger for Patrick deepened, it all still hurt.

She looked over at Henry and went to speak but his cold gaze silenced her.

"What?" he snapped, "It doesn't matter. What's done is done, right, mom?"

His tears cut through her but she stood taller and returned

his cold gaze as the fire roared up above their heads and long into the night. They stayed there longer than they needed to as their fists hung by their sides. Their eyes only blinked when the heat of the fire grew too much for them.

"The doors need replacing," Rosie eventually hissed and walked away.

Henry watched her go before following her. The smell of roasting wolves and ravens was getting to him. It didn't smell like natural meat. He helped his mother pull up extra doors from the cellar when Patrick had made a few extra.

"Just in case," he had said and both Rosie and Henry replied as they realised they were thinking the same thing, "Just in case of what?"

The fire eventually died out when all that was left was ash. The smoke travelled up into the air and the wind carried it east above the Blades and over River's Song. Hundreds of figures approached the bank of the river. Their glowing, silver eyes stared off into the west's horizon. They waited. The bank was an imaginary border. But not for long. From downstream, the shadowy creature marched until it reached the Blades. It stood tall and commanding as it stared across River's Song to the figures.

"Silver Eyes," it hissed. "Come. He is waiting."

The Silver Eyes standing at the bank moved their heads to look down at River's Song. It was as if moving was unnatural for them. Their muscles creaked and their bones cracked. They watched as the crystal, clear water slowly trickled to its last drop. River's Song fell silent.

With the border dropped, The Silver Eyes marched forward

as one. Their feet silently stepped through the long grass until their bodies disappeared by the Blades height. They passed by the shadowy creature as if it were not there. Their eyes, intent on the western horizon, glowed with anticipation. They had been waiting for so long for the time to come, when they'd be free from their prison. Now, they had just one more thing to do.

They had to reach the key to their prison's door.

The Shadow in the Frame

The sun slowly crept above the Lakewood Trees as if its light hesitated to see the devastation that spread across the Edwards' homestead. It had been a few days since the wolves and ravens had attacked and the garden was still dishevelled. Rosie still had moments where she'd stand there and stare at the rotations of work gone in a single day. There were some plants she would have to find the seedlings for in order to replace. For the rarer ones, it would cost her more than she had to get them back. The black worms were still a threat. She'd find one every now and then coming up from the earth. The soil was still infested and there was a part of her that felt the whole garden needed to be upheaved and the soil churned and purified, but this garden had started long before Henry appeared. She wasn't about to give up on it now.

When she wasn't out in the garden, she was helping Silver and Henry with the house. The front and back door had been replaced, but none of them felt safe. For the first time since living there, Rosie insisted on installing locks on the doors. There were a few being used in the cellar to lock away chests full of important papers or sentimental items that were only going to be used once.

"What is this?" Henry pulled a long piece of fabric from one of the chests with dried vines and a few leaves that refused to give up the memory of it.

Rosie waved her hand at Henry and tested a few old keys she had in a drawer up in her room. Two of them fit the locks on the chest perfectly. "Don't worry about that."

"But what is it? It's a weird rope."

Rosie laughed, "It's not a rope. It's a promise." She stopped and felt the cold sting of betrayal lace her heart, "It's a broken one."

"But what is it?"

Rosie unhooked the two keys off of the loop she found them on. She had no clue what some of the other keys were for, but most of them were used to lock some sort of secret or memory away. "Henry, just drop it. It doesn't matter now. What matters is that we have locks to install on the two doors before nightfall."

Henry stared at Rosie until her shoulders heaved and her lips pushed together, "It's a promise two people make to each other. You loop one end around one wrist and you loop the other on the other wrist. The two join hands and in unison they promise each other to always be joined."

She left before Henry could say anything else, so instead, he just looked down at it and dropped it back into the chest full of probably other broken promises. "Oh."

The spiked wolves returned on that night. They heard the howls outside their windows. Not as much as the first time but enough to add new scratches to the door. By sunrise, they'd find more spiked wolves dead. The dam of Entmen had reanimated and now stood randomly around their house. Silver found comfort in them but Rosie knew that their presence here wasn't entirely a good thing. Yes, they were protecting them for some unknown reason, but these creatures were of Blackwood Legends. They guarded the rest of the lands from the shadows that lurked there. If they weren't doing that anymore, then where were the shadows lurking?

Not all the Entmen survived the onslaught of spiked wolves or the teeth ravens. Every now and then, Rosie and Henry would go outside to find another one laying on the ground gray and wilted.

"They won't last forever," Henry whispered and helped Rosie prepare breakfast.

By the next day, Rosie had a lot of moments where she just stood off to the side and watched. Henry surprised her. He was far more self-sufficient than she had ever given him credit for. When Patrick left, she just picked up where he left off. She didn't bat an eye or hesitate. She couldn't afford to, but with Henry and Silver stepping in, she found things got done quicker. It was as if Patrick had never left and their world wasn't crashing down around them. They worked in synchrony.

"Do these speak, too?" Silver asked as he helped lock up the front door and handed the key back to Rosie.

Rosie and Henry went to answer but hesitated at the sound of a distant wolf. The windows had been boarded up so it became darker in the house quicker. Both Henry and Rosie hesitated to use the candles as they found that they were running out of them.

"What happens when the candles run out?" Silver asked a lot of questions and at first it was easy to answer them. As the troubles started to increase and the future of the supplies came into question, it became harder and harder to answer.

Henry disappeared into the kitchen as Silver watched Rosie check the windows to ensure the boards were solid. The boys had spent the first day putting them up while Rosie secured the doors and scouted the perimeter.

"Are we safe?"

Rosie turned around to find Silver standing right behind her. His eyes glinted with worry. His silver hair needed a good wash. They all did. "We are safe enough."

"We really need to return to the community and restock," Henry said as he brought up the last box of candles from the cellar. "Ole Spit will appreciate the business, I'm sure."

"Don't call her that," Rosie hissed and followed Silver back to the table.

"What?" Henry placed the box on the table. The Grand Hall echoed with the remaining light of some dying candles. "She calls herself that."

"Ole Spit?" Silver asked, peering into the box and selecting a few candles. He handed them over to Rosie who lit them and blew out a few that were now just puddles of wax on the mantle.

"She's this little old lady that lives in the middle of the community. She has one eye that peers out of hundreds of folds of wrinkles. Her mouth is just a big gaping hole when she talks because she lost all her teeth. If she's not drooling, she's spitting. Ole Spit."

Rosie laughed loudly, "For the love of gods, Henry, you

are exaggerating! She's not that bad."

"Isn't she?" Henry grinned.

Rosie thought for a moment, "Okay, maybe not. But still, be nice. She's had a tough life. She was Ole Spit when I was a little girl."

Silver helped scrape one of the candles off, "Did she have teeth then?"

Rosie eyed Silver and simply said, "No," before all of them paused a moment in a fit of laughter.

Rosie sniffed the air as the newly lit candles let out their faint aroma. Ole Spit never told them what her candles were made of but they were guaranteed to give off the best glow and cleanse the air of bad omens. Rosie crinkled her nose and smelt herself and then looked over at the boys and sniffed the air again.

"In the morning, we bathe."

Henry and Silver copied her as they smelt the air, too, and nodded in agreement.

By the third day since the attack, Rosie allowed herself to sleep in, even after hearing Henry and Silver whispering to each other as they woke up. It wasn't until another teeth raven killed itself against her bedroom window that Rosie slid out of bed. The windows upstairs weren't boarded up. The frames for the windows and doors kept them safe. It was as if an invisible force kept the ravens at bay. Henry said the same thing was happening with his window in the back. It was as if the ravens were trying to see if the frames Patrick had created would falter. Until then, only during the first light of day, they'd wake up to the crack of the teeth raven's necks and the thunk of their bodies as if they hit a solid wall.

She wondered why Patrick hadn't done the same for downstairs. She wondered about a lot of things when it came to Patrick. "I don't know whether I'd kiss you or kill you," Rosie grumbled to herself as she finally headed downstairs.

The sun kept the upstairs lit just fine but it was a whole other world downstairs. None of the candles were lit so it was as if she had walked down into the cellar. It was cold and mysterious. The back door must have been open because natural light was coming from the kitchen.

"Boys," Rosie called, "you better have taken those baths because I'm next and I think I'll soak for at least an hour." She knew she wouldn't be able to soak that long. They'd need to spend the morning cleaning up the bodies of the ravens and the wolves. Rosie kept some of the teeth of the ravens and a spike from the wolves. She knew someone in the community would be able to explain their transformation to her. At least, she hoped someone could because Rosie had no explanations except that it all started happening after Silver arrived and Patrick sent his note.

As soon as her feet touched the Great Hall's floorboards, Silver appeared to her left pulling at her left arm and Henry at her right pulling her in the kitchen's direction.

They both spoke at the same time. "Mom, you need to come out to the well." "Rosie, there's something wrong in the Cot Cage."

Rosie's eyes looked past Henry and out the back door which still hung open. From where she stood, outside seemed peaceful and normal. The sun was warming the ground. Birds were singing in the distance. There were grass and trees visible. She walked past Henry, sliding her hand across his head and feeling its grease. He had not bathed. She walked slowly through the kitchen and out the backdoor. The sun felt amazingly warm despite the layer of oil and dirt upon her skin.

She followed the path around and twinged at the sight of the garden. Henry must have found a few black worms because a few chunks of their innards were splattered here and there. She kept walking. Her feet lightly stepped across the gravel. She could hear smaller footsteps behind her and knew her boys were following. Her nose twitched and she instinctively raised a hand to itch it. The well stood in the centre of the garden. It was her beacon to each season to know that fresh water from River's Song would fill the garden's forever thirst.

She reached the cobblestone edge of the well and leaned over. Henry had left the bucket just hanging off the side. He must have come out to get their bath water and boil the rest for breakfast. As soon as her hands touched the edges of the well, she knew what she would see.

"Nothing," Henry whispered, stepping around to the other edge and peering in. "The well is dry. How is that possible?"

Years before they had even moved in, there was a drought that had plagued a majority of the lands. Since then, the well had always been replenished. She had fed the soil with her mulch and had travelled with Patrick north to help free the river from the mountains after a landslide. The drought had taken the song away and parts of the mountains crumbled but when the rains came with its tune, the landslide had kept it all to itself.

149

Rosie looked East towards River's Song and then North. What was plaguing them now to take their water away and so quickly? Just days ago, it rained so badly it flooded. She looked around and pointed to a black worm off in the Summer section. Henry nodded and soon she heard the splat of the horrid creature. She smiled over at him fondly.

"Rosie?" Silver snapped her out of her reverie. "The Cot Cage…"

Rosie pushed herself away from the well and started back towards the house. Silver followed quickly and looked up at her. He was always in awe at her height. She was a tall sentinel. He felt safe around her and as he skipped a few steps to keep up with her pace, he no longer felt the dread of returning to that room.

"What are we going to do?" Henry rushed up and matched pace with them both.

Rosie's eyes were on the back door, "WE are going to wash as much as we can with last night's water. I'll use some crystals on it. We will have a dry breakfast. I can't have us getting sick. Who knows what kind of things are on us from handling the ravens and the wolves? Bad enough we burn them and their ashes fill the air."

"But…" Silver rushed after Rosie as she entered the back door and went straight to the kettle.

"I'll split this up. Go upstairs. Change your clothes again."

Silver went to speak but Rosie poured some water into a large bowl and shoved it in his hands. "Go. Now."

Silver looked down at the bowl and back up at Rosie. Henry nudged him, "Come on, Silver. Let's hurry."

Rosie followed them up the stairs as they each returned to their rooms. She washed quickly and grabbed her travelling clothes, her staff, the quiver and bow and her satchel. Just as she walked out of her room, Henry walked out of his, followed by Silver.

"Where are you going?" Henry gasped.

"River's Song," Rosie kept walking straight down the stairs. She could hear Henry and Silver struggle to keep up. She heard their feet land on the floorboards. They must have jumped the last few steps to keep up with her, but she kept walking towards the back door and straight out of it.

"Mom," Henry called out to her, "We're coming with you!"

Rosie shook her head and kept walking. She stepped off the path that led to her garden and straight towards the area that still held signs of Entmen standing at attention. "No, Henry, you will stay here with Silver. Make sure the house is secure. I'd prefer you to stay inside as much as possible but I know you won't do that. So, keep the garden as clear as you can."

"No!" Henry snapped, still following her. "We're going with you!"

Rosie did not falter in her steps, "Do as you're told, Henry. If this garden dries up, our home is lost. If no one is here to upkeep it, our home is lost."

"Mom," Henry tried to argue and it was at this point Rosie stopped and he ran into the front of her as she quickly spun around.

She towered over him. Her eyes held such intensity

that he struggled to keep eye contact with her and in a commanding voice, she said, "If something happens to you, my home is lost. Now, do as I say."

Without waiting for Henry's response, she spun around and quickly marched through the trees and eventually vanished. Henry stood there. His hands were clenched together. His eyes were burning with tears. He stayed there until Silver put a hand on his shoulder.

"Henry, are we going to follow her?"

"No, Silver, we're not." Henry wiped his eyes before he spun around and gave Silver the same look Rosie gave him, "But we're going to help her. She's going to see if something is wrong at River's Song."

"What are we going to do?"

"We're going to have a closer look at that well."

Henry marched past him, taking the same strides that Silver recognised. He watched Henry for a moment before looking over at an Entmen. Two red eyes blinked at him quickly. Scars ran up and down the creature's trunk.

Silver's eyes flashed with mist, "Protect Rosie," before he followed Henry to the well.

The Entmen rose out of the ground. Its roots lifted out of it and pulled it towards the East. The canopy swayed high in the air as it weaved itself past the trees and disappeared after Rosie.

Silver found Henry hunched over the well. Henry didn't look up as he threw a small stone into the well and heard it rattle against stone. The light from the sun showed the bottom of the well where it emptied out into darkness.

"You can lower me down with the bucket. I once had to climb down when the bucket got stuck on a branch at the well's bottom."

Silver looked down into the darkness, "Where is the bottom?"

"Technically, I've never been at the bottom. The well was dug down into an underwater cave." Henry pointed to the east. "There's a point in the river where it splits. One part of the river flows onwards to the Blackwood and the other part flows into the mouth of a cave and fills it. That's how we knew if the river was high or low. The water gets pushed up if it's flooding."

Silver nodded, "Like it did a few days ago."

"Yes, and if it's low, it pretty much just opens up to the roof of the cave."

"How will you see down there?"

Henry looked over at Silver, "Good point. I'll be right back."

Silver watched Henry run back to the house and disappear through the door. There was a slight breeze that rustled the remaining plants of the garden. The sun was fully above the trees now. A few Entmen wandered slowly beyond the trees of the east side of the garden. Silver walked around the well and wished the garden still looked like it did the first day he had seen it. It was something like he had never seen before.

Silver paused and laughed to himself, as he spoke to the well, "I can't remember seeing a garden before."

The breeze suddenly died and with its silence a fluttering cracked the air like lightning and a shadow passed over the sun. Silver looked up to see a flock of ravens dive down towards him from the air. He only had time to naturally flinch and raise his arms in defense before the force of their assault sent him flying over the well's edge.

Henry grabbed the lantern off of the table and went back through the kitchen before he realised he needed to put a new candle in it. With this lantern, he could untie the bucket and replace it with the torch. He'd see if the problem was in the cavern below the well. It'd save his mother some time if she returned with no answers. Entmen were stepping out of the eastern tree-line but Henry ignored them and turned back towards the Great Hall.

"Henry," a whisper startled him as he re-entered the room.

"Mom?" He set the lantern back on the table and looked at the door to the Cot Cage. It was slightly open and a pale light flickered inside.

He waited for a moment. A sound startled him from the back door. He went to go see what it was but the voice returned, "Henry, I need your help." It was definitely his mother. When did she get back? The door to the Cot Cage was open further and the light flickered more intensely.

The back door hit against the house and snapped Henry's attention back to it. An Entmen was at the door. Its branch beckoning to him. Did something happen to Silver?

He held up a hand to the Entmen, "Just a minute, I'll get my mom!" He scrambled past the table and whipped open the Cot Cage door and stepped inside.

"No," the Entmen creaked and groaned.

The door to the Cot Cage slammed shut.

Silver looked up at the circular light above him. His left hand held the end of the rope as tightly as he had held the key. His wrist hurt where it slammed against the edge of the bucket. The palm of his hand still burnt after it slid against the rope. He could feel his legs dangling in the air and each time he dared to look down all he saw was darkness and heard the echo of the breeze as if something was cupping over his ears.

"I don't know how much longer I can hold on." He wasn't sure who he was talking to but he refused to look away from the light. At any moment, Henry would return. He'd have light and he would save him.

The rope jerked a few times and Silver grew hopeful. He tightened his grip one last time.

Silver's heart skipped a beat and he slowly nodded his head. "Henry," he gulped and closed his eyes for a moment as his hand's strength gave way. He fell into the darkness. The circular light grew further and further away until Silver felt the sound of his body crunching against the floor.

"…and they fled the shadows and they fled the dark god," a voice echoed around Silver and his eyes fluttered open. Out amongst the darkness around him the voice continued, "who they blamed for the weird and they cursed for the odd…"

Silver lay in the darkness. He couldn't move anything except for his eyes.

"…and they ran till they were further to pray and to weep…" the voice continued to echo around him. Silver listened. The voice seemed familiar to him, as if it were a faraway dream, "…but you can't run from anything when you sleep…"

"…WHEN YOU SLEEP!!" The voice screamed down into Silver's face, as two strong hands grabbed his shoulders and lifted him up, forcing him to stand on his own two feet. The echoes of the voice's last words drifted further away into the darkness.

"Hello?" Silver remembered the pain of the landing from the fall. He hesitated to move his body but the only pain he felt was the ringing in his ears from the sudden boom of the voice. "Henry?"

He looked up to where he thought the well would be but the circular light was gone. How long had he been down there? And most importantly, who belonged to that voice? It wasn't Henry. It wasn't Rosie. Silver had a thought, "Patrick?!"

His voice just returned to him as his answer. He took a step and felt his feet slide against something slick beneath him. He slowly knelt and blindly felt the floor beneath him. It was slick rock covered in something that slid off onto his fingers. He raised it to his nose and then wiped his hands on his clothing. It smelt like the cellar in the house.
He stood back up and instantly ended up on his backside. He winced. The slight fall reminded him of what it felt like landing. His whole body felt as if it were being electrified for a moment as he remembered the pain. When he remembered that he was fine, he attempted to get up again. The rock floor was just too slippery. He couldn't get his footing.

"I can't see," he whimpered, wishing Henry and Rosie were here to help him. He just wanted to be back in their house and safe in Henry's bed. "I don't want to see Teeth Ravens either, Rosie, or Spiked Wolves or those horrible Black Worms."

Silver felt the presence instantly as the voice returned as a whisper in his left ear. A strong hand returned to prop itself against Silver's left shoulder. "…but you will see the sea and the dead dogs in it, the shadows caw in the edge of what's moonlit, your eyes will cry the innards worm, she'll writhe, he'll die and your silver blood will squirm…"

Silver shuddered as the hand disappeared and all around him he heard the sound of things smacking against the surface of the cave's floor around him. The sound of a hundred small gasps filled the air and like the sound of the Black Worms exploding under his feet, he heard each one of those gasps pop and a spectacular splatter of fluorescent light sprayed around the cave and lit it up spectacularly.

Silver instantly looked around for any signs of the voice, "Patrick? Are you Patrick?"

The smacking had stopped. The gasping was dead. Silver could see as much as the moon could light up the night sky. He could see parts of the cave's floor where he could safely stand up without slipping on what looked like moss of some sort.

"Rosie would do something with this," he said, "I don't know if you can hear me, Patrick, if you even are him…"

He let himself trail off as he looked around and above him. The splatter of light glowed so much that he could see the top of the cave. It seems so smooth and still wet yet

157

no water dripped down at him. There was a darkness that Silver guessed was where the Well's opening would be. Did he sleep until night came?

His thoughts were interrupted by a distant echo of gasps and smacking. In the distance he could see more light appear. "Patrick?! Patrick, is that where you want me to go?"

Silver started to walk towards the light and the closer he got to the edge of the darkness the more the sounds returned and lit his way. The cave was higher than it was wide. He would have been able to go from one end to the other in moments. It wasn't until he had been travelling for what seemed like days that he finally could reach up and touch the ceiling. It, too, was covered in green sludge. The smell that reminded him of the cellar soon disappeared as a breeze travelled down to him from somewhere up ahead. He wanted to quicken his pace and tried to, but the slickness of the rocks forced him to slow.

Two things seemed to happen at the same time. The cave suddenly began to echo with the sound of the breeze and sunlight poured from an opening up ahead. The ground began to incline quickly and Silver found himself sliding backwards, as he fell to his hands and knees to find better footing. The pace was even slower. He'd make progress and then slide right back down. Birds teased him from somewhere beyond the rocks that aligned the opening. Grass grew from the top and only the rocks grew at the bottom. His fingers began to ache and his knees were hurting from the times he slipped and slammed down onto the surface, but it didn't stop him from eventually reaching the opening and pulling himself out onto a dry riverbed. The Lakewood Trees surrounded half of the opening and the other half looked like a pathway that led through the Blades.

Silver rested for a moment, but only for a moment because the drive to get back home led him back to his feet and along the riverbed path. He didn't get far before he heard a few of the trees groan and tilt as an Entmen pushed its way through. It was the same scarred one that he had told to watch Rosie. The Entmen wasted no time in pulling itself forward by its roots towards Silver and scooping him up quickly with a few of its branches.

Silver's head spun for a moment as he instinctively wrapped himself around a thick branch. The Entmen's roots flung forward in their desperation and the Blades was quickly behind them as they flung through the Lakewood Trees.

"Henry," The Entmen's voice groaned up to Silver. "Save. Henry."

Silver had to close his eyes because they were travelling so fast. He called back out, "What about Rosie?"

"Henry." The Entmen insisted and moved his branches around until Silver was now being held in front of it and without hesitation the branches shook him off. Silver went flying until he rolled through the grass and found himself near the area that used to be the dam. "Open the door."

Silver sat up and waited for his head to clear before getting up and looking around. The sun was now well beyond the house and almost heading back down towards the Lakewood Trees. The day was nearly through. The garden was covered in feathers and innards. The well was clogged with the gray body of one of the Entmen sticking out of it. Silver felt a twinge of sadness. He wondered if the creature had died trying to save him. Sitting on the uprooted Entmen in the well sat dozens of what Rosie had called the Teeth Ravens. They seemed to be laughing amongst themselves.

"Go." The Entmen pushed its branches into Silver's back. He was forced to walk until he took the steps himself and the scarred Entmen turned to head into the feathered garden already swinging its branches. Silver went to run to the back door but found another dead Entmen blocking the door. Nothing would be able to crawl through its trunk, not even those black worms that had plagued Rosie's garden.

Silver ran along the house and passed the stump that held the whittling knife. More sadness overwhelmed him as he remembered waking up to learn Henry had burnt all the carvings. Neither Rosie or Henry had spoken of it since, even when Silver tried to understand why they had done it. He didn't understand most things those two did.

The porch was empty and the front door was closed. The window next to it once showed the welcoming hall beyond it. But boards hid the safety of the house within. Silver skipped the few steps that brought him to the porch and ran through the door. It should have been locked but it wasn't. Silver locked it behind him with the wooden latch and the cellar chest's lock that had been left dangling on the loop. He jogged deeper into the room until he was at the bottom of the stairs.

"Henry?" Silver listened for a moment, called Henry a few more times before deciding to run up the stairs. He made it a few steps before his head was pierced with the high-pitched scream of the key around his neck. He fell backwards and landed on the floor.

"I'm tired of falling now." Silver's eyes lifted to the Cot Cage's door. He wasn't sure why he looked to it but something drew his attention and he repeated the words of the scarred Entmen, "Open the door."

Silver got up and walked over to the Cot Cage and grabbed the handle. It rattled in his hand and the door refused to budge. The door was locked. Silver knocked on it, "Henry?"

He pulled and pushed at the door and pounded his hand on it, "Henry? Rosie? Are you here? Please be here? I need you!"

He continued to push at the door until he took a step back from it and stared at it. "Doors don't lock in this house."

He ran towards it and slammed into it. The only thing that budged was Silver as he bounced back and almost fell. His head screamed again and he felt warm liquid drip out of his ears. He didn't have to check to know it was his own blood. His eyes flashed the silver mist as he reached for the door handle. It was as if, for a few blinks of an eye, everything fell into darkness until he was standing there in front of the open door.

Silver whimpered. He hated when he couldn't remember what had happened or what he had said or done. He was too scared to tell Rosie and Henry the truth. What if it were true? What if he was the cause of all this? They'd turn him away. They wouldn't want him anymore. He'd be alone in a world he didn't remember with no one he trusted or loved...and trusted and loved him in return.

His eyes focused into the Cot Cage. He knew what he was going to see. He had seen the room earlier with the strange, glowing glyphs on the walls and they were still there. They had not been there when he first arrived.

"Henry!" Silver ran into the room without thinking and knelt next to the body of his friend, laying within a couple of arms reach from the door. He rolled Henry onto his back and could instantly see he was breathing. A small little snort came from his nose every now and then and Silver pushed his eyebrows together. "Are you sleeping?"

Silver shook him a few times. The glyphs around him almost glowed with the same intensity as the light that appeared in the cave beneath the well. He didn't trust these glyphs, though, like he trusted the lights. He tugged at Henry and pulled him towards the door until they were both out near the long table that sat within the Great Hall. The Cot Cage's door slammed shut.

"Henry."

Henry's eyes fluttered and he stretched as if just waking up. His eyes held that dreamy look Silver had seen every day waking up next to him.

"Silver, what are you doing?"

Henry pushed himself up and away from Silver before realising he was on the floor of the Great Hall and everything came rushing back to him. He scrambled away from the Cot Cage and pointed at it, "That room. It's. I heard my mom, but she wasn't there. Then, I…"

"You were sleeping."

"Sleeping?"

"That room is bad now. I don't like it."
Henry relaxed a bit, "I never did." He looked into Silver's eyes for a moment before widening his own, "My mother!"

"I don't know," Silver sighed, "Teeth Ravens came." Henry got up and pulled Silver up as well, "We need to find her."

Somewhere outside the howl of the Spiked Wolves rose in the air. Silver and Henry shuddered. "We can't go out, Henry."

They both looked through to the kitchen. The back door was completely blocked with a dead Entmen. Henry looked at Silver who nodded, "I know. There are more of them dead in the back. In the well. One of them helped me come home."

"Come home?" Henry asked.

Silver and Henry held each other as the sun seemed to set quickly. The howl of the wolves tormented the walls around them. The body of the Entmen in the back shuddered and shook as the wolves clawed at it. They both looked up the stairs and nodded. They took each step carefully as their fear refused to let each other go. They were alone without Rosie and even though Henry had been alone before, this time felt different.

"The wood frames upstairs will keep us safe," Henry reassured Silver as they went into their room and closed the door behind them.

Silver

The Shadow in the Frame

Silver woke up feeling as if he were falling down an endless well. For a moment, his whole world felt like it was spinning. He grabbed at something and it ended up being Henry, who rolled around in the bed.

"What is it, Silver?"

Silver settled as soon as his eyes met Henry's hazy ones. The windows started to rattle and there were a few sounds of the Teeth Ravens falling to the ground.

"Morning already?" Henry rolled onto his back and lay there for a moment before exclaiming, "My mom!"

Silver watched as Henry bolted upright and looked back down at him. Silver rubbed his eyes and sat up as well.

"Did you dream of her?"

Silver focused his eyes on Henry again and shook his head, "I dreamt of falling down the well."

Henry tried to hide a look of guilt and wanted to apologise again for the hundredth time.

Silver stopped him, "It's ok. You didn't know the Teeth Ravens were going to come."

"So, we are really calling them that?"

Silver nodded, "It's what Rosie calls them."

Henry slid out of the bed. He was still wearing yesterday's clothes. He quickly changed into cleaner ones and dumped the others in the middle of the floor. Silver did the same.

"Something has happened at River's Song for the riverbed to be dry. My mom will figure it out. But we need water here and we need to make sure her garden doesn't dry out. The water in the well's cave was very important."

"Where do we get more water?"

Henry shrugged and opened the bedroom door with a loud creak and pop. Henry looked surprised for a moment as Silver walked up to him. "It's never done that before."

They walked downstairs slowly, listening to the sound around them. At the bottom of the stairs they found splintered wood. They looked at each other and drew the other closer to themselves as they took each step down into Patrick's Great Hall. The room was dark except for a soft glow of light coming from the kitchen. The dead Entmen may have blocked anything from coming in through the back door, however, it couldn't hold back the natural light of the rising sun over the eastern horizon. They tiptoed across the floor to the table and started lighting the candles around the room until both of them gasped at the sight of the Cot Cage door. It had been blown apart. It no longer existed and the Cot Cage itself looked as if it had been burnt from the inside. Everything was black and charred as they stood at its doorway and peered inside with their candles.

"What happened?" Silver took a step back and raised his

candle up. "It hasn't burnt out here."

Henry nodded slowly and pointed around the door frame, "It's charred a little but that could be from the door exploding outwards. How did we not hear this?"

They checked the front door and the boarded-up window until they were satisfied they were safe before pushing themselves through the dried leaves of the Entmen into the kitchen to fix themselves some breakfast.

"I don't know how we are going to move them," Henry said leaning against the counter and watched a dead leaf rattle at a breeze seeping from somewhere between bark and branches. He stuffed his face with some bread.

"I don't think we are supposed to move them. I think they died knowing nothing would get through." Silver took a large bite out of his bread.

"Not even us."

"Not even us," Silver repeated and took another bite. "It's better with strawberries."

Henry nodded and pulled Silver out of the kitchen towards the front door. Both of them eyed the charred remains of the Cot Cage as they passed. Silver unlocked the door while Henry raised the wooden plank and put it in the corner. Both of them pulled the door open and peered around the edge of it outside. As soon as they felt it was safe, they stepped out onto the porch.

"We'll clean up any ravens and wolves and then I'll show you this plant to the west my mother showed me." Henry jogged down the small steps that led to the yard and both of them walked around the grounds and dragged a few of the wolves to the area for the bonfire, just beyond the whittling stump.

"Watch for Teeth Ravens," Silver warned, eyeing the sky.

The sun was fully above the Lakewood Trees by the time the bonfire was done. Only one Entmen stood near the house now. It was the scarred one in the garden. Its red eyes blinked at them as they kept passing it.

Henry thanked it for bringing Silver back. "Do you know where my mom is?"

The Entmen pointed a few of its branches to the east and then closed its eyes. Somewhere beyond the garden towards the Blackwood they heard the caws of the ravens and both boys left. As they passed the whittling stump, Henry pulled out the knife that waited for him.

"We'll need this," Henry whispered, as the caws sounded like they were coming closer. "Quick. Let's get into the Lakewood Trees. It will give us cover. I'll show you the plants I was talking about."

Silver nodded and followed quietly as they left the stump behind and walked towards the porch where Henry turned right towards the west and ducked into the trees. Silver felt comforted knowing the canopy of the Lakewood Trees were hiding them from the ravens.

"What about the Spiked Wolves?" Silver reached out and grabbed Henry's hand that wasn't holding onto the whittling knife.

Henry squeezed Silver's hand, "The plants aren't that far. Besides, the wolves have only come out at night, remember?"

Only the distant caws reminded them that they weren't safe. Around them stood the peaceful Lakewood Trees. Beams of sunlight shared itself where the canopy allowed it. A warmth hummed with the grasshoppers and the crickets. Every now and then a buzzing of some insect would startle Silver and Henry would have to explain. He smiled to himself and wondered if this was what parenting was like.

"I know what all of this is," Silver finally said, "but I don't. It's like…when you explain it to me I know it's true…like I had known the whole time."

"Like the voice in the well?"

Silver looked over at Henry expecting to see a look of blame or distrust but he didn't. Silver lost himself in Henry's eyes as if they were the tall, green grass of the Blades. "I didn't do this. I wouldn't hurt you or Rosie."

Henry felt his own shock travel head to toe as Silver's words sunk in. "No. Silver. I don't think—we don't think that."

A crystal clear tear formed in each corner of Silver's eyes. "I can't remember things."

"I know," Henry sighed, still pulling Silver through the ferns and bushes that covered the floor of the forest. What seemed like a loud explosion burst out from one of the ferns was only a deer. Henry knew they'd almost be there where the wildest of ferns grew. The world around them burst with wildlife and unlike the ones living in Blackwood, these living creatures were timid and shy.

"No, not before, Henry," Silver was struggling to keep his breath under control. The deer had sent his heart racing and he made sure he was as close to Henry as he could be and still have the freedom to walk. "There are times, like at the table, when you both took the key, I…I don't remember. Moments of shadow."

Henry listened and slowly nodded as he turned a bit to make sure they continued west. If they spent the rest of the day walking, they'd arrive at the community before dark. There was a part of him that wanted to go there and climb up the stairs that led to their gates and beg for mercy and help.

"Do you think the voice was Patrick?" The question Silver asked made Henry stop in his tracks.

"I don't know, Silver. Things are happening so fast. I don't know what to think. I just know we need water. We can't dehydrate."

"If it was Patrick," Silver continued as they stepped through a spread of ferns and into an area tinted bluish gray. It was as if they passed through an invisible border into a new land. Silver trailed off, "then he saved my life… what is this place?"

Henry grinned, "In the community, they call this The Shale, but don't ever let them hear you call it that."

Silver let go of Henry's hand and slowly explored the area. The trees were the same around them, just more sporadic but off in the distance, Silver could see the bark start to change into a lighter tone of colour and the leaves became more rounded, until eventually, the horizon just seemed to be a blue mist. The grass threaded itself through the ground like a thick rug. It no longer held the deep hew of green Silver had grown accustomed to.

"Why can't we call it The Shale?"

Henry knelt down near a small round bush and rifled through it before getting back up and walking over to another one. These bushes held gray leaves and only grew underneath the trees. "Well, we can't even say the name of the community. Community is a word my dad came up with. The people that live there are a sacred people who do not believe they are like us."

"Like us?"

"Landwalkers."

"They fly?"

Henry laughed, "If they could, I think they would, but no, they cannot fly. But they've never touched the soil. Their people have lived in their village high above their grove's canopies. Everything they need grows up there. Everything they want gets traded with them. It's a beautiful place to visit. Not everyone is allowed up to their canopy, but my mother and father can, so that means I can, too."

Silver stood over Henry as he examined another bush and got excited with it. "What are you doing?"

Henry lifted up a handful of berries. "When I was little, I called these Water Berries, but you know Rosie, she made me call them by their correct name: umSwi. My mom uses them for many things for different people for trade. It can be used to clean clothes. It can be used to make wine. It grows beneath The Shale trees only. My mom says the plant is a parasite to the trees. Its roots dig their way into the roots of the trees and feeds off of their water and nutrients. The water is collected into the berries. Eat one. They'll explode in your mouth. It's fun."

Silver picked one up and studied it before casually popping it into his mouth. The berries were as big as his fingernails and as blue as the sky, which hid well behind the gray, round leaves of the bushes they belonged to. Henry wasn't wrong. The berry exploded in his mouth the moment he bit into it. His tongue almost curled at how sour it was and for a moment, Silver wanted to spit it out.

"Don't spit it out," Henry laughed and popped one in too until his face twisted up as well.

Silver laughed with him. "My mouth," he said in between chews and swallows, "filled with water."

Henry nodded. He had already finished his and popped in a few more, "Find enough of these berries and we will have water for days. Though, if we eat too much we'd be shitting and pissing all the time."

Silver fell backwards onto the ground in laughter. Henry joined in making noises and joking about how that might be their weapon against the wolves and ravens. After eating a couple handful of berries and joking about their weapons of excretion, they found themselves laying side by side in The Shale's grass staring up at the round leaves of the trees.

"You live in a beautiful place," Silver sighed happily and moved his head till it touched Henry's shoulder. He felt Henry stiffen and moved it away again looking over at his friend. "Are you okay?"

Henry's face was red and he nodded, "I was just thinking. I never had a friend my age before. I always wished we lived with the community or further into town just so I could know what it was like. When I'd visit these places with mom and dad, I'd always watch the kids and be so jealous. For a while, I hated where I lived."

Silver nodded and looked back up at the leaves in silence.

"But now," Henry continued, moving his head till it touched Silver's shoulder, "my home is in trouble and all I can think about is how to save it. It's dying and I don't want to have to go, but maybe my dad is right."

"Your dad?" Silver asked, moving his head to touch Henry's.

"We are to meet him at Moon's Edge, aren't we? Don't you think he knew? He knew this place wouldn't be safe forever. Isn't that why he wanted to go? My mom didn't want to go. I blamed her, you know, for him leaving. But now, I don't know. I think I blame him. But maybe we should have left with him?"

Silver whispered, "But then you wouldn't have met me."

Silence blanketed over them like the soft rays of the sun that kept them warm. Something in the distance walked casually through the trees. Neither of them moved. They just enjoyed the peace The Shale brought with it. The longer they stayed in that spot in their silence the more the fauna started to appear. The birds nestled in their branches and sang their songs. A few creatures darted up and down the trees as they climbed them. Silver wanted to know what they were but he knew his voice would take the life away. Henry felt the warmth of Silver more than he felt the warmth of the sun. He had spent many days in The Shale here alone wondering how life would be away from his mom and his dad and his home. But now that he had Silver there with him, he just wanted to be home with

Silver and his mom. Henry still didn't know how he felt about his father. He'd have thoughts of running up to his father and hugging him and crying into his short, strong arms, but then he'd feel this anger inside of him that just wanted to yell and scream and curse him.

Whatever was walking in the distance was getting closer. It was as if a breeze was coming through the trees and the leaves were dancing in it. None of the life around them flinched from the noise. Henry watched two squirrels chatter to each other as the sound was just beyond the western portion of The Shale, back where Henry and Silver had come from. Silver was watching a few rabbits dart in and out of a bush, their teeth gnawing at probably the same berries they had eaten.

Henry and Silver sat upright as an Entmen appeared between two trees and approached them. It hovered over them with red, blinking eyes but nothing more. The silence came back again. The squirrels and the rabbits had darted away the moment the boys sat up. Henry wondered if they wouldn't have if he wasn't so fearful.

The scarred Entmen closed its eyes and stretched its branches beyond its body until it created a new layer of leaves and branches above the boys. Its roots slowly sunk into the ground as if nothing had happened. It looked like a normal tree only slightly bigger than the rest. After a while, the grays and blues of The Shale seeped up into the body of the Entmen. They watched in silence as it soon looked just like the rest of The Shale trees.

Silver laid back down and put a hand on Henry's shoulder, "Tell me again about the Entmen."

Henry stared at it for a little while longer before he allowed

Silver to pull him back down with him. He softly told Silver the legend of the Entmen in the Blackwood Trees. Sometime during the soft lull of Henry's story, Silver fell asleep and despite the encroaching dangers that haunted his dreams, Henry joined him.

The branches of the Entmen slowly stretched over the sleeping boys. Its shadow slid across them like squirming fingers hungrily crawling across. The Entmen knew what was coming. It knew of the horrors these boys would face and all it could do was shade them from the sun piercing its canopy.

Every now and then a small creature would leap from the trees onto the Entmen's branches. It would open its eyes, an effort that was getting harder and harder to do. Though Rosie's salve had helped it, the newer wounds had still taken their toll on it. Each moment it attempted to heal was more energy that sapped away. The Entmen's red eyes blinked slowly at the joy of the squirrel leaping through its arms and tickling its bark as it ran around and around playing with the other squirrel that had joined it.

The Entmen ruffled its leaves at the feeling of the tiny little claws and both squirrels leapt through the air and abandoned it for the safety of the tree. The Blackwood did not hold such joyous creatures. The time within those black trees were spent keeping the darkness at bay.

Silver slipped into his dreams almost instantly. They plagued him each night and by the time morning came, he didn't feel rested at all.

He'd always find himself in the same place, standing next to the man at the scrying pool. The more he studied the man the more he could see a bit of Henry in him.

Sometimes he could move about in his dreams and he'd walk around the large scrying pool and look around. The room was in darkness. The scrying pool was very much like the well behind the house. It was made of stones but was wider. There wasn't a bucket or windlass but it seemed like a very familiar place to Silver.

"Let go of my son!" a voice would rise from the waters and each time Silver felt himself drawn to the cobblestone edge with a sweaty Patrick. The man was muttering under his breath but no matter how hard Silver listened, he could never hear the actual words.

The silver waters in the scrying pool always showed the same scene of Rosie fighting a darkness that had long, sharp claws holding onto Henry. Silver and Patrick winced at the same sight of blood appearing at Henry's throat. A part of Silver wanted to dive into the water and swim to stop it all from happening, but he could never move. He was as still in his dream as the image of his body near the stump appeared.

Henry dreamt of something entirely different but still just as real. He was a young boy in his bed. It was during a really bad winter that had brought a terrible fever that had him stuck in bed for days. Patrick was still there helping take care of him while Rosie was out somewhere in Blackwood trying to hunt down a rare flower that would heal him.

Patrick kept returning with a washcloth damp with well water to ease Henry's discomfort. He would hum his lullaby but in these dreams, Henry heard him sing.

> *"You'll raise a bird who'll hunt you down*
> *the huntress will come after,*
> *the silver tongue will guide their path*
> *and the gift you give thereafter."*

In his dream, with the fever raging against his forehead, Henry would thrash about asking his father what it all meant but Patrick didn't seem to hear him. He'd just sing it and leave, returning with a new damp, wash cloth and singing the verse over and over again.

The Entmen reached down towards the boys and nudged each one before starting to pull its roots from beneath the ground and dragging itself back towards the house.

Henry's eyes snapped open as the branches of the Entmen rose back up into the air and started to move away from them. In Henry's arms, Silver slowly sat up and watched with him as the tree creature started to head back towards the house.

"I guess our time here is done," Henry sighed, standing back up.

Silver joined him and both boys followed the Entmen slowly through The Shale before returning to the Lakewood Trees. They made sure to gather more of the umSwi on their way. The journey home was slower. They allowed the Entmen to set the pace and Silver was able to explore a bit more, asking questions about the creatures back in The Shale and the community that lived beyond them.

By the time that they returned home, the sun was high in the sky and the boys found themselves hungry.

"Do you eat?" Silver asked the Entmen, who found a place at the edge of the Lakewood Trees to nestle its roots into the ground. The yard that held the whittling stump just beyond it.

The Entmen leaned itself over the boy and blinked its red eyes slowly, "The soil. It feeds. Go. Stay."

Henry pulled Silver away from the Entmen and both of them ran across the yard and through the front door. The Entmen waited till the door was closed, latched and locked before it allowed its roots to go deep, beyond the blackening soil and to what was left of Rosie's mulch that had once spread its magic through the region. Soon, the worms would destroy what was left and the Edwards' Homestead would fail. The Entmen's red eyes grew heavy. Not much longer. It would not be able to protect them for much longer. The red eyes quietened and it slumbered once again.

Henry prepared lunch while Silver went to light a few candles before Henry poked his head through the doorway, "Why don't we eat in my room? The dead Entmen in the kitchen door are making me feel weird. We can finally play Tabs until my mom gets home!"

Silver nodded and helped Henry finish preparing lunch, which was the last of the stale bread, some conserve spread on top and a few pieces of jerky, before they both bounded up the stairs and walked into Henry's room. Henry laughed at the sight of Silver's face. The strawberry conserve was spread all around his lips and the bread was gone.

"What?"

Henry continued laughing and shook his head, "Nothing. You really like the bread!"

Silver grinned, "I really like the conserve."

Henry juggled his food in one hand and pulled open the top drawer and grabbed the bag of Tabs, "Remember me telling you about this?"

"You said the children don't play this anymore and your

father got them for you." Silver slid to the floor with Henry, who dumped the contents of the bag out onto the floor. Three different types of coins rattled across the area.

Henry quickly finished his food and wiped his hands on his pant legs. Silver had finished everything but his jerky.

"You never really eat the meat, do you?"

Silver shrugged, "I just don't like it. I'm sorry."

"No. No," Henry said, snatching it from him and laughing, "It's okay. It just means more for me."

They laughed as Henry stuffed his face and turned his attention to the coins. "You definitely need to have the Silver ones. I'll take the Gold ones. The wooden ones are really old. No one definitely plays with those anymore."

Silver piled up his coins into two even piles of six. He sat on his knees and rested his hands on his thighs watching Henry slide the wooden ones aside and placing the gold ones into a pile and picked one out to hold onto. Silver brushed his hand against the two piles until they crashed into one pile like Henry's.

"So you pick one. I always have a lucky one in each pile."

"Is it that one because it has a chip in it?"

Henry paused, "Um. Yes. I mean, no, of course not."

Silver grinned, "What do I do with it? Do I need to put it aside?"

"Yes," Henry nodded and pointed to the rest of his pile,

"The rest gets put into two rows. The back row will have six. The front row will have only five with a space empty. You get to choose. Where the empty space goes."

Silver copied Henry, who started to push his rows closer to Silver, "Now we need our rows to be only one space away from each other. So push yours closer but leave a spot between."

Silver moved each coin one by one as Henry sat across from him in silent patience.

"A little bit closer. Like one coin space away. That's our battlefield."

Silver smirked, "To battle!"

Henry smirked back, "I'll win but that's okay. I know how to play."

Silver raised an eyebrow, "Oh? You will?"

"Now you take your lucky coin and put it in one of the empty spaces between our front row. I'll go first." Henry placed his lucky coin in a spot across from Silver's empty space. "I put mine here because you won't be able to jump mine. That's called being strategic, my dad would have said."

Silver studied Henry's move and tried to understand his instructions. Henry pulled out a string from one of the bags and surrounded the coins. "This is so we don't make the battlefield too big. It can only be six coins long. So now we can only pick the coins from the back row to always move forward and what you want to do is try to trap one or more of my coins between two of yours. It's called jumping. When you jump someone else's coins, you get to keep it. Then at the end we count up all of our coins who survived moving forward and all the ones we jumped together. Whoever has the most wins!"

Silver nodded and after only a few more questions, Henry counted up 13 coins. Silver only had 11. "I told you I would win."

"Again," Silver nodded, "and explain the rules again."

This time Silver asked more questions. "Can I move this one backwards?"

Henry shook his head, "No, you can only go forwards. Not even if you can jump. But you can jump sideways."

Silver nodded, "So I can put it here because I can jump?"

Henry nodded and grinned, "But now I can jump diagonally and get two. Thank you."

"I can't move backwards but I can move sideways if I can jump?"

Henry nodded again.

"So I can do this?" Silver moved a piece to the back row, "And that will take your whole back row?"

Henry squinted as if he was having a hard time seeing. His nose scrunched up so much it wrinkled. "Um. Yes. Yes, you can."

"And all those coins are mine?"

Henry's shoulders dropped, "Yep."

They played a few more rounds. "If we can't jump backwards, what happens now? We can't jump sideways."

"We get to keep our coins. They survived. Now add it all together."

"I got 14."

"I got 10."

"So I win?" Silver grinned as Henry started to already set them up. Silver won the following game as well and the one after that. "I'm really getting the hang of this game."

Henry grew more and more quieter until Silver put a hand up to his chin and lifted his face up until their eyes met, "Thank you for teaching me this game, Henry."

Henry blushed and pushed the empty bag that went with the silver coins, "Here. You keep the silver coins. They're yours."

Silver's eyes lit up, "Really? Forever?"

Henry didn't think it was even possible to blush even further, but he discovered the truth. His whole face felt like it was on fire and he wondered if blushing so much could cause a fever.

"Thank you, Henry."

Henry put the rest of the coins back into their bag and put them away.

"What are we going to do now?" Silver asked as he followed Henry down the stairs.

"I think we should try and clean up the garden before nightfall. It'd help my mother out. I hope she figures out why the well is dry soon."

"What if she doesn't return today?"

Henry paused for a moment. The thought hadn't occurred to him. He just automatically assumed she would come back. She always came back. He looked over at Silver, suddenly frightened. "I don't know, Silver."

There was no more dam of the Entmen left. All of them had risen again to continuously fight off the onslaught of wolves and ravens. The ravens were fought off the easiest, however, their bodies would only burst out more until they were burnt or pummelled so badly that they were no longer recognisable. It was the wolves and their claws that ploughed the Entmen down one after another. Their wounds were poisonous to the Entmen and even though they'd hold them off, they'd eventually gray and wither.

As the boys tried to clear out the garden and fix up the well, the day faded closer to night until they quickly retreated back inside where they gathered up food and stayed in Henry's room, knowing the frames would protect them if anything made it through the front door.

In their haste, however, they failed to notice the glowing eyes appearing in the eastern horizon. The Silver Eyes. Pale, ghastly beings that slowly stepped closer to the house. Their steps were slow as if it were an effort to move forward. Their frail looking bodies leaned into each step as if fighting against an unknown force that tried to prevent them from moving forwards. Thin wisps of silken clothing barely hung from their skin as their gaping mouths, long forgetting how to swallow, dripped with the same silver substance that flowed out of their lifeless eyes. Their clothing only hinted to what they once were as they marched with each step in unison with one purpose softly whispering in their collective minds.

"He is waiting."

Already some of the Silver Eyes had fallen. Their legs could not withstand the force of each step and pull it took to make another. Their hips tore apart with a few as they toppled forward and shattered into small particles of dust. The stronger ones forged ahead with their eyes intent on the prize. At first their prize was each horizon. The water's edge of River's Song until it finally dried up. The edge of the Blades. The Lakewood Trees. None of them faltered when one fell. Their determination fuelled when the trees were behind them and their first step hit the edge of the gardens and grassy yard of the Edwards Home.

They had heard the boys first until they saw them. The Silver Eyes gaped at them and watched them run around to the front of the house before they were able to take their next step. Their heads tilted upwards at the lights that appeared at the framed windows. Finally, each mouth closed as both feet stepped into the yard. Their footprints left a puddle of murky silver mist behind.

The first Silver Eyes to step onto the property adjusted its jaw and the pressure of each step stopped.

"He is here," it growled and waited for more of the Silver Eyes to step through. Their mouths snapped open and closed and their bodies loosened as each one enjoyed the freedom in their steps.

"He is waiting," a Silver Eyes responded to the first, who

then responded to the next and so on until the air filled with their voices.

A shadowy creature crawled out of the well, blasting the Entmen that had sealed it aside.

Silver

The Silver in their Eyes

They rose out of the ocean screaming as the air ripped down their throat and filled their lungs for the first time in hundreds of rotations. Their chorus of horror rattled the eastern beaches as the tides retreated. Their steps painfully slow as their screams died down to a whisper.

"Mine!" a voice trembled up into the clouds.

They struggled to step through the sands and stones that littered between the depths of the ocean and the expanse of white sands of the eastern beaches. The ocean kept its tide back. The waves stayed silent as if they were letting their screams have their turn to slam against the shores.

They were called the Silver Eyes. Hundreds of them stepped out of the ocean and took their turns to scream in the winds that refused to die down despite the pain they were bringing. Sailors capable of sailing above the depths of the ocean would tell tales of people swimming the seas unafraid of the darkness that loomed around them. Their eyes would glow in the moonlight with silver streams. Some sailors claimed that if they looked into the silver eyes for too long, they'd be allured to fall into the depths of the ocean and join their ranks.

But these were just tales and the truth was even darker still. The Silver Eyes hated the Wind Screamers, who seemed to abhor silence. They would sing within their ships or plague the shores with their incessant discussions with each other. The sound of their world would echo into the depths to where the Silver Eyes would live. Their coral towers would tremble at the sound of the constructions, songs, speeches and destruction of the very world in which they lived in. Their wars would plague the oceans and spill into their homes when one of their ships would sink. Wind Screamers were a pollution.

Wind Screamers were thieves.

Their screams were not from the pain, as their lungs begged for the ocean's water, but from the rage they felt that they had to leave their homes to retrieve what rightfully belonged to them.

Many of the Silver Eyes were not prepared to breathe in the air. They stood there screaming until their bodies popped into silver ash. Others could only take a few steps before their legs and hips separated and their bodies fell forward and vanished. It disgusted the rest that their fates could just end up in the very wind in which they detested. But the rest of the Silver Eyes did not falter. They would continue forward, not backward, even if it meant only one returned to the coral beneath the sea and they could live in their darkness and their silence for eternity.

The Wind Screamers would have to pay first for their treachery and the thief ended their life with the same screams and the same tearing of flesh as the Silver Eyes had already faced.

"They call themselves The Oiden," the frail, little creature whispered, rubbing her long whiskers as she huddled beneath a shawl her granddaughter had woven for her. She had taught her many rotations ago. Her granddaughter nestled close to her listening intently to her tale and tracing the threads along the edges of the shawl. "But like most humans, they rename things and claim them as their own."

"But not the Woman in the Woods, right Chembere Hove?" her granddaughter squeaked.

Hove rubbed her little brown nose against her little pink one. "No, my little Kush, not her."

Hove peered beyond her sleek nose at the other little ones that gathered around her. Her eyes stopped at a group of them lingering near the entrance to the hut. "The humans call them Silver Eyes, but I like Oiden better. It is a name that comes with a warning. Do not swim too deep into the ocean and do not gaze in their eyes or you will be drawn to them. Once their hands grab you, they begin to pull out your very soil."

The group of little ones sniggered at the entryway.

Hove would have stood up and stretched out her long, slender body that made it easy to dive into the ocean and torpedo through the waters as if it were air, but she required a cane these days. She couldn't stand tall like a tree and act all menacing with chirps and squeaks like she once did to predators from the Blackwood.

But she still had her voice and she still had the Mhuka temper. She spoke quickly and loudly. All the other Mhuka's ears flattened as her shrill squeaks filled the hut, "And what is it that you are giggling about over there? Don't think I hadn't notice you slowly trying to sneak out! If you have something to say then have enough fish guts to say it to a Chembere."

At the use of the last word, she knew she called for respect and they'd show it if they knew what was best for them. One of the little ones at the door stood tall. He was always mouthing off at her.

"Oh, Muromo, I should have known. Well, what pointless chirping do you have to say today?"

"My name is Zeve," the young Mhuka corrected her like he always did. His sleek fur stood on end like a trail from the top of his head down to his tail. "And Oiden are just stories you tell us to stop us from swimming out too deep!"

"Oey Oey Oey!" Zeve's friends chanted around him.

Hove rolled her small beady eyes, "You know why I call you Muromo? Because of your big mouth. He always boasted about being the best until his mouth got so loud the felines of the northern fields got him."

Zeve rolled his eyes back at her more dramatically, making sure to keep standing on his hind legs so that he was taller than what he appeared to be when on all fours. "Don't chitter at us, Chembere Hove! Your stories won't scare us. The only thing that lives in the sea are the fish we eat! You're just an old lure!"
Everyone gasped at the insult, even Zeve's friends around him.

Hove pushed herself up with her cane and squeaked so loudly Zeve fell back down on his front legs and whimpered. "Quiet, you little scamp, I am no lure but a warning that you are in a grave danger. Pipe down, all of you, you little pipsqueaks! And you, Muromo, snap those traps before I drag you by your tails and find one to snap you in!"

Hove felt a paw on hers. She looked down at the cane in which she struggled to hold on to. She didn't do much standing unless necessary. Her granddaughter looked up at her. Her pink nose had not browned yet. She was still so very young and yet so wise. Hove caressed her granddaughter's whiskers, "My sweet, Kushambira. My Kush. I shall sit."

As soon as Hove sat down, Kush turned around to the rest of them. Her little whiskers twitched and she chattered angrily. It was a good thing she didn't see Hove because the old Mhuka quickly hid a smile. The young ones did not sound as fierce when they tried to show the Mhuka temper. It came out more like a stuttered squeak that caused more giggles than regret. "No! No no! You will not talk to a Chembere this way. Never! It is bad! Yes, she is old, but so are your parents' parents! This is not our way! We listen to Chembere. We respect Chembere and we look after Chembere. And the Oiden are real! Even the humans talk about them! They are lures. Not Chembere Hove!"

An albino Mhuka suddenly stormed into the hut, "Hove! Hove! They! They walked onto the shores! They're eating! They're here! Oh, Hove, what do we do?!"

"Chembere Chando, what are you on about?" Chembere Hove struggled to stand up but it had taken all of her energy to do so earlier. She pushed her long neck out and pointed her nose at Chando.

"The Oiden!" Chando screeched, "They're screaming in the air!"

Hove choked back tears, "Impossible."

* * *

The Oiden's steps, slow and determined, reached the boundaries of the small, fishing village. A few creatures dashed from behind stone that breached the sands. They were small, slender beings that dared not ride their rafts out above the true depths of the ocean. They normally had no need for the Mhuka, but the steps were not easy and if they were going to make it to the Lakewood Trees, they'd need sustenance.

"Chando!" one of the creatures screamed as they tripped and fell. The snowy, white creature stopped and looked back until the silver eyes of the Oiden threatened to lure him into their grasps. He looked away and continued running even as he heard the high-pitched squeals of his mate dying.

The fishing village was just little mounds of sticks and grass. Nets and cages piled vicariously around each one. To the Mhuka a large bonfire rested in the middle of the village where they'd gather together to cook the fish and distribute it around until everyone was fed. To the Oiden, the Mhuka were tiny creatures but they had big souls. Their energies would last them many more steps afterwards.

As soon as the Oiden took their first steps into the village, it exploded with a bunch of tiny creatures sprawling out every which way. Those who were foolish to look up and match their gaze were lost in a foggy haze until the Oiden plucked them up and breathed in their essence until they faded away into dust.

One little one, tiny in comparison to the others, climbed up onto one of the huts and started chattering up at them until their eyes met and they fell silent and then in one swoop of the Oiden's big hand, the tiny one faded into dust like the rest of them. The Oiden grew stronger and the steps were easier.

* * *

"Come. Come come!" Kush whimpered at the doorway, not daring to look up even as Zeve was taken up and all that was heard was his painful squeals. "Chembere Hove, come!"

Hove held the door frame and peered sadly down at her granddaughter before thrusting a satchel into the little one's arms. "Oh, my sweet Kushambira, go. Find the Woman in the Woods! Tell her the Oiden are coming. Tell her the Silver Eyes now scream in the air like the rest of us! Go!"

Kush dashed away a few steps before turning back with one last whimper, clutching the satchel to her chest as she tried to stand tall and strong on her hind legs, "Chembere Hove?" A shadow began to loom over her.

Hove's fur stood on end and with one last effort she tossed aside her cane and scrambled out to her before turning her back to Kush and looking up, "Kushambira, we listen to Chembere. We respect Chembere but sometimes, Chembere looks after you! Now, run! Their steps won't catch you!"

Hove's body seemed to hang like a fish on a string and Kush knew it was too late. She nodded her little head and held the satchel in her mouth and dashed away. The satchel was difficult to hold and it tasted funny in her mouth. This little satchel was not made of the barks or the grass. She had tasted feline before on a dare and this satchel tasted very much the same. Kush had seen humans before and they had held one much like this but much bigger. It took a few dodges, weaves and some really good hiding spots before she could get the satchel around her body until it

193

seemed to be riding on her as she ran a bit more freely away from the eastern shores.

"Be a good Mhuka, Kushambira," she squeaked as tears rolled down her whiskers, "Listen to Chembere. Listen. Listen." And so she did, she listened to all of them around her as she ran. She listened to the squeals and screams as the Mhuka learned that the Oiden were very real. Her kin had laughed at Hove's dreams and stories, but they trembled about them now.

* * *

Their feed lasted for days as they took their painful steps towards the River's Song. The terrain was still difficult for them and many of them still fell. With each step in unison, they covered the rocky shores and seeped into fields riddled more with stones than grass. The memory of the Mhuka blazed in their eyes. Every so often they'd see one ahead of them, leaping from rock to rock, never looking back, but always running in the same direction as they were. As the sun stroked many more Oiden, they fell to dust and as the moon strengthened their determined steps, they broke free of the rocky plains and marched through a plethora of flowers that seemed to have replaced the stone. The vibrant life of the flowers repulsed the Oiden. They stood at the edge of the field and stared across from it. Soon their forces gathered together as they stood at the flower's edge.

Near a cluster of purple flowers that hung like dew drops, a small creature poked their nose out and smelled the air. Their eyes were closed but the Oiden were too far away for their gaze to affect the little Mhuka. Their heads turned in unison to watch the creature. A few of the Oiden closest to the border of flowers that lead to the purple cluster signed to the others. Their hands slid through the air along with their legs. Some of the words they couldn't sign because it required both legs. The buoyancy of the ocean was missed and it made communicating difficult. They began to moan in frustration. The very sound brought them pain as the air filled their lungs like the sharp edges of shrapnel that floated down to them from wrecked ships.

Why…our…?

…to warn…?

Gaze…and devour…

…not…pass…

* * *

Kushambira could smell them. She had dared to sleep amongst the pretty flowers and regretted it, but she had not slept for days. The field was called The Wilden, named by the Woman in the Woods. Hove had told of times she had met her and unlike the other humans seemed to be more attuned to the flora than most.

"She is as tall as the north-eastern mountains but as gentle as The Wilden's petals we like to garnish our fish with. Her voice is like the crashing waves but as tender as the flesh of a plump fish. Only the Tora can go to The Wilden and I just so happen to be one of the best."

"Used to," Zeve sneered from the back of the hut. "You're a Chembere now."

Hove shook her cane in the air as her fur stood on edge and her voice turned to a high-pitched squeak, "And you won't ever get there, Muromo, if you keep it up you tiny little pip-squeak."

Kushambira hugged the satchel to her chest. It had grown heavier with each day but it still wasn't as heavy as the thought of Hove and the others. Their memories filled her head just as much as the scent of the Oiden did as they approached. She woke with a start.

Now that she felt rested, she was hungry and wondered if she'd ever get to eat fish again. The scent of the Oiden was still distant and so she opened her eyes for a moment before snapping them shut again. They were gathering on the horizon at the edge of The Wilden. She opened them again and tried to stand tall. Some of the flowers were still taller than she was, especially the purple ones. That's why she decided to sleep within their bundle.

She watched as the Oiden moved around to each other. Hove had explained this was how they communicated in the depths of the ocean. Their arms and legs would move around in different ways to mean different things. She chittered nervously as she looked away from them. She knew she should run for it while she still had the chance but she also wondered why they didn't come into The Wilden.

"Chit chit. Maybe they can't?" Kushambira whispered to the flowers. "Hove always said you were not only beautiful but you all had different things you could do to help us. The Woman in the Woods taught the Tora that. I wonder if she will remember Chembere Hove."

Kushambira's whiskers vibrated as she came to a sudden realisation, "Oh. Oh oh. She is not a Chembere anymore. Or the rest of them. Or will be. They are the Akafa."

Hove's words echoed in Kushambira's mind as she bowed her head, "Sometimes we do not reach Chembere. I was lucky, little ones, that the cold winters or the felines of the fields did not take me. I get to sit here with you and tell you all that I know. It is the way of the Chembere."

"We're lucky you're here?" Zeve muttered, but still loud enough for all to hear.

Hove's fur began to bristle but she thought better of it, "I will not spar with you today, Muromo, because becoming an Akafa is a sacred space."

Kushambira's tears rolled down her whiskers as she whispered what she had asked that day, "But you won't become an Akafa, right Chembere Hove?"

"One day," both the memory of Hove and Kushambira said as she huddled back into the safety of the tall purple flowers. "But not yet, my sweet Kush."

The Oidens started to make a horrendous sound as if they had been holding their breaths for too long and were desperate to gulp in the air. Kush peeked out again as clouds began to form in the sky. The sun quickly disappeared and the winds started to howl its warning through the petals of the flowers. She watched as the flowers shivered. A voice suddenly etched The Wilden like a crack of lightning.

"Come!" its voice hummed and lingered and following it, came the rains.

The rain pelted down onto the flowers as they drooped lower to the ground as if curling up to defend against the oncoming attacks. Kush watched the rain mingle with the ground before she squeaked at the sudden pain of something striking her. She flicked her long tail up to shield her head as she reached a paw out to grab a small black stone. It was one of many that was falling from the sky. It began to move and uncurl as the dirt and water absorbed into her. She flung it away and jumped in place a few times.

"Chit. Chit. What is this? This?"

Out of the ground large black worms the size of her started to rise from the ground. She squealed in fear but the black worms didn't seem interested in her. They were devouring the flowers. With each blink of her eyes, she saw sections of The Wilden disappear all around her.

"No. No no!" Kush gasped as her little paws covered her pink nose. She quickly plucked a couple of the purple flowers and stuffed them into the miniature satchel she had been given by Hove and jumped out of the dying purple flowers and through the rest of The Wilden.

That's when she heard the steps again. The Oiden were coming and could take more and more steps as the flowers disappeared. She squeaked again as she leapt in fear in the air and tumbled forward with an added haste. No time to eat. No time to sleep. She listened to the sound of the black worms eating the flowers. It was another sound she ran away from. First, the squeals of the now Akafa and now the munching of the petals of The Wilden.

* * *

The Oiden watched The Wilden disappear before them and they delighted in it. The Wind Screamers delighted in such beauties and scoffed at the darkest of the algae. Coral was a more beautiful and permanent beauty as long as the Wind Screamers kept away from them. The Wilden held the warmth of the sun and its soil lacked the salt of the sea.

It was just as thick and suffocating as the air in which it thrived upon. The ocean floor was purer and more lasting. It fed on the waves of the ocean to keep it forever moving and mingling. Soil was stagnant and it repulsed them that they had to step above it.

"Come!" the voice that had called them from the depth of the ocean repeated itself.

The Oiden took a step forward and found the power that kept them at bay had waned. They stepped through the empty patches of flowers, inevitably stepping on the very things that were helping them through. The Wilden was dead and the rhythm of their steps returned, however slower. The strength they had gotten from the Mhuka was wavering. They would need to feed soon. Some of the Oiden eyed the creature that darted away. It was still heading in the same direction. Curiosity hit some. Hunger hit most.

...walk…not stand…time…

The Oiden passed the same signs to each other but without being able to move freely in the ocean most of them gave up trying to speak. Silence spread across them and their silver eyes flared with a newfound anger. Not just one thing was taken from them but two. They lost their own unique voice. Cursed to step foot on land and scream its air but also cursed to not fully be able to express themselves. Anger fuelled them and hatred of their new surroundings brought about a viciousness they never thought they'd ever be capable of.

Kush was tired of running and when she saw the Lakewood Trees in the distance her whole body suddenly decided it couldn't run anymore.

"No. No no. Chit. Chit. Not safe, Kushambira! Keep going! Through the Lakewood Trees. Over the River's Song. Then the Woman in the Woods. Go. Go go. Now. Run!"

But she faltered. Her paws seemed to drag against the ground. The satchel was hurting her back and her head was having a hard time lifting up. The Lakewood Trees seemed to stay in the distance. Just as she was about to go over the last hill that led down to the trees, she collapsed. The grass around her blanketed her and the night breeze soothed her sore and tired body. Her eyes refused to stay awake but the wind brought the scent of the Oiden. They were still quite a distance away but fear that they'd find her while she slept kept snapping her eyes open.

"Sleep. Little. One," a deep voice loomed over her as the ground shifted. She felt herself lift into the air as her eyes closed again. When she opened them, the stars were hidden beyond something above her as she felt herself nestled between an archway of some sort. "We. Will. Slow them. We will. Hasten. You."

She slept to the lower hum of the being that carried her and the gurgle rolling around in her stomach.

When she woke, she was instantly blinded by the sun and she felt her tail wet. She allowed herself a moment to remember what had happened before her eyes snapped open and she found herself next to a river running between her and the longest blades of grass she had ever seen. She stood right at the shores of the river. Her tail was completely drenched along with her hind legs. She just stood up in the water and gazed down at it. Her heart leapt at the sight of tiny fish darting through her legs. Instantly her stomach took over and she threw her satchel aside and dived in. She was used to the depth of the ocean and found herself scraping the bottom of the river and finding it hard to move at first. But her skills in catching fish and swimming had her gnawing away at the fish. She patted her full belly.

"Good. Eat. Wait. She is coming."

Kushambira's hairs immediately stood on end and she hopped around in quick circles hissing and spitting until she saw what was speaking to her. Two large red blinking eyes stared down at her from a tree that stood a few feet away from her.

She cowered back a bit and burped, spitting out a few fish bones.

The tree stood tall and a low chuckle vibrated the ground before its roots pulled out from the shore. She watched as the ground seemed to heal itself from the tree's movement as it looked unscathed. She watched as it slowly moved a bit closer to her.

"Mhuka," it said.

"Entmen," Kushambira's eyes widened and she bowed her head, "Hove told us your stories."

"Cross. Swim. Warn her. She cannot face them. Alone," it said before it turned around and all the trees she had thought were Lakewood Trees suddenly stood up and moved away from her towards the scent of the Oiden.

She kept staring at them, reaching a paw blindly to find the satchel nearby. She patted the ground a few times, her eyes unblinking, until she found it and looped it around her until it was on her back once again. She hated the thing but knew it had to get to the Woman in the Woods.

"Akafa Hove, I'm listening," she whispered and found a way to leap from stone to stone across River's Song without drenching the satchel. She felt a sense of pride calling Hove an Akafa now but a sadness that clutched at her tiny heart. By the time she crossed the river, the Entmen were gone. She dove into the blades of grass and felt even smaller in a world that already made her feel tiny.

* * *

The Oiden stopped taking steps the moment the Entmen appeared along the horizon. The Wilden was a barren field of dead soil. They went through the hills beyond the field that showed the mountains at their far right distance. The looming trees of Blackwood at their far left. But those places were not their location. Beyond the hills they could sense him.

"Come, he is waiting," the voice now said.

By the time they made it through to the last hill before it dipped down to River's Song, the Entmen appeared. They formed a single line and planted their roots deep into the ground. Their branches spread long and their canopy stretched high.

Feast…wall…

By the time the front line of the Oiden made it to the wall of Entmen, their branches swung out and struck them to dust. Wave after wave of Oiden became part of the wind as it wound around the hills deceptively playful. Soon the Oiden made their own wall at the bottom of the hill as they peered up to the Entmen. The sun was well past the hill and would soon disappear. The Oiden would no longer be blinded by the light and the moon would empower the tides that raged in them. They stood there and stared at the wall of trees as their hunger grew the closer night came.

And with the night, came the sound of wolves.

* * *

The night brought a sense of dread to Kushambira as she ran through the thick, tall blades of grass, avoiding thick bushes of tiny flowers. By the time the darkness came, she was absolutely lost. Her running slowed to a pace and she let her nose guide the way. She couldn't see well in the dark. The colours turned to shades of gray and seemed to merge together. She always listened out for the steps of the Oiden. It was like how she had to be if the felines of the fields were on the prowl. Kush stopped and took the satchel off her back and placed it next to her. She curled around it and whimpered. If she tried to travel any further, she'd run the risk of losing her way completely.

She found comfort in her memories.

"Patience," Chembere Hove whispered to her audience in the hut, "is the key to fishing. The Mhuka are a very clever people. We can hold our breath for a very long time. Much like the whales that dance above the waves when they travel past our shores. Hold your breath, little ones. Though our eyes are not suitable for the dark, they are like the felines in the fields in the ocean. Alert. Ever listening. Smelling. Seeing. We float like the algae and when we see the school of fish swim past our nets and our traps…"

The whole hut screamed, even Kushambira who followed her scream with laughter, as Hove screamed, "AND SNAP, we catch the fat fish and GOBBLE THEM UP!"

Kushambira pulled the satchel closer to her as she smiled

at the thought of Akafa Hove. Kush took a deep breath and she held it. Her shade of fur matched the soil. Her heartbeat slowed. Her body became completely still. She watched the shades of gray around her. She listened. Her pink, little nose wriggled at all the different scents. Some animals liked to stalk at night, like the felines. The Oiden seemed to be faster in the dark too nor did they seem to need rest. She titled her head slightly and looked up at the stars peeking through the monstrous blades. They even seemed bigger than how she felt right now and they had so many more around them. For the first time in her life, Kush understood what loneliness meant.

Suddenly the blades around her erupted with howls and gigantic beasts much larger than the felines suddenly ran through. She tightened herself up against the satchel and continued to hold her breath. Patience, she thought to herself, let them dash around me. Listen. Smell. See. The beasts bounded above her. They were furry with sharp fangs that hung out of either side of their mouth. Spikes grew out of the back of their bodies. She had never seen or heard of these creatures. She wondered if Hove would have recognised them. Just as they appeared, they were gone. Their howls faded in the distance as they ran towards something. She could sense their hunger and the immediate danger she was in if they discovered her. But she had been patient and her nose told her that they faded away towards the smell of the Oiden. Her head darted up and she unravelled herself around the satchel and put it back in its place before darting off. Smell. The smell told her the right directions. The Oiden, and now those beasts, were that way. So were the Entmen. All she had to do was run in the opposite way and she'd be heading towards the Lakewood Trees and hopefully into the safety of the woman who lived among them.

* * *

The Oiden stood at the bottom of the hill looking up at the wall of Entmen that stopped them from moving forward. As little pods growing up, the Oiden heard stories of the world once ruled by the oceans. The lands were beneath them and the winds were controlled by the waves forever churning. Then one day the floor of the ocean erupted upwards. What used to be parts of the ocean's floor were now part of the wind's floor. The lands defied the waters and rose up to reach the winds and join together to spread the seeds of growth until there were the Entmen. The monstrous trees roamed the newly formed lands. Magic, once exclusive to the ocean, spread and the creatures who grew curious of the land betrayed the water and chose to walk the lands and breathe the air. A rift was formed, much like the one that now stood opposing on a hill between what was once The Wilden and River's Song. An endless war began.

As the day faded and the moon's power rose, the Oiden finally smiled up at their old foe. The howls rose up behind the Entmen and, in the moonlight, the Oiden watched as the living trees twisted around to defend themselves against the onslaught that erupted behind them.

"Come. He is waiting," the voice called down to them.

The Oiden took a step up the hill. The wait had been trying for some and they faded at first step, but where one fell, more seemed to appear from behind their ashes. They continued upwards in painful steps until they were able to join the wolves in their attacks. Within moments, the Entmen fell. Gray bark turned to dust as the Oiden fed on them and then turned to the wolves, who were submitting themselves before the pale ocean walkers.

"Come," the voice continued to beckon as the Oiden

fed on the multitude of wolves that kept pouring out of the horizon just to be fed upon. They did not falter nor whimper. The wolves seemed to know that this was to be their fate.

Step by painful step. Determination still outweighed the anguish. The Oiden reached the River's Song and stood at its edge. The force that tried to repel them was strongest here. The ones at the front line dared to step foot into the waters, after all, they belonged to it, didn't they? Their haste proved fatal and instead of turning to ash, they melted into the river as the salts of the tides boiled out of them. The rivers and the lakes were another abomination brought on by the war between land and sea. Some of the oceans were captured and separated. Their salts separated for some and the waters roamed free across the lands. Some of these rivers even dared to run back into the ocean and try to mix their fresh water with the salt of the seas. Futile, but offensive nonetheless. The River's Song came from the northern mountains where the lands reached up to meet the air. They mingled until together they created their own water until it cascaded down the slopes and through the lands to disappear beyond the Blackwood.

The Oiden aligned along the river and hissed down at its blasphemous sounds. The current of the river against the rocks tried to emanate the sounds of the ocean but failed. It was a pathetic attempt and the Oiden screamed in rage as they were forced to bide their time to the one that led their charge. A few attempted to disobey their orders, refusing to have to kowtow to a shadowy creature that was still a wind screamer despite its loyalties.

Go, the Marina had danced vehemently through the water as she commanded her people, *retrieve what is mine*.

The Wind Screamers would refer to her as the Oiden's

Queen, but she was more than that. The coral crown bestowed upon her brow was adorned with gems from beneath the ocean. These gems were what the land proclaimed as its own. But what ate away at the lands or compressed it together to make such gems if not the ocean's ebb and flow? The Marina was more than just a queen to the Oiden. She was worshipped. Her dances changed the currents. Her songs brought the sun and the moon. Her very presence was a hurricane and her coral crown was its eye.

Follow the voice for now, the Marina's movements caused such a strong current, the mass of Oiden that watched her from the sea floor struggled to stay in one place. *No one steals from an Oiden! Do not falter in your steps! Make the Wind Screamers pay for making you one of them! Go! He is waiting!*

"Silver Eyes," it hissed. "Come. He is waiting."

The Oiden gave a collective groan at being referred to as Silver Eyes, a name given to them by the humans in their ships. They looked down at River's Song and watched as the abominable water suddenly began to shrivel away from the banks. They looked to the north where the mountains stood mocking them and the Oiden took a moment to mock the mountains in return before gleefully taking a step into the dried-up bank of the silent song.

If they did not have the pull of the shadowy creature's voice, the Oiden would have lost themselves in the Blades. The western horizon beckoned to them. The essence of the Entmen and the wolves strengthened them and their eyes poured out their silvery mist. Just one more step and the key to their prison would be the Marina's once again and all the Oiden would be free.

* * *

Rosie watched as the scarred Entmen seemed to search the Lakewood Trees for a moment before returning south. She had almost called out to it but something told her not to. Her nose itched and she just knew he was needed elsewhere.

"Oh please, let Silver be okay." She stepped around a couple of trees. She wasn't worried about Henry as much. He could take care of himself. Silver was a big unknown. She wasn't sure how much more the young boy could take. She could see he was starting to feel that everything that was happening was all his fault. "Perhaps they are in a way, but I'd be a right sac if I held that against you."

She could see the Blades just beyond the horizon of the Lakewood Trees. "Silver is just another victim in all of this, isn't he? Now Patrick on the other hand, now if there's a finger to point, I'd flick it his way." She jutted three fingers up into the air.

A small bush growing sideways off of a tree exploded and Rosie hissed as something clawed its way up her right leg, around her back and dug itself into her shoulders before a little claw pressed against her lips.

"Chit. Chit. Come. Shhh. Come. Go. Go go. That way," a voice whispered in her left ear. The claw on her mouth momentarily pointed to a group of trees with a thicket hiding their bases. "Chit. Chit. You are tall. Very tall and I am small. Crouch. Quick. Quick quick."

Rosie went to say something but the tiny creature's paw returned to her mouth and the others dug into her shoulder insisting that she listen. Her nose twitched as well and something inside of her was drawn to the thicket, as if the flora itself was calling to her.

The whisper continued, "Woman in the Woods?"

Rosie's heart leapt and she instantly knew what this creature was and smiled beneath the little paw. It tightened its little grip on her lips. Rosie slowly nodded and quickened her pace until she was able to crawl her way into the thicket and hide. The creature began to shiver against the back of her neck as her claws dug in deeper. Rosie went to hiss at the sharp pain but a shadow passed by. Rosie looked through the leaves and stifled a gasp.

Silver

The Woman in the Woods

Rosie tried to wait till the Silver Eyes passed, however, they just kept appearing out of Blades and took a step through the Lakewood Trees and towards her home. Rosie noticed with each step they appeared to be in pain. The little creature that had warned her of them still clung to her neck and head.

Rosie couldn't stay there. She had been gone longer than she had wanted and now that she knew the Silver Eyes were coming, her worries over River's Song dissipated. It wasn't as if she hadn't seen Silver Eyes walk upon the land. It was rare, almost a legend, but after seeing the Entmen walk out of Blackwood, she thought twice about shrugging off legends.

But in all the legends she had heard, none of them spoke of this many Silver Eyes stalking the lands. This was as unnatural as the wolves, the ravens and the worms. She waited for a few moments longer before silently repositioning herself and heading north. The Silver Eyes seemed to be following a direct path. They were not spread out but grouped together as if they were like migrating ducks in the sky.

She quietly crawled her way out of the thicket that had hidden her well and slipped through the northern trees until the Silver Eyes were out of eyesight.

"Thank you, Mhuka, for warning me of the Silver Eyes," Rosie whispered to the creature on her shoulder.

The Mhuka unwrapped itself from Rosie and leapt off of her and onto the ground with a roll, "Chembere Hove said I would find you. She is almost never wrong. I am honoured to meet you, Woman of the Woods."

Rosie sighed, "You can just call me Rosie."

"Oh no. No no. I couldn't. You are the Woman of the Woods."

"I see Hove still insists on calling me that."

"Chit. Chit. Of course, you are the one that talks to the trees and understands the plants!"

Rosie smiled, "And who might you be, Mhuka? You seem to know a lot about me. I'd like to know a bit about my little rescuer."

"Oh, oh oh. I am so sorry. I am rude. My name is Kushambira, grand-daughter of Chembere Hove. I have come to give this to you." Kush held up the miniature satchel.

Rosie peered down at it until her eyes widened and she straightened, "Why, that looks like mine!"

Kush held it out to her for a little longer before she realised the Woman in the Woods wasn't going to take it. She wasn't going to admit it, but she didn't want to carry the annoying thing anymore. She placed it next to a Lakewood Tree.

"What is going on here?" Rosie wasn't expecting an answer.

She certainly had none. She pointed to a patch of dark sprouts. "Pull those up and gather as much as you can. They're full of nutrients. Good for when food is scarce."

The small creature happily obliged, running a full circle around a patch before digging them up from the ground. "Chit. Chit. And the small satchel? I do not need to carry it anymore?"

Rosie eyed it still sitting at the base of the Lakewood Tree, "Oh. That. No. No you don't, but I guess I should see what's inside."

"Yes. Yes yes. I am glad that I do not have to carry it. I am free."

"You might be," Rosie muttered and picked up the small satchel that barely fit in the palm of her hand. "But I seem to be being haunted…"

Kush hugged the sprouts to her chest and shivered, "Sol-haunted? By spirits? Oh. No. No no. None of that for me."

Rosie chuckled, "Not by spirits. By my husband, Patrick. You see, he made me my satchel when we were very young. One of his first gifts to me. And this little satchel you've given me, well, I can tell it's made by him, too. But when did he visit the Mhuka? How did Hove get it?"

"Oh. Oh oh. I don't know," Kush said as she waddled over to Rosie with a handful of sprouts, "Is this enough?"

Rosie nodded and used her finger and thumb to unlatch the miniature satchel and opened it. Inside was a small rolled up scroll and petals to a dried up red flower. The scent of the petals hit her and she gasped, "These cannot be…"

Her fingers unravelled the note and she read, "I trust you'll know what to do with these when the time is right. I wish you had come with me. Patrick."

"When did Hove get these?" Rosie asked, putting the red petals into her own satchel, tucking the note into one of its pockets and tossing the small satchel aside.

"Chit chit. I do not know."

"It has been awhile since I have visited Mhuka. I shall have to make the trek when this is all over." Rosie placed the sprouts into her satchel and started to stand.

"No. No no," Kush said, running easily up the length of Rosie's body and onto her shoulder.

Rosie winced at the nails digging into her slightly but turned her head to look into the creature's forlorn face.

"There is no Mhuka there. They are Akafa now."
Rosie frowned, "All of Mhuka?"

"When they started walking to Mhuka…" Kush whimpered. "The Oiden's eyes got them. Akafa Hove. She…I am the only one."

Rosie watched as the small Mhuka rubbed away tears with her small paws. Rosie nodded and started walking, "All the more reason for me to get back. The Oiden are marching for a reason. They would not leave the depths of the oceans for just anything. Something has happened. Even the Entmen have marched out of Blackwood. The ravens and wolves have become these twisted creatures. Black worms fall out of the skies to eat away at my gardens. I cannot let my house fall."

Kush nodded and wrapped her tail around the back of Rosie's neck, "Yes. Yes yes. You are Chembere, no? You are the Woman in the Woods. You will save. Hove told me of your powers."

As Rosie weaved through the trees, she eyed Kush, "My powers?"

"Yes. Yes yes. You speak to the plants. They commune with you. Tell you of their secrets like no other. Not even Hove knew of all their secrets. But you do!"

Rosie blushed and was glad that Kush's position on her shoulders prevented the Mhuka from seeing the reaction. "The Woman in the Woods was a name given to me by the Mhuka purely from exaggeration."

"Chit chit. No. No no. I know the story. Akafa Hove told me. She would not lie."

Rosie froze for a moment, holding a hand up to Kush. Both of them watched as an Oiden took a few steps off in the distance. Rosie altered her course further west before veering south again.

"They are not far. I can smell them. They are like the salts of the ocean but bitter," Kush chittered in Rosie's ear. "But I am with the Woman of the Woods. She will guide me."

Rosie leaned against a tree and looked over at Kush, who was cleaning her ears with her paws. "You need to stop that. Just call me Rosie."

"The Woman in the Woods was deep within the Wilden. Chit. Chit. She was talking to the plants and asking them lots of questions. Some of the Tova swore they heard the plants answer back. Hove was there, before she was a

Chembere. Before she told us all of these stories, she was there as a Tova and she saw you talking to the plants. Even as you picked them, you spoke fondly to them. Some of the Tova said that the Woman in the Woods does not pick flowers. No. No no. The flowers jump out of the ground for her. Hove was the only one who dared to dart across the Wilden and speak with you. You were kind and gentle. You talked to Hove like you talked with the plants."

Rosie smiled, "The Mhuka are a peaceful people and were so kind when I ventured out as far as the Wilden, especially Chembere Hove."

"Yes. Yes yes. Hove liked you. Taught you some of our words and our ways and in return, you taught us some of the things the plants taught you."

"Not always, Kushambira. The Mhuka taught me about the tsvuku," Rosie absentmindedly put a hand on her satchel. Those red petals were to be protected and used sparingly. They created a healing salve like no other. "I am sorry for your loss. My son, Henry, always wanted to travel to the Mhuka. I am sorry he will not see the great fishers of the sea at work."

Kush nodded, silent tears slipping down to the tip of her nose, "Chit chit. Me, too. Wait. Wait wait. You have a son? You are a Mubereki or Chembere?"

Rosie turned her head towards her shoulder where Kush perched, "Remind me what the other word is?"

"Mubereki? Chit chit. You are with child."

"I have a child, yes."

"And your child has a child?" Kush quietly asked.

Rosie laughed, "Oh no. He is still very young."

Kush squeaked, "He is with Mubereki?"

Rosie shook her head, "No. I am the only Mubb… Moob…"

"Mubereki."

"I am the only one."

They were silent for a moment as they heard footsteps in the distance and veered quickly to the left and kept walking in that silence until Kush whispered, "Then why leave your child alone? How would he eat? How would he drink?"

Rosie knelt behind a tree for a moment and looked around before whispering back, "Henry is quite capable of taking care of himself."

"Then he should have children and teach them. You become a Chembere. Chembere of the Woods. Yes. Yes yes. That sounds nice."

"As honoured as I would be to be a Chembere, I—"

A small paw pushed against Rosie's lips as another paw appeared and pointed further west, "Tsere. Tsere tsere."

Rosie nodded and made her way through the trees kneeling as close to the ground as she could. "What do you see?"

Kush leaned over Rosie's shoulder and out until her nose pointed in the direction her little paw had been pointing. Long whiskers twitched in the air for a moment before she pulled herself back and put her little face in front of Rosie's.

"The Marina," Kush whispered.

Rosie's heart caught in her throat and a new fear rose from her gut, "Here? Impossible. The Marina does not dare walk!"

Kush shook her head, "No. No no. Something else. Tsere!" The young Mhuka pointed back towards the direction she wanted Rosie to go.

Rosie slipped through the trees following Kush's directions. She knew where they were headed. She just wasn't sure what Kush wanted her to see.

"Tsere! Tsere tsere!"

Rosie came across the crater that had been left within the Lakewood Trees on that day she had found Silver. She stood and looked over at Kush, who intently looked down into the soil's new dimple. "Here, Kushambira?"

"Mwari," Kush whispered. "Mwari Mwari."

Rosie's heart thudded in her chest until it echoed in her ears. Her words barely cut through the pounding, "You said The Marina."

"Zvimwe," Kush whispered.

"More than The Marina?" Rosie asked, but she didn't wait for Kush's answer. She broke into a run and smashed her way through the thicket that blanketed the floor of the Lakewood Trees.

Kush squealed and hugged Rosie's head but that didn't

stop her. Rosie kept going. Her feet against the ground was like thunder to the Mhuka.

"Woman in the Woods is worried?"

Rosie yelled up at her, "No, Kushambira, she is terrified. I need to get home! Silver!"

Each footstep was precise and planned. Rosie could have walked through this portion of the Lakewood Trees with her eyes closed. It became harder, though, to navigate through when she came across the gray forms of Entmen newly weaved amongst the trees. It wasn't panic that rose to her throat and gripped it tightly. It was something else entirely. Kush tried to ask about Silver but the thoughts that flashed through her mind were like the many trees that she had to get through before breaking out of them into her backyard where the whittling stump sat alone and unused. Henry and Silver called out to her from the porch as an Entmen, thee Entmen she had healed so many days ago, tore through the yard towards the horde of Silver Eyes that burst through the trees from the eastern edge.

Henry and Rosie at first ran towards each other, until Rosie pulled out the bow that had been fastened on the back of her. She drew an arrow and nocked it before letting it fly through the air and hit its target: an Oiden burst into a silvery ash.

* * *

The Oiden's steps were no longer painful the moment they stepped onto the boundary that made up the Edwards' property. They immediately started to sprint across the grassy yard with an ear-piercing scream, "Mine!"

Silver froze at the top of the stair of the porch that led back into the house. His head turned slowly towards the waves of Silver Eyes that poured out from the trees. Their eyes flashed silver and as they screamed, a silver frost poured out of the corner of their mouths. Silver's hand squeezed the railing and he whispered back, "Mine."

* * *

The Entmen swung out its branches in front of it until a handful of Silver Eyes burst into their mists. Its red eyes flashed brighter and for the Silver Eyes that dared to meet their gaze with it, they disappeared, too. This was it. This is what it woke up to do.

"You. Will. Not." The Entmen groaned and dug its roots into the earth and up and around a few more Silver Eyes and squeezed until they vanished. Long had it stood with its people. Wanderers once. Wanderers again. Wanderers no more.

It growled as the Oiden refused to stop pouring out of the trees and those that escaped the Entmen's grasp, they poured around it and across the yard to where Henry met with Rosie. It did not hesitate but it did not like that they passed it. It must not fail.

"I. Will. Not."

* * *

A few fell to the arrows until Rosie decided they were getting too close and she dropped her bow onto the ground and pulled her staff out from the back of her. Her other hand dug deep into her satchel until her fingers found what they were looking for. She pulled out the small bulbs and threw them in front of her. The moment they touched the ground they fed upon the soil beneath it. Long threads of ivy spread across the yard and slowed the Oiden.

Rosie swung her staff around her as it connected with one until she quickly swung herself back again to hit it once more. The Silver Eyes vanished into mist. She saw Henry just stand there and swung her staff at him as she snapped, "What are you doing? Fight!"

* * *

Henry ducked as her staff swung around her and connected with a couple of Silver Eyes. They faded away. He continued to weave behind her until he was able to find better footing and brought out the whittling knife. He had thought for a moment that Rosie was going to pull her into his arms. He cursed himself for expecting it. Like with the spiked wolves, Henry moved with speed and grace, a trait taught to him by both his mother and father, mostly his father. Although, he had to admit, she was impressing him now. Of course she had held back her skills. His father didn't. He insisted on practising.

"Why do I need to know how to do this?" Henry had asked his father between practice.

"Though the Lakewood Trees bring us security, thanks to your mother of course, there are evils out there and nothing lasts forever. One day, they will come and I want you to be prepared." Patrick had grinned, wiping the sweat from his bald head and flexing his muscles. He was small but he was tough.

Henry had looked his father in the eyes. Henry was already his father's height at twelve but he knew despite how short his father was, his speed and agility made him a threat. "What will come, dad?"

221

Patrick's eyes had grown distant as if he was seeing something a world away, "I wish I could tell you," before he had blinked his eyes and returned his son's gaze, "Now, weave like a needle through the thread. Step and twist as if you were dancing with the wind. Like this…"

Henry weaved from the Silver Eyes webbed claws and took a few steps before twisting his feet to change direction and found himself behind them.

"And like the hook in a fish's lip, jab here," Patrick had poked at Henry's sides, causing the boy to giggle, "And here," and continued to poke below the ribs, "But hopefully they don't collapse into a fit of giggles."

Henry turned his wrist until he could jab upwards until the Silver Eyes faded and danced his feet around until he was able to jut the whittle knife again up into the ribs of the other.

"But don't stop there," Patrick had warned, "Keep moving like the tides. Stay low and out of reach as the mice do with the eagles."

Henry ducked and darted through a few more Silver Eyes.

"But strike like the eagle, make them the mice, and fly around again until the foolish ones are caught."
Henry swiped his knife at one but missed. His feet responded by side-stepping and helping Henry spin around until the knife struck out one more time before the Silver Eyes turned to mist.

"He really liked comparing me to the animals," Henry muttered, slightly distracting himself until a Silver Eyes slammed its hand into his chest and sent him flying backwards.

"And when he falls?" Rosie had said, walking up to them practicing one day, "Because he will fall. We all do at some point."

Patrick had grinned and jabbed a finger into Henry's chest, "My son? No way. After I'm through with him, no one will catch him."

Rosie had walked up to Henry and looked down at him. He always wondered if he'd reach her height one day. She had looked him over and sneered down at him, "You will fall."
Henry had gotten so angry at her then. He had looked over at Patrick but he was looking away again as if revisiting that other world.

"What then?" Rosie had asked. "Huh? What then?"

Henry had returned his gaze up to her and snapped, "I don't know."

"Simply, Henry," she had said, before pushing him down to the ground, "don't let them catch you."

Henry rolled as the Silver Eyes lunged down at him. He swung the hand around that held the whittling knife and stabbed it into the back of the Silver Eyes as a couple more lunged at him.

* * *

"Rosie swung her staff just as she watched Henry roll out of the way of another only to create an opening for a few more. Her staff connected with them and they vanished. She called out to Henry, "Don't let them catch you, Henry!"

Henry rolled one more time before curling up and flipping

223

back onto his feet and stabbing another one that ran towards Rosie, "Simply put, mother, they won't!"

They grinned at each other before Rosie nodded her head towards the house, "We need to stick together! To the house!"

* * *

Kushambira watched from a Lakewood Tree as Rosie took on a few more Silver Eyes. The boy she protected belonged to the Woman of the Woods. She could see her in him.

Kush had never seen the Oiden walk so quickly upon the ground. She had never seen them walk to begin with, but to see the pale, haunting images of them rushing towards the Woman in the Woods was absolutely terrifying. Her whole body trembled as the hoard grew large and larger. The Entmen was taking most of them out. She watched in awe as it swung its branches out and took out a whole group of Oiden. She wished the Mhuka had an Entmen to protect them when the Oiden came ashore.

Kush watched as the Woman in the Woods fought off a few Oiden that tried to attack the boy she called Henry. Her whiskers twitched as he headed towards a structure that only by Chembere Hove's description did Kush know it to be a house. Her eyes fell on another boy standing on the porch and she pushed herself closer to the ground.

"Mwari…"

* * *

Silver slowly took the second step and then the last before Henry reached him. He tried to look at Henry, but his eyes could not stop watching the Silver Eyes as they swarmed around the Entmen. Rosie fought off those who passed the living tree and a few were heading in Henry's direction. He could hear their voices like a song humming in his ears long after it had finished. The sight of them weighed heavily on his shoulders and chest. His hand gripped the railing tightly as if letting it go would mean he'd float away.

"Mine," he whispered, his eyes beginning to flare with silver, sparkling mist. The same kind that appeared when the Silver Eyes were defeated. Blood began to drip from his nose and ears.

"Silver!" a voice called out to him, but it seemed so far away. He took a step onto the ground. It was suddenly extremely painful as if he were walking on shards of sharp stone. Hands grabbed at his upper arms and shook him. He blinked and the voices died down and his eyes focused on Henry's face. His voice always seemed to calm the ones Silver heard whispering in his head.

Henry stared back at Silver in concern, "Silver! Silver! I'm here!"

"Henry," he whispered his name but meant it more like a question.

"Yes, Silver," Henry said and felt the whoosh of something brush past him from behind. He spun around and saw Rosie attacking a couple of Silver Eyes that had almost reached him. "Silver, come on!"

Rosie gave Silver a quick nod and called out, "Can you fight?"

Silver blinked, "Sol-who me?"

Rosie raised her voice, "Silver, can you fight?!"

225

Silver's eyes blazed with the silver mist. The key around his neck hummed and he bowed his head. All he heard was her voice now. She really needed to stop silencing Henry. The Silver Eyes were coming and he started to hear the whispers again.

Henry heard him whisper, "I'm so sorry," before he raised his head again and stepped out into the chaos.

"I'll take that as a yes!" Rosie grinned and swung her staff into the head of another Silver Eyes.

Henry watched Silver and tried to scream out to his mother, but it merely came out as a whisper, "Mother…"

Silver screamed, "MINE!!"

Rosie went flying through the air and slammed into a Lakewood Tree and fell limply to the ground. Henry flung backwards and his body skidded across the western yard before laying still. The Silver Eyes froze, even as the Entmen continued its assault and destroyed more of its ancestral enemy.

Silver stood there. Blood from his nose flowing freely. His eyes were completely silver. His hands outstretched with his fingers bending through their own mist. The Silver Eyes stood silently, their own silver mist flowing from their eyes and around their bodies.

"No, young one," a crisp voice cracked the air and a dark cloud descended above the Oiden. Its long shadowy claws dancing in the air towards Silver, "Mine," and the shadowy beast flung through the air and slammed into Silver's chest.

* * *

The Oiden took a step and seemed to awake from their haze. Silver's body flung up into the air and slammed back to the ground closer to the whittling stump. The Entmen roared and flung itself into half of the Oiden.

Kush rushed over to Rosie and pushed herself against the Woman of the Woods' head, "Chit chit. Get up, Mubereki, get up. Oh. Oh oh."

"Destroy the cursed tree," the shadowy creature hissed looking proudly down at the limp body of Silver. The creature's long claws held tightly the key on the silver chain as it watched all of the Oiden turn and attack the tree.

"Yes." The Entmen groaned and fell sideways into the ground, "Come."

The Oiden all piled on top of the large tree and tore away at its branches. The Entmen reached out with its roots, desperately digging into the ground beneath it, to pull itself into the soil and the Oiden with it. "Mhuka! Red! Petals!"

Kush pushed herself up with her hind legs and stood tall. The Entmen's words echoed in her small ears. She put both her paws on her mouth and nodded. She scrambled around Rosie's body and pushed herself underneath her until she could reach the satchel. Within moments, she came back out clutching onto a red petal and shoved it into the Woman of the Woods mouth.

Rosie's eyes snapped open and she pushed herself up as Kush dashed back to the safety of the Lakewood Trees. She watched as the rest of the Oiden seeped into the soil with the gray body of the last Entmen.

"Come. Oiden. Let our war. End."

Rosie's heart sank until she looked around and saw Henry's body across the yard closer to the Shale's border. She got up and ran towards him until the shadowy creature dived down and grabbed Henry's body and flew back towards the whittling stump. Something fell from Henry and landed a few feet away from Rosie's feet.

"Let go of my son!" Rosie roared and ran towards the shadow. She quickly swiped up Patrick's whittling knife and roared again as the shadowy creature squeezed Henry's neck and drew blood. Silver's body lay near the stump. Rosie wondered if this would all end if she just plunged her knife into him but the sight of the key in the shadowy creatures' other hand told her that that was the answer. She needed to get that key back.

As Rosie got closer, the shadow lowered, "I am Sol."

"I don't care who you are," Rosie hissed, stopping next to the stump and Silver's body, "You don't lay a hand on my son."

Sol turned its crooked mouth towards Henry. Its glowing eyes squinted and its claws gave one last squeeze before he tossed Henry off to the side and sank lower to Silver, "A trade then, Lady Edwards. Henry for what is mine!"

"You know," Rosie spat, "I'm sick of all this mine sac."

* * *

Kush watched from the trees as Rosie left Silver's side and dashed over to Henry, leaning over him and shoving something into his mouth. She watched as the creature, calling itself Sol, hovered over the other boy.

"The Mwari…" she whispered and took a deep breath

before scrambling out of the trees and slinking through the grass before jumping onto the stump. Her fur stood up on all ends and her voice turned high pitch, "No. No no. You sent the Oiden and they killed my people and you killed the Entmen but you won't kill the Woman in the Woods because the plants love her and so do the Mhuka. Stay away from the Mwari!"

Sol turned its head slowly towards the little creature and a low chuckle slowly formed into a loud laugh, "You? A Mhuka? A baby? Challenge a demon?"

Kush gasped. She had heard that word before but never knew what they looked like. Ignoring her sudden dread, she screamed, "I am Kushambira, grand-daughter of Chembere Hove, and I am not a baby. I! Am! A! Tora!"

She flung herself into the air as if she were torpedoing through the ocean after fish and dived towards the silver key Sol carelessly held onto. She felt herself roll and tumble through the grass before she continued running towards the Woman in the Woods. "A Tora gets what it is after! Chit chit!"

Sol howled in rage until its eyes rested back on to Rosie as she stood proudly in the yard holding onto her bow. She smirked, "A demon, aye?"

She nocked an arrow and aimed. The arrow's tip dripped with a milky substance. "It just so happens, in my satchel…"

The arrow flew through the air and struck the demon through its crooked mouth. Sol howled, trying to reach for the Mhuka and the key that dragged behind her. The silver chain lay between Kush's sharp teeth. Sol arched backwards as its long fingers clutched at its head as its howl cracked the air one last time before the demon faded.

229

"…I have the milk of the Trinity flower." Rosie let her arms drop to her side. The bow held tightly in her hand. "If it had been anything more than a Lesser Demon…"

Henry stood next to her with the whittling knife in his hand in case the arrow hadn't worked, "What would have happened?"

Rosie stared at the space in which the demon had been hovering, "It wouldn't have worked and we would have had one upset Greater Demon."

"Silver," Henry gasped and went to run to him, but Rosie held up an arm to block him.

"No, Henry, stay back," Rosie hissed.

"Mwari," a voice squeaked from their feet, "Mwari Mwari. Chit chit."

Rosie knelt down and took the key, "Thank you," and continued to walk towards Silver holding out the key in front of her. "Silver, I don't know if you can hear me. I have your key. I'm coming to you. I know it's yours. I'm just giving it back."

"Mom," Henry called to her but Rosie ignored him.

"Silver, the key is yours. Here it is," she slowly knelt beside him, "I am dropping it near you now."

"Mom!" Henry called again, stepping over the little Mhuka.

Rosie stared down at the key and the still form of Silver.

"Mom, I can't hear the noise. Aren't we supposed to hear

something when he doesn't have the key?"

"I know what I could do," whispered Rosie, "I just don't know if I should do it."

"Red. Petals."

Rosie turned and saw Kush peeking through Henry's legs. She twitched her nose and her whiskers fanned out, "Red Petals," she repeated.

"But this is more than the Marina. Mwari, you said."

"What's a Mwari?" Henry asked.

"Yes. Yes yes. Mwari. Zvimwe Marina."

"Mom, what's she saying?"

Rosie looked down at Silver and watched him for a moment. She saw the startled little boy she had found in a crater just lying there in silence. He looked weak. She looked over at Henry who was kneeling down and running his hands through the silver hair.

A soft voice travelled with an unnatural breeze, like the hum of a honey bee and before Rosie could stand up and apologise to Henry, the words held her attention:

"You see a stick I say a snake
the music you hear I say is fake
you cannot blink, you cannot think
your will falls deep to sleep, to sleep."

Rosie's eyes felt heavy as the words repeated over and over again inside her head. She knew that voice. She had heard it before. The more she concentrated on figuring out where she had heard it, the heavier her eyes felt.

"Mom, can you help him?"

She wanted to say no. She wanted to apologise but she just wasn't sure if Silver was safe. It was still unclear to her who Silver had attacked, but his power and the Mhuka's responses to him…she had to protect her home. She had to protect—

Silver opened his eyes and Henry pulled him into a hug.

Rosie blinked her eyes rapidly, "What did I—"

Henry looked up at Rosie and grinned, "Where did you get those petals?"

A slow hum started to vibrate next to Silver until it quickly escalated to a high-pitch scream before he grabbed the key on the silver chain and put it around his neck. He looked up at Rosie, who was standing above him staring at him with a look of displeasure.

"It wasn't me." Silver allowed his head to collapse in Henry's shoulder and sobbed.

"No. No no." Kush scrambled up Rosie's body and leaned over her shoulder and pointed at Silver, "Kiyi. Mwari."

Rosie looked over at Kush, "The key?!"

Messages Within Keys

As night rose and the shadows that loomed against the trees fell onto the ground, fingers started to appear like gray worms between the torn up grass of the yard turned battlefield. Splinters of wood, pieces left of the last Entmen, crackled up with the hands. The ivy left over from Rosie's bulbs began to get torn apart as the hands broke the natural bars to their graveyard cages. The hands treated the soil like water and they pulled up a head and then a body with them, as a silver mist burst out all over the place like geysers.

A dark shape emerged from the sky and descended down above them. A black skeleton emerged from that darkness and its expressionless face rattled down as its teeth clattered together. Its bony fingers waved into the air as it weaved its spell and the shadow demon that had once been destroyed now reformed.

"Come back to me, Sol," a voice bellowed from the breathless, black rib cage of the skeleton. "The Blackwood is finally free to spread. The Oiden have done well. Haven't you, slaves?"

The Oiden painfully pulled themselves back onto the top of the soil and collapsed. They hungered for their watery home but they could not rest until what was lost to The Marina was found and returned.

The skeleton shook as the voice within its cage laughed and a long bony finger pointed to each of them, "She promised me. That is why you have returned to your march. Get up, Oiden, and fulfil her promise."

Sol looked down at its shadowy claws and back up to its master and hissed, "Thank you, Blackwood. I will not fail you again."

"Oh," Blackwood waved Sol off with a long, rattly arm, "this is not entirely your doing. The Messenger is in the wind. I heard him. I did not expect him to interfere, but it seems they grow desperate. I will silence him."

Blackwood's skull flew backwards and thousands of tiny black worms exploded out of it and into the sky, as the stars quickly disappeared above thick clouds. Each of its bony arms flung off to the side and thousands of ravens flew out of it. Blackwood dropped down to the ground and as soon as his feet touched the ground a few dozen wolves leapt out from between his legs. The rib cage and the hip bone of Blackwood cackled.

"Take this, Sol," the voice echoed beneath the black worm rain, "And become greater for it."

Sol felt itself being pulled suddenly and its shadowy form melded with the bones. Sol stretched and grew until thick arms and legs sprouted out and it landed onto the soil with the Oiden. A dark shape formed where Blackwood's skull used to be. A bald head with silver eyes and long, sharp jagged teeth. It grinned until the edges of its mouth reached its ears.

"Tear this place apart," the voice of Blackwood echoed and faded away like a roll of thunder and like a crack of lightning, the black worms seeped into the soil and destroyed Rosie's mulch; the spiked wolves surrounded and assaulted the house as it clawed away at the doors and walls; the ravens slammed into what was left of the windows and pecked away at Patrick's frames; the Oiden climbed and tore into the house by any opening created by the ravens and the wolves.

Sol, once again living, walked up the porch steps one by one with its awful grin. It waited as the wolves tore the door apart and stepped aside so that he could walk in. It looked around and grinned at the charred remains of the Cot Cage, remembering the time it spent weaving Blackwood's spells. As it walked past the long table in the Great Hall, Sol slammed its fist down and marvelled at how quickly it broke in half.

Sol studied his fist and grinned, "It's great being greater."

The wolves and ravens tore the Hall apart. The hearth collapsed. Sol watched as Oiden poured in from the backdoor. The kitchen filled with the sounds of cupboards being smashed. Sol was pleased by the destruction as he climbed the stairs to a hallway already filled with ravens. It kicked in Henry's door, knowing the magic of its frame had long since vanished. The room was empty for only a moment before the wolves and the Oiden ransacked it.

Sol walked slowly to Rosie's bedroom door. The frame was still intact. It waited as he listened to the sound of pecking and wood being torn apart and the sound of a wall exploding before it kicked the door in.

Ravens flung around the room searching and Sol spun away from the destroyed door and made its way back down the stairs.

"They are not here!" Sol howled, "The cellar?"

A couple of the Oiden shook their heads and Sol screamed before heading out to Rosie's garden, "Flatten this place!!"

* * *

Rosie watched the house fall before she slipped back into the shadows of the Lakewood Trees and stalked quietly through the darkness. Her lips pushed together against her teeth as she held the rage inside. Years of hard work were gone in a matter of moments. It was as if it were all inevitable the moment Patrick left. Or was it from the moment she found Silver? She couldn't decide who she wanted to blame more. She was careful not to leave a trail and had used spores to hide her scent. She knew the boys were waiting for her near the Shale.

After a moment, her teeth could no longer stay clenched and she took a moment to hide behind a tree and lean against it. A little bit at a time she allowed the whimper to tremble passed her lips. The burning tears soon followed and Rosie quickly wiped them away before making her way forward again.

Henry and Silver were sitting around a bush with Kushambira sitting on Henry's lap when Rosie arrived. Kush was stuffing her face and talking to the boys at the same time as Rosie watched them quietly from the shadows. A small fire kept them in a spotlight.

"I have not had umSwi in oh so very long. No. No no. My grandmother, Chembere Hove, would cook these and make them into a—I am not sure what the word is. Chit chit. I only know my word. Chingwa."

Henry stopped petting Kush and grabbed another handful

of the water berries. The Mhuka watched him for a moment and waited till his hand was free before pushing herself against it, demanding more pats.

"Rosie is going to come back, right?" Silver suddenly asked and looked towards the direction of the house.

Rosie held her breath. She wasn't ready to be seen. She wasn't ready to act like an adult and pretend everything was going to be okay because quite frankly, she didn't think they would be…not with Silver and his key around.

"Of course she is," Henry said, spitting bits of water berries from his mouth as he struggled to swallow. "She's just making sure we aren't followed and probably collecting herbs and stuff."

For a brief moment, Rosie imagined them falling asleep and coming in and scooping up Henry and stealing him away, but shame struck her like a punch to the gut. Silver was just a boy. He had no idea about that key either. Unless he was just pretending this whole time. Rosie absentmindedly reached for her staff and pulled it out. It hit against the tree and the boys went silent. Kushambira scrambled up onto Henry's head and made herself look tall.

"Ow," Henry whispered, "Kushambira, you're hurting me."

"Chit chit!" Kush's hair lifted and stuck outright and her voice went high and shrill, "You come out right now whoever you are or I will come out there and find you and I will bite you. Mhuka have a terrible bite and it will hurt for days and you will cry a lot and wish you had never scared a Mhuka!"

Silver put his hands over his ears and winced. Henry was trying to pull her back down before her claws scratched up his head even worse. Rosie couldn't help but crack and smile and stepped forward.

"Hush now, Kushambira," Rosie chuckled, "It's just me."

Kush peered into the darkness at the voice until the light of the small fire illuminated Rosie and the Mhuka nodded and clambered back down into Henry's lap and insisted on my pats.

Henry rubbed his head.
"I wasn't sure if you were going to come back," Silver said, trying to make eye contact with Rosie, but she just couldn't get herself to give it to him.

"Of course, I was going to come back. I just had to check on a few things, make sure we weren't followed and I grabbed a few herbs and such on the way."

"See, told you," Henry smiled.

"Try and get some sleep," Rosie whispered, "we will trek through The Shale tomorrow and reach the Community by nightfall."

Kush gasped and put her front paws over her mouth and nose, "Sleep? Oh, no. No No. What if the Oiden come?"

"They will not come this way," Rosie sighed and slowly sat down next to the fire and stared into its flames. "I told you, I have made it seem as if we have fled north to the mountains."

She refused to tell them about what she had seen, the one known as Blackwood, the demon being summoned and created stronger, the Oiden rising from the graves the Entmen had created or the origins of the cursed ravens, the black worms and the wolves. She didn't have the heart to tell Henry that all that he had ever known now lay in rubble.

"Rosie?"

Rosie automatically looked up and finally caught the eye of Silver. She couldn't fight the automatic scowl that formed and the moment Silver turned away fighting back tears, the shame hit her in the gut again.

"Yes, Silver?"

"Nothing," Silver muttered and used a stick to poke at the fire.

Rosie's eyes fell to the key that hung loosely around his neck. Her nose twitched and she looked at Henry instead.

"You did well back there," Rosie said, reaching out to scratch Kush's head, "You still remember your training even after all these rotations."

Kush kept giving out short little squeaks as she pressed herself into his hands. It was almost as if a chirping bird was caught in a quake. Henry looked down at her and laughed.

"I never thought I'd ever get to meet a Mhuka. You'd never take me over River's Song. Kept saying I wasn't ready. Do you still think I'm not ready?"

Henry looked up at his mother, who frowned and scratched the back of her head, "It doesn't matter if I think you're ready or not, Henry. The world is different now. We have to keep moving."

Henry nodded, placing Kush on his shoulders, "Where are we going? Just the community?"

Rosie shook her head, "We will go there to gather supplies. I have grabbed as much as I could of value that will help us barter and trade. After that, we will head into town where I have coins to keep us going."

"Going?"

"To the only place I know where we will find some answers."

Silver lifted his head, "Moon's Edge?"

Rosie nodded, "This all started when I found—when Silver—when I got the letter from Patrick."

Henry furrowed his brow as Silver went back to stoking the fire with his stick, "This is not Silver's fault."

"How do you—" Rosie quickly asked before snapping her mouth shut.

"How do I know it's not his fault?" Henry snapped back, "because he's my friend and you've seen what that key does to him. If anything, it's the keys fault. Do you just want us to hand the key over then and be done with it?"

Rosie stared at the key swinging back and forth slightly from Silver's neck.

"Chit chit. No. No no. Kiyi. Mwari," Kush suddenly said,

dropping off of Henry's shoulders and hesitantly taking a few steps towards Silver.

Silver tried to reach out to pat her head but Kush bolted backwards into a stumble and then stared wide eyes at the silver-haired boy. Silver sighed and returned to the fire.

"You keep saying that, Kushambira. You say it is more than The Marina. Then you call it a god. Then you say it is a key. What does that all mean?"

Kush slowly blinked, watching Silver closely before turning to Rosie and shrugging, "Chit chit. I do not know. Chembere Hove did not tell those stories. I just know. I feel it. It is Oiden magic. It sings like them. It sings of The Marina. When we fish, we hear them. Deep. Deep deep. They sing like the key."

"Then why does Silver have it? How did he get it?" Henry asked.

Kushambira sprawled her front paws up into the air, "Chit chit. How am I supposed to know?"

Rosie sighed and patted the bedroll closest to her, "Perhaps we will get the answers to those questions in Moon's Edge." Henry watched her lie down and looked over to Silver, "Don't worry. We will figure this out. I promise."

Silver nodded and let himself sink into his bedroll and turned away from them. Kush watched him for a moment before returning to Henry's lap.

"Don't worry, Kushambira, Silver is a friend. He is good."

"Hmmm. Yes, he is silver," she said quietly as Henry

turned to pat his bedroll. She balanced herself as he began to lay down and crawled along his side until she hopped down in front of his face, "Yes. Yes yes. You sleep. You sleep. I will watch."

"Aren't you tired?" Henry yawned.

"I am," Kush whispered, "but I will watch and tomorrow you will carry me and I will sleep."

"Oh okay," Henry yawned again and laughed lightly. He closed his eyes and tried to let sleep take him.

Kush looked over to the already snoring Rosie and then whispered to Henry as she curled up next to face, "What's it like to have The Woman in the Woods as your Mubereki?"

Henry, already half asleep, whispered, "My what?"

"Your mubereki. Your mubereki. I do not know the word."

Henry opened an eye, "Why do you call my mother 'The Woman in the Woods'?"

"Yes. Yes yes. That is the word. Mother. She is the Woman in the Woods because that is what she is. Chit chit. Okay. Okay okay. You go to sleep and I will tell you what Chembere Hove told me."

Kush rested her head on her front paws and began her grandmother's tales all the while watching Silver closely as his shoulders and chests heaved and bounced and a few sobs escaped him.

Silver watched his sparkling tears drip off his nose into the purple grass that marked the beginning of The Shale. He imagined himself in each one just floating along inside of it till his body splattered against the ground. Sleep overtook him. He dreamt of whittling on the stump with Henry's arms around him. He felt safe and secure. He dreamt of Rosie coming out and ordering them to help in the garden. Henry groaned but Silver quickly agreed. He saw himself helping Rosie planting seeds in the small crevices she created and covering them with her mulch. She was happy. Henry was happy. Most importantly, Silver was happy.

Then out of the sky a large tear appeared and landed on him. He was floating around in it as it rolled south away from the garden. Rosie and Henry chased after it but it kept rolling faster and faster until he found himself in the thick, cursed trees of the Blackwood. Out of the sky a large, black skeletal hand reached down and plucked up the tear with him in it. He tried to scream but only small bubbles came out of his mouth.

A deep voice cracked through the darkness with one simple word, "Mine," and the skeletal hand clasped its fingers together until the tear splattered and Silver felt himself tumbling down into the Blackwood trees. It was then that he could scream and so he did.

He screamed until he was suddenly shaken awake by Henry and it was morning. Kush's tail was sticking out of Henry's backpack that he had brought from home. A small snore was coming from it. Rosie stood off in the distance leaning on her staff watching him closely.

"What did you dream?" Henry asked, helping him pack up and put his own backpack on.

Silver muttered, "Nothing." He heard Rosie grunt and

watched her begin to walk deeper into The Shale without them. "I'm sorry, Henry."

"Don't be. It's okay. Come on. We'll catch up."

"She hates me now," Silver muttered.

Henry grabbed his hand and pulled him along, "She does not. She's scared and my mother does not like to show that she is scared. She also doesn't like not knowing everything. That key is a mystery that she can't solve."

Silver reached for the key, "I hate it."

Henry looked over at Silver and smiled, "It frustrates me, too, but we'll figure this out together. Just ignore my mother. She can be a big baby."

"I heard that," Rosie called back to him.

"Well it's true!" Henry snapped.

When Kushambira woke and peeked out of Henry's backpack, she gasped in awe and shoved her front paws onto her nose. Her round eyes went wider and she took a moment to wipe them.

"Chit Chit. Henry. Henry Henry, what is this place?"

Henry seemed surprised by the sudden voice that whispered in his ear from the backpack. He stopped for a moment and put a hand back for her to crawl into his arms. He held her as he continued. Rosie had walked in silence since the morning and Silver was much the same. He didn't understand why his mother started to distrust Silver. After all, wasn't he a victim of the key more than they were?

"The Shale," Henry whispered down to her.
Kushambira shivered, "Runako."

"Runako?" Henry repeated.

"Chit chit," Kushambira whispered, "Runako," and looked down at the thick grass. She marvelled at how deep of a green it was. It was almost like the deepest algae she could almost reach in the ocean. She wondered how the grass tasted.

The trees were more spread out than the Lakewood Trees and the round leaves seemed to dance together almost in a twirl as they spiralled on their branches. A blue mist darkened the horizon.

"Dark? Night?"

"No, Kush," Henry whispered, "The Shale."

"Oh. Oh oh. Runako."

"Dark?" Henry asked. "Runako?"

"No. No no. Runako," she repeated, pointing to the grass, to the trees and to the Woman in the Woods as she repeated the word.

"Pretty?" Henry asked.

"Yes. You learn quick like a Mhuka. Good."

Henry looked over to Silver and whispered, 'Runako,' suddenly blushing. Kush looked up at him and tilted her head, following his gaze. She stretched out a paw and said aloud, "Yes, Runako. But also, Mwari. Very dangerous."

Henry looked down at her and quickly snapped, "He is not dangerous!"

Kushambira slapped her forehead, "Chit chit. You think like Woman in the Woods. Your mubereki. Kiyi is Mwari. Different but same. More than The Marina."

Henry huffed, "But Silver is not dangerous."

"He is silver," Kushambira replied.

Silver turned slightly and looked back at Henry, who quickly looked away. Kushambira kept her gaze upon Silver until he turned back to face the direction Rosie was silently heading. Silver felt an emptiness within him that mirrored the key against his chest. He had tucked it away. Every time it was out, he caught Rosie staring at it and he hated it. He looked up at the back of Rosie and found it hard to breathe. He just wanted to run to her and beg her to like him again.

Silver sighed and looked away deep into the trees of the blue of The Shale. A movement out of the corner of his eyes caught his attention. He stopped for a moment and looked a bit closer to his left.

Henry caught up to him, "What is it, Silver?"

"I thought I saw something. Someone. Moving from tree to tree."

"Keep moving," Rosie called back, "We must reach the community by nightfall."

Silver shrugged and slowly continued to follow.

Henry followed with him, glad to be walking side by side

again. Kush chirped lightly as Henry caressed a spot on the back of her head between her ears. Her paws twitched slightly at the sensation. Her eyes tightly closed. She could fall back to sleep. She wondered why the Mhuka didn't do this to each other before. It was fantastic. The most her mubereki did before the felines got them was lick her clean vigorously. This was nothing like it.

"You only see what you want to see." Rosie jumped and turned around. Silver was looking at her with the steel of his silvery blue eyes. She turned back towards her chosen path and listened to the sound of footsteps. "Why can't the boy be what he's meant to be? You're twisted and I see right through you."

"You're so confused about what you don't know." Silver looked up and saw Rosie glance back at him with a warning in her eyes. When she returned to facing forward, he was left with a lump in his throat. He dropped his face back down to his feet listening to them drag themselves through the grass. "You're locked away and don't know where to go. You're frightened and I know your secrets."

"You crave for love but you're full of hate," Henry turned to look behind them. There was a brief moment he thought he saw someone go from tree to tree but the mists just swirled and he turned to find Rosie walking faster and Silver walking slower. He sighed. "Why carry a heart that holds such weight? You're sinking and I have what holds you."

The mist slowly flowed anticlockwise across the horizon as a hum consumed The Shale. The round leaves of its trees twirled to the soft lullaby that filtered through the branches.

"If I could tear you apart, I'd taste your heart. Give yourself to me and I'll take care of the key."

"Now, which way will you point the blame?" Rosie clenched her fists and roughly pushed a branch out her way. It snapped back as soon as she let it go. "What you don't realise is they're one and the same. You're twisted and I can almost taste you."

"You think you're broken and cannot be fixed," Silver flinched as a branch slammed into his chest. He felt the heaviness of the key and the tears started to well in his eyes. The silver mist flared as he stared at the back of Rosie. "Your water and her oil cannot be mixed. You're frightened and I can almost reach you."

"Who would you miss more if all of them left?" Henry tried to reach out to Silver before the branch snapped into his chest but failed. Henry clenched his fists much like his mother was doing and stormed after her. "How much more can you lose before you're bereft? You're sinking and I can smell your sorrow."

Three hunched shapes emerged from the trees and rotated with the mist. Their pace quickened as they passed each tree. They cackled to each other as their grotesque appearance was slowly replaced with beauty.

Kushambira gasped and jumped back into Henry's backpack and whispered, "Muroyi."

 "You are the huntress and he is your hunt, we both know what happens to runts. You're twisted and I'll be the one to twist you." One of the shapes approached Rosie slowly, its haggardly hand reaching out and slowly its flesh smoothed.

"You are the bird and soon you will fly, let go of them or

you, too, will die. You're frightened and I'll be the one that takes you." Another shape approached but slowly slid itself towards Silver, its face gnarled and unkind but with each step softened and smiled.

"You have the silver and won't let it go…"

Kushambira bit Henry hard in the shoulder and then scrambled up on top of his head. Her hair stood on end and her voice became shrill, "Muroyi, you are old and ugly and mean. I do not like you and I will not let you hurt the Woman in the Woods. I will not let you hurt her Henry and I will not let you become a Mwari. You smell like mushrooms and your clothes look like the guts of a feline!"

Henry blinked and stumbled forward. A sharp pain spread through his shoulder and up through his head. Blood ran down his forehead. His ears screamed and he reached out to Silver to steady himself. Henry wiped the blood away and looked around in time to see a shape reach out to him.

"Don't look at me!!" Henry heard as his eyes fell upon two halves of a face that did not meet evenly in the middle. Pus oozed out of sores and a foul stench seeped out between blackened teeth. Two hands with gnarled fingers flung up and blocked its face before it screamed in horror and retreated back into the trees.

Two other gnarled figures stumbled forwards towards Rosie and Silver before Henry looked at them and they screamed in horror. Both of them retreated to the trees and Silver and Rosie both lifted a hand to their head and groaned.

"Muroyi. Muroyi muroyi!" Kushambira squeaked and she scrambled back down to Henry's shoulder.

249

"Hags?" Rosie moaned. "Beyond the Blackwood border? Impossible!"

"Muroyi. Chit Chit." Kushambira shuttered and hugged Henry's head, "I am sorry I hurt you, shamwari."

Rosie turned around quickly, "Shamwari? You honour my son. Thank you, Kush, for saving us. Here, Henry, Silver, take these and do as I do with them. Keep your eyes around us as we walk. If you see one, point to it. Acknowledge that she is here and she will not approach!"

Silver and Henry took what seemed to be a cluster of moss Rosie had taken out of her satchel and watched as Rosie stuffed hers into her ears. She nodded at the boys and they obeyed.

"Their words will not affect us, but if they grow too near and touch us, we are lost. Move! Quickly!"

Rosie jogged forward, rotating her body around clockwise from time to time to watch the horizon. Every now and then she'd point, "There you are, hag! I see you! I know you!" and the trees would echo a horrific scream.

Silver pointed to the north, "I see you, hag! I know you!"

"Good, Silver, keep going! Stay close!" Rosie called back and Silver smiled and quickened his pace. He had to run to keep up with her job.

"There! There there!" Kushambira pointed to the south.

Henry called out, "I see you, hag! I see you!"

As they ran through The Shale, it echoed with the frustrated cries of the hags as they desperately tried to reach for them.

"Keep going! Do not falter, my boys!" Rosie yelled and pointed to a cluster of trees, "I see you, hag! Back to the Blackwood in which you were lost!"

Silver and Henry pointed to another together and shouted, "I see you, hag!"

They both shared a quick smile and grabbed each other's hands as they bolted after Rosie. The trees were gathering more and more into clusters. Their trunks were getting thicker and they began to stretch higher and higher into the sky until it started to become impossible to see the branches and their circular leaves.

"I can't see through the trees!" Henry screamed but briefly saw a hag, "I see you!"

"Rosie, we can't see!" Silver reached out to her as she turned around and pointed behind them and prevented a hag from approaching. She looked down at Silver's hand and took it.

"We're almost there, boys! Do not worry! I have you!"

A figure stood before them raising a staff above their head. Silver gasped and pointed at them, "I see you, hag! Go back to Blackwood, you ugly worm!"

The figure's staff faltered a moment before a strong voice said, "Excuse me?"

Rosie put a hand over Silver's mouth and pushed him forward, "Eldar, he does not know you! But hags, they are here in the forest!"

Eldar pulled back her hood revealing her short, white hair. Her staff returned to its original height and her voice boomed beyond the trees, "I see you, hags! Return to your coven!"

Screams cursed their names before they turned to sobs before they faded and the mist around them settled.

"Dark days," Eldar muttered and waved an arm at Rosie.

Rosie grinned and released Silver before stepping forward and into the arms of the one she called Eldar. "It is good to see you again. I brought Henry, of course."

Eldar pushed Rosie away and waved Patrick over, "Well get over here and give old Eldar some love!"

Henry grinned and skipped over to her. A small squeak came from his backpack and Eldar held him out in front of her.

"And what is this?" she asked, peering over into his bag.

Kushambira peeked out and Eldar put a hand to her face, "Well if my old eyes are deceiving me let them! Is this a Mhuka?! I am blessed to meet you."

Kush blushed and bowed her head.

"And who is this thing that said I was a hag?" Eldar huffed and neared Silver before her eyes widened and she stepped right up to him and studied him closely. "Well, boy? Speak up! It's not every day my feet touch the soil. It is sacred, you know!"

Silver looked to Rosie for approval who nodded her head. He returned his gaze to Eldar and gazed into her eyes. A green mist swirled around her pupils. He gulped, "They call me Silver."

"He is silver," Kushambira squeaked and Eldar turned to her with a fond smile and the Mhuka giggled madly before dropping into the backpack. She squirmed around as the embarrassment overtook her. "Runako. Runako runako."

"Well, Silver, I am no hag. I am Eldar. Welcome to The Shale," she said and embraced him.

Silver

In and Above

The cauldron began to boil over; its liquid oozing over its sides. The house filled with delightful laughter and the sound of urgent footsteps. In the rafters of the room, wooden keys and long bones hung loosely and clattered together, though there was no draft. Three figures emerged from their rooms and trampled across the balcony overlooking their cauldron below and rushed down the stairs. They scrambled passed each other, their gnarled hands clawing at whatever they could grab off of each other. It was important to them to be the first to reach the cauldron.

"Sisters. Sisters!" another figure appeared at the front door right under the balcony. "Calm yourselves. We all know that I will drink from it first, after all."

The three eyed each other and started to squabble over being too loud and if they had been sneakier they could have reached the cauldron first.

"Sisters, three, eyes on me!" the lone figure hissed and the three jolted upright, heads turning towards the speaker as their bodies rose until their toes barely touched the floor. "In the beginning, we were discarded. Forgotten. Accused of selfishness and cruelty until we finally embodied it. Out of the six, you three have stood by my side. I owe you my thanks. But not today. Not now. After hundreds of rotations, this brew finishes. I," she said delicately, "will not share it with you now."

The three howled, all begging, "No, Hagatha. No please. Forgive us, sister!"

"Silence!" Hagatha snapped and pulled the hood of her cloak backwards and glided to the cauldron. The three sisters hung in the air helplessly. "I will drink from it. Four times. Not one! Four! You will stay there and watch what words could have been yours!"

Hagatha's hair hung haggardly on either side of her neck. Her beauty held together by the enchantment of the pouch that hung around her neck. She looked with disgust at the appearance of her rotting sisters.

"We have stayed prisoners within the Blackwood for far too long. The Feygods blamed us for the Calamity. Though I played my part in it, we all know who is really to blame, don't we? But Hagatha was prepared, wasn't she?"

Hagatha approached the cauldron and pulled off a large spoon hanging off of a hook on the mantle of their hearth. She grinned, her mouth widening, as she dipped the spoon into the boiling liquid and then brought it up to her lips. She spun again and gazed at the three sisters.

"Hagatha, you owe me," the one wearing wolves' teeth around her neck hissed.

"Tut tut, Hylandra. Your wicked words won't work on me."

"But, Hagatha…" another whimpered as worms poured out of their pockets.

"Nope, not even you, *Nanna* and your pathetic attempts will persuade me." Hagatha sneered at Nanna for a few moments before turning to the last of the hags that remained silent. "No insistence from you, sweet sister? Surely the intrepid Akra has something to say."

The one called Akra shook her head, the black feathers that decorated her clothing fluttered softly to Hagatha's spell. Hagatha grinned and took a sip, "Good girl, Akra."

The magic of the cauldron made Hagatha's veins rise up through her skin and blacken. She closed her eyes for a moment and when she opened them they cried tears of tar. Her lips parted and she said,

> *"Water, Earth, Fire, Sky.*
> *The Dark. The Light. It all will die.*
> *But as the barrier of death doth fall.*
> *The silver one rises to stop them all."*

The house shook around them, bringing down the dust that clung on top of the rafters. The three sisters screamed in delight and then in anger as Hagatha dipped the spoon into the cauldron again.

"The Feygods will die," Hagatha chuckled, "That's music to my ears."

She brought the spoon up to her blackened lips and gazed over at the others. She sighed and slowly stepped over to Akra. "I suppose you were silent when you needed to be, sweet Akra. Perhaps I can give you a taste."

She leaned over and brought the spoon to Akra's lips and then quickly brought it back to her own and swallowed. Akra howled as Hagatha stumbled backwards. Her eyes darkened like the night skies.

"You cantankerous cow that was mine!" Akra howled.

Hagatha spat out black blood and spoke,

"Silver silver strands of hair
the oceans are choking
and the lands are bare."

Hagatha choked on her words for a moment until she was able to turn them into a chuckle before limping over to the cauldron and spooning out more of its liquid. Although she had had only two spoonfuls, the cauldron was now almost practically empty. Its magic being drained down Hagatha's gullet. She turned to Nanna and raised it into the air.

"Cheers, Nanna, to what could have been yours if not for your constant whimpering!" Hagatha gulped the liquid down. Her head flung back and her illusion that held her beauty fell. Her face returned to two halves of a face crookedly displayed upon her head. One ear hung loosely at her jawline. The other stood high but decaying.

"Eyes of frost and mist and light
it's all of our secrets
he dreams in the night."

Hagatha fell over and slammed into the large table that held their mixtures, their salves and potions. Glass shattered everywhere. The potions hissed and evaporated instantly. Some of the mixtures combined and burst together like bubbles colliding with a needle. Hagatha moaned.

"Hagatha, please, it's not too late," Hylandra howled, trying to fight against the magic that held her there. "Akra and Nanna are not worthy, but I am, Hagatha. I am!"

Hagatha's body suddenly stood upright in one swoop and she flew towards the cauldron madly with the spoon still in hand. She scraped the bottom of the cauldron and shoved the spoon into her mouth as she stared at Hylandra defiantly.

Hylandra screamed, her mouth cracking apart and her dilapidated eyes bulging, "You sac. You sanctimonious sac!"

Hagatha's ears poured out more of the black blood that was being forced into her system as a shadowed veil seemed to fall over her. She screamed in agony,

> *"The Blackwood, The Lakewood,*
> *The Blades and The Shale*
> *will all lie down if he fails if he fails."*

Their front door exploded inwards and all the hags fell to the floor in a heap. Hagatha held her throat and tried to breath as the last of the cauldron's brew seeped into her system. A skeleton stepped into the home of the hags with its constant grin.

Hagatha choked out before collapsing herself, "Sol."

"We are free," the skeleton watched her fall, "Tenebrus will be waiting."

Hagatha felt the last of her breath leave her as her eyes filled with the cursed blood and lay open, staring over at her sisters. Hylandra, Akra and Nanna all stood up and brushed the dust off of their stained cloaks and burst out laughing.

"Leave her. She has played her part. It is time for mine and time for yours," a voice boomed from the rib cage of the skeleton.

The hags followed the skeleton out into the clearing amongst Blackwood and cackled even more loudly at the dark shadow that formed in the sky above them.

"The Oiden walk," the skeleton pointed off to the northeast. "You will help me end the march of the Entmen, spread your curses and begin your travel to The Shale..."

Hagatha watched them disappear in the cursed trees of the Blackwood. Her gnarled hands clutched at the door frame for a moment as her wicked grin simmered into a smirk, "Yes, go. Play your parts, for then Hagatha's reign over the realms will begin."

The door closed quietly as she slid across the floor and waved her hands above the cauldron. A spark ignited within its emptiness until a whiff of smoke spun around filling it up with whispers, "Sisters, we are free. Our coven can reconvene."

* * *

"Welcome to The Shale," Eldar said to Silver as they approached a large tree that had stairs spiralling up like vines growing into the thick canopy above.

Silver felt comforted walking with the white-haired stranger. He wondered if she had silver hair at one point before age changed her. He wanted to speak and ask questions but he felt like he was wearing the seashell necklace again and his voice was trapped inside his throat.

"We welcome all visitors, Silver."

Eldar's voice was gentle, almost a hum, but there was a strength behind it that suddenly intimidated him. Still, he started to take the steps with her.

"It has been many rotations since my feet have touched the soil you normally walk upon, but I was told Rosie was coming…with a guest…"

Rosie could take a few steps at a time and caught up easily. Silver looked over at her and watched her try to patiently take one step at a time to keep pace. He laughed to himself after clearly seeing the pained expression on her face.

"You've never greeted us before," Rosie commented with a hint of snark to her tone. She was using her staff much like Eldar was using it. They both tapped them against the steps as they walked.

"We both know, dear Rosie, that this time your arrival is much different. Besides, I welcome you with open arms at the Gates of Krysa every time you come."

"Krysa?" Silver asked, his sudden muteness overcome by curiosity.

Henry gasped, "Silver…"

Eldar paused on the steps and turned to Henry and lifted up her free hand, "It is alright, Henry. I doubt you have had time to educate him on our ways. An adventure I will insist on hearing once we are inside."

Silver nibbled on his bottom lip, "I said a name I wasn't supposed to, didn't I?"

Eldar lifted an eyebrow and eyed Henry, "Curious. Yes, Silver, Krysa, our Holy Mother, a name that cannot pass your lips ever again. Same with The Shale, for it marks the boundaries in which most of us cannot walk passed. Follow me and I'll explain."

She held up an arm to put behind Silver's shoulders as they continued walking up the steps, "You see, Silver, my people have walked these lands since the oceans separated themselves from them. We are the children of Krysa herself until the Feygods themselves created their Calamity."

"Calamity?" Silver eyed Rosie, who shook her head slowly, but continued to walk up the stairs slowly. Henry walked on his left side, with Kushambira nestled in his backpack and Silver heard him gasp again.

"Though I appreciate your questions, Silver. Understanding is important. I get that, but I will request that you hush now despite that. You ask of things you cannot."

Silver nodded, "I'm sorry."

Eldar looked up the flight of stairs, "I know. I will answer you, though I should not. Something tells me that I should." Eldar paused once again to study Silver, "Certainly Curious," and continued walking as well as explaining, "The Calamity was the Feygods first mistake. I will allow you access to our scrolls later."

Even Eldar seemed surprised by her statement. Rosie just shook her head.

Eldar sighed, "For now, know that if the Calamity had not happened, the Gates of Krysa would not exist as it does now. The Calamity sealed the Feygods away but in the Holy Mother's last few moments walking The Shale, she grew this very tree to lift us up and protect us. My people vowed to never to walk the lands again, though they quickly learnt how difficult that would be. We still needed to harvest and hunt the lands Krysa helped create. So, our boundaries widen to The Shale. Some chose to walk farther still. At great cost, mind you."

There was an awkward pause before Eldar spoke again, "When we arrive, you will enter what is known to us as the Common," she smiled over at Rosie before returning her attention to Silver, "These words you may use without offending my people."

"The Common is where you trade with others?"

Eldar ran her hand absentmindedly through Silver's hair. It was only when she felt the pricks of static that she withdrew her hands and stopped once again on the stairs to look down at him, "You are a curious one. But yes, we welcome most visitors in the Common, but it is the Gates of Krysa which most are not allowed to pass. The Edwards are part of the few that can enter these gates. Today, you will be entering them as well. But first, Abitha would like to meet you."

Henry grinned over at Rosie, who couldn't help but share a smile with him. They walked the rest of the way with Eldar asking questions about the last few days before quickly insisting that they not tell her until they were inside.

"Then why ask?" Henry laughed.

"Silver is not the only one curious," Eldar said with a wink.

The stairs wound around the tree a few times before they stepped into the thick canopy of The Shale's round leaves. They wound around the tree a dozen more times before the stairs broke free of the canopy. A stone path ended the stairs and led into a village that surrounded the road. The houses looked similar to the Edwards' house.

"How are we back on the ground again?" Silver scratched his forehead and took a few steps onto the path.

"Isn't it beautiful? The Holy Mother made it appear as if we never left the lands. But what you see before you is the Holy Land, the first Shale."

Silver stomped a foot onto the ground with such fascination it caused the other three to burst out laughing.

Out of Henry's backpack an exasperated Kushambira clawed at Henry's shoulder before perching herself against his head, "Chit chit. This is amazing. Oh, Woman of the Woods, thank you so much for bringing me to this place! Akafa Hove told me such stories!"

Henry put a hand on Kush's side to keep her balanced as he followed Eldar further towards the village. Kush took that moment to get a few more scratches from him.

Two guards, dressed in thick, leathery garments, tapped their staff against either side of the pathway in which they stood, "Welcome back, Sister Eldar. Welcome, Landwalkers. Lady Edwards."

Silver remembered Henry explaining that's what they called those who lived below. He nodded his head after he saw Rosie and Henry do the same. Henry looked excited and spoke quietly to Kush, however, Rosie's lips were pushed together.

Eldar looked to Silver, "Rosie has never been fond of returning to the Commons."

"It's not the community I have an issue with. I quite like visiting and trading," Rosie said as a couple glared at her and went into their house and closed their door, "It's some of the people I'm not fond of."

Silver looked at the houses and the people before returning his questioning gaze back to Rosie.

Eldar noticed, "You have not told the boy? So many secrets and questions. None of that, though. Silver, all you need to know is that The Shale was Rosie's home once."

"Yes," Rosie muttered, "once upon a time."

They walked a few more houses down the pathway, getting closer and closer to the large gate at the end of the path. Two trees grew on either side of it with what looked like more guards standing nearby. Beyond the gate there seemed to be a tall temple and beyond that a large, wooden statue seemed to grow out from behind the temple with its back to them all.

Silver felt a hand on his shoulder and Eldar's whisper in his ear, "That is the last gift The Holy Mother gave to her people. She stands watch. My people believe that she points into the direction in which she will return to us. Come, Abitha's house is this way."

Within moments of entering the smallest house they had come across in the community, Silver was pushed to the centre of the one room house. He eyed Henry, as a little old lady hobbled around him peering up at him with one large eye. He wasn't sure if she had two of them. A fold of wrinkles covered where the other one should have been staring. Her mouth hung open and an uncomfortable gurgle and hum rose out of the gaping hole where two rows of teeth should have been. She had gotten up from an old creaking chair that Eldar helped herself to once she moved. Rosie stood next to Henry with her arms crossed.

A gob of drool slowly seeped out of the corner of her gummy mouth and stretched to reach the floor, "I see you."

From the stories Henry had told, he thought he knew who this was that was inspecting him over. "Ole Spit?"

Rosie winced and elbowed Henry, "I told you not to call her that."

Ole Spit froze and tried to stretch herself up to his face much like her spit was trying to stretch to the floor. Slow. Almost calculative. She cackled and looked over to Eldar. "It knows my name!" She wiped her spit away with a long sleeve that draped over gnarled hands. She had a deep voice that sounded as if her tongue kept getting in the way.

"I-it?" Silver watched as she drew closer and continued her rotation around him lifting each arm up in her inspection

Henry, rubbing his ribs where he was elbowed, stepped towards Silver.

Rosie put her arm up across Henry's chest and slowly shook her head, "Watch."

"Wicks. Get me my wicks!" Ole Spit howled and hobbled quickly over to a table pushed against the farthest wall.

Silver looked over at the table with curiosity. Henry grinned and told Kush this was where Ole Spit would make her candles, salves and other items that she'd say would 'cleanse the world around you'.

"They do at that," she said, slurping up another line of spit.

"Abitha," Eldar said, leaning her staff against the chair and folding her fingers together, "This is Silver. Henry and Rosie you know. And the Mhuka I have not been introduced." Eldar gave Rosie and Henry a look of displeasure.

Abitha peered beyond Silver, her gnarled hands holding his hips, "What? Henry? Rosie? Old news. Want to buy my wicks and wares?"
Rosie nodded, "I shall return later."

Abitha waved her away and peered closer at Henry, "A First One. Here. In Ole Spit's hubble. Well, Mhuka, come. Let the First Ones reunite for we have not crossed paths in many rotations."

Kush obeyed and leapt off of Henry's shoulder, stumbling across the planked floor of her house a bit as her claws struggled to find footing. She scrambled up Silver's side, much to his dismay, and perched herself on his shoulder, peering down at her. "Chit chit. I am Kushambira but you can call me Kush. Akafa Hove told me the stories of this place. How words are forbidden. How you don't walk on the land and I asked her if you swam and she didn't know. So I am very excited that I get to ask. Do you swim, Abitha?"

Abitha peered up at her with her one eye as drool plopped down onto the ground, "Mhuka. Always were her favourites, though she will never admit it. This one does not know my name. She does not know if Ole Spit can swim. I can swim. Yes, of course I can swim. Just because my legs do not go beyond The Shale does it mean they cannot swim. Much to learn, young one. Much. You've come to the right place. Buy my wicks and wares and you'll be better for it."

Kush pushed her front paws over her nose and nodded, "Oh. Oh oh. Thank you, thank you. But how will I buy them?"

"Ah," Ole Spit slurped from the corner of her mouth, "not all things need coin to purchase. Knowledge, little one, knowledge."

"Ow!" Silver exclaimed as Ole Spit poked his side, "This is new. Very new. Silver, you say your name is now? Interesting. It suits you."

Abitha glared over at Rosie, "Like Ole Spit suits me!" and as she spoke a blob of spittle flung across the room.

Eldar slowly stood up, using her staff to support her, "Well, I have done you this favour, Abitha. You have seen the boy. Now we will continue through to the Gates of Krysa."

"Fine," Abitha spat, "I'll get my things. Much to discuss."

"Excuse me?" Eldar replied, almost spitting herself, but instead choking on the hard swallow. "You'll what?"

Henry and Rosie shared a look. Silver took this moment to slip away and return to them. Kush remained on his shoulder.

"You heard me. Yes, you heard me fine."

"You have not entered the Gates of Krysa in a hundred rotations!" Eldar held her staff tightly.

"Oh? Only that long? I had hoped longer."

268

Rosie grinned despite herself.

"Nothing should surprise you about Ole Spit," Abitha said, now poking at Eldar's side, "Nothing. Now close that mouth. Let's go. Come on. Get out. Get out!"

Ole Spit motioned for them to get out, pushing Eldar harder than she needed to push.

Eldar stumbled out of the house and looked to Rosie before muttering, "Dark days indeed…"

Rosie stood awkwardly outside of Ole Spit's cottage and dared to look around. Though she'd never admit it, she did find comfort in returning to The Shale, after all, it had been her home for so long. The Commons was always a magical place for her as a little girl, darting through the crowds that would come during the Fey Festivals. She closed her eyes and listened around her. She could hear the murmur of the few people that passed by and tried not to imagine the slurs that escaped their lips. She opened her eyes and found Eldar looking over at her.

"You are always welcome here. No matter what they say or you think," Eldar put an arm around Rosie and pulled her towards the Gates of Krysa. "Let them see Sister Eldar welcomes you each time. As far as I'm concerned, it was your parents that chose to walk away from us. Not you."

Rosie's eyes stared at the back of the statue that loomed over them all, "But I chose not to stay."

"Will you now?" Eldar stopped and looked deep into Rosie's eyes, "Your home has been lost. A darkness looms on the horizon. The hags roam again. The Blackwood is free. Here you are safe."

269

Rosie quietly slipped a note out of a small pocket and handed it to Eldar, who silently took it and read it. She finished just as Henry and Silver walked up with Ole Spit in tow.

"Hurry it up, boys, there's many things I must tell you and teach you," Ole Spit laughed, her small walking stick tapping on the stone path. "But first," she hissed, "we need to get that key off of you. And Ole Spit has got the trick!"

Eldar looked up at Rosie and silently returned the note to her before sighing, "Moon's Grove. No sooner? No later? So be it. But you will stay here for the time being."

Rosie arched an eyebrow. She could hear the shift in Eldar's tone, one she hadn't heard since she was a child. Eldar was commanding her.

"We will help prepare you and hopefully find some answers."

"Are we staying?" Henry asked, eyeing the note that passed between Eldar and Rosie. "Really? But we've never stayed—for how long?"

Suddenly a menagerie of birds sang around them. Ole Spit yipped, "We have our answer! The phoenixes have spoken! Through to the Gates of Krysa! May the Masalta cringe knowing that I step through her gates once more!"

A few people stopped and gaped at Abitha as she made a scene.

Silver followed Ole Spit closely, just as intrigued with her as he was with Eldar and this place. He didn't belong here but it seemed neither did Ole Spit or the Edwards. He looked back briefly, watching Rosie and Henry quietly talking. Eldar looked beyond them as if she were looking through a window to another world. Kush's tail was the only sign that she had returned to Henry's bag.

"Do not fret over them right now, Silver. Let them have their reunion. There is history here for them. For some, a visit to the past is an awful lot of climbing but to stay there, well, that can be an impossible mount."

Silver walked with Ole Spit for a bit more before he hissed, "It's mine."

Ole Spit chuckled as they approached the guards that aligned the path leading up to the entrance, "Of course it says that. Oye," she used her walking stick to tap the spears the guards used, "move aside, Ole Spit is coming through. That's right. Watch those eyes; they might just leap out of your skull! And this one is with me so don't you even ogle him or you bunch of sacs will see what else this walking stick can do!"

Beyond the gates was a large temple made of twisted trees. Vines grew up around the archway of the door and continued up and around windows before spreading out beyond the steeple above the second floor. Silver felt a heaviness over his chest.

"I knew it," Ole Spit hissed, "It grows heavy. I can see it in your face. There is great power here and it responds to it. Masalta Krysa once lived in this very temple before she lifted this place up above The Shale. Powerful magic. Coveted." Ole Spit stopped at the entrance to the temple and sat upon its steps.

Silver turned to see the rest of them still travelling up to the gate where the guards started greeting Eldar, "It is mine. It is…if you take it, I think it will hurt them…him."

271

Eldar whacked Silver across the legs with her walking stick, "Sit down, boy. Ole Spit is no fool. I told you that I had tricks, didn't I?"

Silver sat down next to her, rubbing the back of his legs, "What tricks?"

Ole Spit laughed and held up a hand. In it was Silver's key still hanging from Patrick's chain. Silver gasped and clutched at his chest. The key wasn't hanging around his neck. Before he could reach for the key, Ole Spit pulled out a bag made of leather and hair and tucked the key and chain inside before tightening it closed with twine. She tossed the bag to Silver.

"There. They will not find you for now. My bag has bought you time. I told you not all things require coin." Ole Spit smirked and tossed her walking stick onto the ground and watched it slither away.

Silver tried to catch his breath, "How did you—"

Ole Spit watched Eldar eye the walking stick as it slithered out the Gates of Krysa and approached the two, "What have you done, Abitha?"

Ole Spit let a glob of drool seep out of her mouth and onto her chest. She stood up with ease and seemed to be taller. Definitely proud of herself, "I was tired of all this mine, mine, mine. Old news."

Silver held the bag as if it smelled horrible. Actually, he sniffed, it did.

Ole Spit watched Henry approach Silver and she giggled, "But these two. This is new."

"Are you alright, Silver?" Henry asked and Silver lifted up his shirt and showed his bare chest. Henry blushed crimson. "What are you doing?"

Rosie gasped, "Silver, what did you do with the key?"

Silver held up the bag with his finger and thumb, "Abitha put the key in here. I do not hear it. I do not hear its whispers."

Henry lifted his eyes to meet Silver and they both grinned at each other.

But Rosie eyed the bag and glared at Abitha.

Ole Spit paid no attention to Rosie but glared at Silver muttering, "I take the key and the boy still calls me Abitha. And yes, Rosie, the eye is now closed. A trick you could have had if you had not hidden our name."

Eldar frowned at the bag in Silver's hands, "I do not like what I am seeing, Abitha. This magic is not welcome here. You know this. They—"

"Don't you start with me," Ole Spit howled, pointing a finger at Eldar, as she made her way up the stairs to the entrance of the temple rambling all the way. "If Krysa herself had an issue with my magic then why can I step foot in her temple still?" She stopped at the two guards posted within and looked each one in the eye, "Huh? Ever think of that? After everything I've done against her name? Out there they shun me. But here I am, in here. Whenever I want." Her rambling continued as she continued into the temple, randomly shouting at people, "Shun me?! Bah! Is it against her will, though?! Think on that Sister Eldar."

Rosie watched Ole Spit disappear before ascending the

stairs to the temple herself and stopping at its door frame. She winced at the sight of the door frame, but ran her hand across it, before following Abitha.
Silver and Henry followed and Silver whispered, "Patrick made these frames."

Henry nodded sadly and entered the temple silently. Eldar stopped at a chair in the middle of the foyer and sat upon it.

"Aren't you coming, Sister Eldar?" Silver asked as he watched Henry quietly follow after his mother.

Eldar shook her head, "My family's place is here, but please follow Abitha and pay your respects to the Holy Mother and her children. We have time later to talk." She ran her hands through Silver's hair before nodding him through, "Simply curious."

As Silver walked into the next room that held a stone altar with seven pillars growing out of the back of it. His eyes wandered curiously around as he approached the three standing before the stone structure.

"How were you able to hold the key? Didn't you hear it?" Henry asked.

Ole Spit laughed, leaning against the altar. A few worshippers glared at her but she paid no mind. She just smiled fondly at the boy and gloated, "Simple, Henry. I made that key."

* * *

Far beyond the western hemisphere a roar echoed throughout the darkened sky of Moon's Grove. High in a tower, Hagatha stood next to a large altar shaped as a hand holding a bowl. She grinned up at a monstrous shape that billowed above the bowl and cursed Rosie's name. The water inside the scrying pool exploded as a thick, crimson hand slammed down into it. The room echoed with the roars of frustration.

"Careful," her voice cracked through the darkness, "this scrying pool's magic is powerful and hard to replace if it is damaged."

A deep voice reverberated throughout the room, "Do not lecture me, Hagatha."

Hagatha leaned against the edge of the large bowl. Her eyes were still blackened from the deadly brew. She shrugged, following a finger along a bulging vein on her arm, "Merely a warning. It would take me many rotations to bring this eye back to its full potential."

"Your sisters failed to stop them from reaching The Shale."

"That is correct. It is why I drank the Black Blood and they did not. They're incompetent."

"Fail me again, Hagatha. Fail me again," the voice grumbled and deep footsteps faded away into the darkness.

Hagatha rolled her eyes and looked over at the feeble prisoner whose eyes finally opened. His arms wobbled terribly before he collapsed, sending Hagatha into a fit of laughter, "Oh Patrick, how completely and awfully," Hagatha laughed, holding her gut as she moved closer to him, "wonderful it is to see you this way. Chained to my altar. Your eyes, our eyes."

Patrick tried to lift himself up again to defy the hag but as the rotations moved on the chains attached to the floor grew heavier. He saw himself pushing himself up with a strength that he once had. He imagined standing tall despite the fact that he was short. But that's all he had, dreams, because in reality, his arms gave out and his face slammed into the moss-covered stone.

Hagatha fell sideways and leaned into the scrying pool with more fits of laughter, "Like the crack of a tree as it tumbles to his knees! A carpenter's irony. What's it like, Patrick, watching your beloved Entmen fall one by one? What's it like being chained to this altar so that your eyes show us what we want to see? To know that with all your clairvoyance, you did not see this coming?"

Hagatha stepped over him until each of her legs were on either side of his thin, frail body. She kicked him in the ribs once before squatting over and pulling his head backwards, "You should really eat something. You're wasting away. Perhaps a little bit more of my latest brew? I can see it in your eyes, you know. That hope of yours. It's because of what I said? What was it? Oh yes…

> *You'll raise a bird who'll hunt you down*
> *the huntress will come after,*
> *the silver tongue will guide their path*
> *and the gift you give thereafter."*

Hagatha slammed his head back down onto the floor and stood back up, "The scrying pool will eventually show us where they are headed, Patrick. It's been reported they have fled north to the mountains. But we both know that's not true, don't we? We'll find them, Patrick, your eyes will deceive you eventually. Tomorrow perhaps. Your snivelling god, Masalto Edar, won't be able to protect you forever."

She pulled his head up by his hair and licked his bloodied forehead and smacked her lips delightfully, "Yes, my delicious dwarf, open those eyes! For that silver-haired boy will be mine!"

End of Book One

Books by the Author

In-Rel Trilogy
Book 1 - Silver
Book 2 - Coming Soon

He Was a Boy Who Smiled
Book 1 - Phoenix Rising
Book 2 - Phoenix Falling

Shorts
A collection of short stories

We Need To Talk About This
Hanging On The Wall
Inclusive Love
Silenced Violence

Novella
Apartment 1B

About Michael

Michael Stoneburner lives in Sydney, Australia with their husband Joel. Michael was a primary teacher for almost 10 years before focusing all of their time on their writing. They donated their time to the local writing groups where they helped organise publications, radio shows and public readings.

He Was A Boy Who Smiled Book One and Book Two are now available. Book Three is on its way! They also wrote a series of short stories called Shorts that bring inclusive characters from the LGBT+ community, something they wished they had more growing up.

Michael enjoys observing humanity and interactions and it shows in Apartment 1B. Michael recharges their psyche with poetry and has released a collection of poetry. They also released Book One of their In-Rel fantasy series, Silver.

Michael is an advocate for mental health, working as a Peer Support person and has worked extensively with survivors of Domestic Violence, Inequality and Mental Illness. Each of these topics are addressed in their poetry anthologies. Michael continues to work on their website where they released free to read poetry, fan fiction, guest bloggers and personal thoughts and self-reflection.

Visit michaelstoneburner.com for more.